1

Wolves

"THERE ARE NO WOLVES IN NEWFOUNDLAND." The guide tapped the lit glass case with a curled index finger. "Except this one. This is the only complete skin of a Newfoundland wolf in existence." Waving his hands, he explained that the government had placed a bounty on the wolves, and they were hunted to extinction a hundred years ago. "Newfoundland wolves were a distinct sub-species—that is, they were different from all other wolves found anywhere else in the world." He rested a hand on the glass case and bowed his head. "Gone, forever."

Peter wondered if the guide performed a mini eulogy for every tour group.

His classmates jockeyed for the best spots to view the stuffed wolf standing on the raised platform. Mrs. Walsh reminded them not to touch or lean against the glass case. Not wanting to elbow it out with his classmates, Peter remained in the back.

After the students had gawked at the wolf for a while, a couple of class jokers howled at an imaginary moon. Mrs. Walsh shushed them right away.

The guide gestured with his hand for the class to follow him to another room. "Now, let's have a look at the caribou." Peter lingered behind, watching his classmates walk into the next room, before approaching the glass case.

The mottled fur, golden and brown in colour, had lost its lustre long ago. Peter peered at the wolf's face and caught his own reflection in the glass. Under his dark wavy hair in need of a cut, his grey eyes looked bright. Just beyond, a pair of amber glass eyes stared back. Peter pictured the wolf running through the boreal forest, its fur thick and bristling, its long snout exhaling white puffs of breath in the cold winter air. Many more wolves came into his picture—beautiful and healthy, eyes alert, bodies powerful, running and running.

Did my ancestor, the legendary bounty hunter, kill this wolf?

As Peter turned toward the doorway, his clumsy long legs stumbled, and he dropped his question sheets. He crouched to gather them up.

A loud crack.

Peter spun his head and stared at the glass display case. Short, delicate lines inched out from the bottom right corner. He stood and took a step forward. The subtle lines gave way to deep jagged ones as they fanned out. Peter looked around for his teacher or the guide, but the entire group had already moved on and he was alone in the room.

All at once, the case shattered, sending glass flying. Peter jumped back, then froze as everyone rushed into the room, led by a beefy security guard who pointed a sausage finger and accused him of hanging back to break the glass. All Peter could do was stare at the wolf, now speckled with glistening shards.

Mrs. Walsh vouched for Peter, saying that he was not the kind of kid who'd vandalize. Besides, there wasn't a single object that could've been used to break the display case. All Peter had in his hands were the question sheets. Still, the guard looked unconvinced as he filled out the report.

Two months later, another unexplainable incident occurred.

While fishing with Grandpa, Peter saw something move on the other side of the pond. Squinting to block out the rays of the setting sun, he aimed his fishing rod at the bristling creature so he wouldn't lose sight of it.

His heart began to beat faster. "Look! A wolf!"

Grandpa shot him a look of disbelief, then fixed his gaze on the pointed fishing rod and followed it to the woods on the far side. His crinkly eyes darted from tree to tree, then came to a rest at the place where the dark grey creature stood.

Are wolves good swimmers? Peter wondered.

A black raven flew low overhead and squawked a piercing alarm. Grandpa stepped back and knocked over his tackle box. By the time they looked again, the wolf had receded into the shadows of the woods.

Grandpa said, "It must be Ben's mutt, Willow. She's as big as a wolf and wanders all over the place."

"Willow is part sheepdog and looks nothing like a wolf." Peter's face was flushed. "I know what a wolf looks like because my class went to the museum and saw a stuffed one up close." Although this alive one was bigger and a different colour.

Grandpa continued to gaze across the water and shook his head. "It can't be a wolf. There's none left on the Rock."

"That's what the museum guide said." Logic told Peter he couldn't have seen a wolf, but his pounding heart hinted otherwise.

Grandpa reeled in his line. "Best get going so Lily can fry up these fish for supper."

"What? We're not cooking them up here over a fire?"

Grandpa sorted the spilled contents of his tackle box back into their compartments. "Cold mist moving in." He nodded at the clear sky.

Peter didn't argue further. He wasn't sure he wanted to hang out in the dark with the mystery animal lurking around, and besides, Grandpa knew weather.

As they walked through the woods back to the house, Grandpa seemed troubled. Once, he stopped in his tracks and stared back toward the pond, scratching his beard. Peter was deep in his own thoughts. *How could a wolf be here?* Newfoundland was an island. A wolf from somewhere else couldn't just walk over. Even though he couldn't think of anything that wasn't outlandish, dreaming up the possibilities put Peter in good spirits. Not paying any attention to where his oversized feet stepped, he tripped and fell, painfully scraping his bare knees. With an arm wrapped around Grandpa, he hobbled the rest of the way home.

They found Peter's mom at the dining table engrossed in one of her many books about herbs. With her long chestnut hair tied in a neat ponytail, Mom looked a lot like Grandma Helen in the photo in Mom's bedroom. Standing in the adjoining kitchen, Grandpa held out the brook trout. "Change of plans, Lil. We're having supper at home."

Mom raised her pale oval face. The crescents of permanent dark circles under her intelligent eyes hinted at trouble with falling asleep. Her gaze dropped and she saw the blood dribbling down from Peter's dirt-caked knees. She stood up so fast that her chair almost fell backwards. "What happened, my honey?"

"Just scrapes," Peter said, even though his knees throbbed and burned.

"The boy doesn't know the size of his own feet. He tripped just walking." Grandpa plunked the fish in the sink.

"Go wash out the wounds." Mom rushed off to the greenhouse in the backyard. Peter knew she'd pluck the right combination of herbs to ease the pain and would pound them into a smooth pulp with her well-used mortar and pestle.

Peter sat with his legs stretched out on the couch as Mom applied her concoction to his knees. Upon contact with the herbal paste, Peter exhaled a sigh of relief. The burning pain stopped, and the blood coagulated. "Mom, your green thumb works magic."

2

Reindeer

PETER SHIVERED IN THE CRISP MORNING AIR. Toast crumbs stuck in his throat. Grandpa had just rushed him through breakfast and pushed him onto the porch. Ben, wearing his rain jacket and rubber boots, came around the side of the house followed by Willow, the stray mutt that Ben had adopted a couple of years ago.

"Morning, Ben!" Grandpa said with too much enthusiasm for the next-door neighbour they saw all the time.

It took only a few strides for long-limbed Ben to reach the base of the porch. Willow made her way up the steps, and Peter scratched the shaggy dog under her collar. *It definitely wasn't you at the fishing pond yesterday.*

Ben planted a foot on the first step. He wore a cap over his nearly bald head. "A fine morning for a drive, I must say. I'm thinking of going down to my cabin, you know, just for the day." Ben snapped his fingers. "Say, would you b'ys like to come with me?" Ben had the smiliest eyes of anyone Peter had ever met.

"What do you think, Peter?" Grandpa asked.

Peter looked back and forth at their faces before answering. "Sure."

Grandpa leapt to his feet and rubbed his hands. "Get your rain jacket and boots, son."

"Is Willow coming with us?" Peter asked Ben.

As if she understood, Willow shook her head and loped back toward her house. "Willow likes to go on her own adventures," Ben said.

Grandpa wore his bright red rain jacket lined with white fleece that poked out at the collar and the ends of his sleeves. When Peter was a preschooler, he had called it the "Santa jacket" and was delighted to see Grandpa wear it. With his thick, silvery-white hair and beard and black rubber boots, Grandpa did look like a slim Santa.

A big red button on the Santa jacket hung at the end of a thread. "Grandpa, one of your buttons is gonna fall off."

A weathered hand searched for the loose button, yanked it off, and put it in the jacket pocket. "I'll ask Lily to sew it on when we get back."

On the beautiful drive down to the Southern Shore, the narrow highway undulated up and down, left and right, revealing delightful views of clapboard houses with clean sheets billowing on washing lines, steepled churches jewelled with stained glass windows, lonely lighthouses watching for ships, and the grey-blue ocean dotted with small, verdant islands.

Cold rain began to splatter the windshield. Grandpa was never wrong about the weather.

Ben's cabin came into view and Grandpa pulled up alongside it. Ahead of the small structure, the trees cleared to reveal an open area. To Peter's astonishment, he saw a herd of caribou foraging there. There must have been more than a hundred of them.

"Well, look at that." Grandpa raised his thick eyebrows in an effort to appear surprised.

Noiselessly, the two grey-haired hunters retrieved their hunting rifles from the back of the truck.

"You guys just happened to have your rifles?" Peter looked over at the two men, who didn't meet his eyes. The weapons must have been packed in the truck before Ben's "spontaneous" suggestion that they go down to his cabin. Although Grandpa had been disappointed that Peter had shown no interest in hunting, he always said that all Connorses were hunters, and when the time was right, Peter would see that hunting was in his blood, too.

As Grandpa put his arms through the straps of his rucksack, the two hunters discussed their strategy.

"Guys," Peter said, "it's August. The legal hunting season doesn't start 'til mid-September."

Grandpa said, "It's allowed when the caribou come onto your private property."

That didn't sound right at all. Ben kept his head down.

The hunters led the way through the patches of trees that edged the boggy grounds. The reluctant young apprentice followed, dragging his feet.

When they were level with the caribou, Grandpa nodded to a cropping of rocks outside of the tree patch. Hunched over to avoid being seen, they inched toward the rocks. A few of the caribou, still chewing, lifted their heads up and sniffed the air, but the hunters were downwind, and the animals remained unaware of their mortal danger.

Grandpa placed the rucksack on top of the rocks and securely balanced his rifle on it. He peered through the viewfinder.

Ben said, "John, do you have a clear shot of the bull by the alder bushes?"

"Not quite. C'mon big fella, turn."

Peter screwed up his face, bugged by the anticipation in Grandpa's voice.

Nosing for more food on the ground, the bull took a few steps and turned perpendicular to the hidden threesome.

Grandpa made an almost imperceptible nod to Ben.

Ben nodded back. "Peter, would you like to take the shot?"

Peter crossed his arms.

Ben looked at Grandpa.

Grandpa let out a small sigh and undid the safety latch. Peter covered his ears to muffle the sound of the rifle.

Bang!

All the caribou started running and Peter breathed a sigh of relief. "You missed, Grandpa."

"No, I didn't."

Sure enough, a caribou faltered and fell. He tried to stand up, but his shattered shoulder was unable to support the weight.

"Darn it! I was aiming for a clean lung shot." Grandpa hurried toward the animal with Ben close behind.

Peter passed the two hunters. He didn't know why he was running so hard. There was nothing he could do for the caribou. He certainly didn't want to look at the dying animal. But when he got close, he couldn't stop himself. To his horror, the alert bull lifted his head and their eyes met. The guileless face of the doomed beast, wet with cold raindrops, accused him of being an accomplice.

Grandpa took aim. Peter turned away and suctioned his palms to his ears.

"Reindeer is another name for caribou," the museum guide with the expressive hands had said. "And they're also native to Newfoundland."

Peter wished Grandpa wasn't wearing his Santa jacket to slaughter a reindeer.

3

Caribou Stew

"I CAN'T EAT THIS STEW."

"If it's too hot, give it a good stir." Mom said, demonstrating with her own.

"No, it's not that," Peter replied.

"Then what's wrong, my honey?"

"I saw his eyes."

Grandpa lowered his spoon. "Whose eyes would that be?" His sarcastic tone indicated he knew where this was going.

"The caribou in my stew," Peter huffed.

At the square dining table, in mismatched chairs, the

family of three sat together for supper. On the table were three bowls of stew containing bite-sized potatoes, carrots, onions, herbs from the greenhouse, and the star ingredient: the fresh caribou meat. Grandpa's and Mom's bowls were half finished. Peter's was untouched.

"You love caribou meat," Mom said.

"Well, I never had one look at me before it was killed and chopped up." He gave Grandpa an accusatory glance.

"Hunting is the traditional way to get food," Grandpa said. "You have to kill to eat any kind of meat. Or do you think meat is born in Styrofoam trays in grocery store coolers?"

"I know how we get meat." Hot prickles erupted on the back of Peter's neck. "But he looked at me."

Grandpa shrugged his shoulders. "So, he looked at ya."

"The caribou was scared. I saw it in his eyes!"

"Fish have eyes," Mom said, trying to cool the family discussion. "You catch and clean fish. And you certainly like eating them."

"When you catch a fish it flops to one side, so you see one eye at a time. The caribou looked at me straight on with both eyes." Peter pointed to his own eyeballs with two fingers in a *V* shape.

The weather turned, as it often did in Newfoundland. Clouds covered the evening sky and raindrops tapped on the dining room window.

Grandpa spoke in a calm but upbeat voice. "You know, I got your mom her first hunting gun when she was thirteen."

Mom was somewhere far away, looking at the empty blue chair across from her. Peter extended a leg but held back from kicking it.

Grandpa said to Mom, "You got a clean shot on your first time out, as I recall."

"Hm? Yes. I sure did." She beamed.

"Ah, we had some wonderful times, eh, Lily?"

She nodded with a smile.

Grandpa turned to his grandson. "You've been thirteen for a while now. I've got to take you on your first hunting trip soon."

"You mean my second." Peter glared at the stew.

"Yes, you're right." Grandpa leaned back in his chair. "I did take you on your first hunting trip." He drew out the next words. "Now, if by some chance I can't take you on the next one, Ben will."

"That's a strange thing to say, Dad," Peter's mom said. "Of course you'll take him."

"Well, none of us are getting any younger."

Something sharp tugged in Peter's chest. Even now, as mad as he was with Grandpa, he wanted Grandpa to be around for a long time. Peter pushed his bowl away, as even the smell of the stew was starting to bother him.

"Do you want the leftover rice and fish?" Mom said. "I don't want you to go hungry."

"No, Lil! This is ridiculous. Peter, you're descended from generations of hunters. My grandpa, your great-great-grandpa Connors, held the record for killing wolves." He pointed his spoon at the ceiling. "Upstairs, I have the certificate the government sent him, thanking him. He was a hero and a legend."

Peter hung his head and rolled his eyes, having heard about the family hero many times. "The Newfoundland wolf was a distinct subspecies and should not have been wiped out," he mumbled and stole a glance across the table without lifting his head.

Grandpa's clenched jaw barely moved as he rumbled, "Don't you feel pity for them wolves. A hundred years ago, they were thieves and killers, terrorizing farms and decimating the caribou population." He pointed his spoon at Peter. "Hunting is a part of who we are as human beings, just like eating and sleeping."

Peter thought about this. "Newfoundland wolves were hunters, too. It was who they were."

Grandpa slowly lifted a big spoonful to his mouth and chewed and chewed, thinking. "Your great-great-grandpa saved a toddler from being dragged away by a wolf."

"Oh, that sounds like an old wives' tale." Mom gave Peter a wink.

Grandpa banged his spoon down on the table. "Ask Ben's cousin in Pouch Cove. It was her great-grandmother who was saved. She'll tell ya her great-grandmother had ugly bite scars on her arms and back."

Mom touched his hand. "Calm down, Dad."

Peter fought the urge to blurt out that the museum guide had told the class there was no evidence that wolves attack or kill people.

With his jaws still clenched, Grandpa said, "Now young man, you're gonna sit there until you finish the stew that I provided for you. You're a mighty ungrateful lad."

"Dad—"

"Now. I mean it. Wasting food, that's a sin." Grandpa took his empty bowl to the sink. He started washing the dishes, mumbling about a sore throat and a headache.

With beseeching eyes, Mom pushed the bowl of stew a couple of inches closer to Peter. She stood up. "Let me make you some herbal tea."

Later, Peter nodded off at the dining table. When his head jerked forward, he opened his eyes wide and sat up straight. The clock on the wall showed it was almost ten o'clock. The cold stew had not been touched. He was determined to stay up all night if he had to, but soon his head started to bob again.

The next thing he knew, Grandpa was tapping him on his back. "Time for you to go to bed, son." His voice was hoarse and he smelled like lemon and ginseng.

Sleepy and disoriented, Peter raised his arms, thinking for a moment that he might be picked up. His ears reddened. It had been many years since he was small enough to be carried. He was already taller than Grandpa.

When Peter had slipped into his bed, Grandpa stood at the foot of the bed and searched his grandson's face like he was trying to memorize every part of it. Just before switching off the light, he said, "You don't have to go hunting if you don't want to."

Peter partially sat up, leaning on an elbow. "Thanks, Grandpa."

Closing the door, Grandpa mumbled, "Stubborn boy."

What just happened? This was like striking gold when he wasn't even looking for it. Grandpa had a stubborn disposition himself and he was particularly obstinate on the subject of hunting. Never in his wildest dreams had Peter dared to hope that he'd be off the hook from the long-standing family tradition of hunting. Grateful, he drifted into a peaceful slumber.

Next morning, Peter was roused by the muffled sound of a panicked voice from the next room.

"Dad! Can you hear me, Dad? Dad!"

Peter flew out of his bed and ran to Grandpa's room. At the open doorway, he stopped and grabbed onto the door frame.

Mom, bent over the bed, was shaking Grandpa by the shoulders. Grandpa's eyes remained closed, but his waxen lips were parted slightly as if he were about to speak. Mom turned her head to the doorway, pale as a day moon. "Call for help, Peter."

Peter's fingers held a death grip on the doorframe.

"Peter?" She walked unsteadily over to the big oak desk as if her legs were asleep, fumbled for the phone, and pushed three buttons.

Our father who art in heaven…thy kingdom come…give us our daily bread, forgive our trespasses… Peter couldn't remember any more. His family went to church twice a year, on Christmas and Easter, which was enough exposure to religion to know when it was time to bargain. *Dear God, please don't let Grandpa die. Let him live, and I will memorize the Lord's Prayer in English and French. I will get all A's. I will clean my room—no, the whole house. I will not talk back to Grandpa at supper or any other time. I will finish all my food. I will…I will…go hunting.* Tears streamed down his face.

Light-headed, he floated toward the ceiling. Looking down, Peter saw himself let go of the doorframe, walk over to the bed, and hug Grandpa. He was jolted back into his body when he felt Grandpa's cold face against his hot, tear-soaked cheeks.

It was too late for bargaining.

4

a Strange Visitor

PETER, WEARING A BLACK JACKET, STOOD IN front of his living room window. He pushed his mop of hair from his damp forehead and loosened his tie. Earlier in the day, the minister from the neighbourhood United church had performed a short funeral service right at the cemetery as per Mom's request. And when his mom's left shoulder started twitching, Peter held her hand and reminded her that they'd be home soon.

The casket was lowered into a grave that held a few inches of rainwater. The white flowers on the casket did not make the dark, rectangular hole look any less lonely. Engraved on the matching headstone next to Grandpa's were the words

HELEN HONG-CONNORS
WIFE OF JOHN CONNORS
MOTHER OF BEATRICE,
AGNES, AND LILY

Grandma Helen had died before Peter was born.

Now, at the reception at home, about thirty guests remained; many more had filtered in and out. Grandpa had lived in the same town forever, and he was known and liked by all of the old-timers. The town, once considered remote but now riddled with new homes in various stages of completion, was growing like so many others around St. John's.

A pumpkin-coloured upholstered couch faced Peter and the window. It looked new with the three seated ladies covering all the threadbare patches. Between sips from their teacups, the ladies, who had grey hair with subtle tints of violet, smiled at Peter encouragingly.

By the front door, Mom and Ben talked quietly. Ben had driven Mom and Peter to the hospital, speeding after the ambulance with Grandpa inside. When the emergency doctor informed them that he had officially pronounced Grandpa deceased, Peter, full of remorse, blubbered that he had caused Grandpa to get upset. While Mom rubbed Peter's back, the emergency doctor had explained that Grandpa was old and it was his time, nothing more.

From a soft leather briefcase, well-worn from his law clerk days, Ben pulled out some papers. As Peter approached them, he heard Ben say, "Your sisters know."

"Mom, what are you guys talking about?"

Mom touched the double heart charm on the delicate chain around her neck. "Grandpa left the house to me *and* my sisters."

"Why? They're rich. They don't need it."

Ben shrugged. "John came to see me after supper on the evening he passed and asked me to change the will."

"Did Dad say why?" Mom asked.

"No. He refused to sit and kept straightening the salt and pepper shaker collection on the shelf. Just wasn't himself, but was so insistent." Ben fidgeted with the buckles on his briefcase. "I'm sorry, Lily, to be the bearer of bad news."

Mom gave him a tired smile. "I'm sure everything will work out. Thanks, Ben."

From the living room, someone called for Mom. Peter held the front door open for Ben and eyed the well-trod path across the road that led into the woods and to the pond where he and Grandpa had spent countless hours fishing, talking, and enjoying each other's company. From his pants pocket, he pulled out the big red button that no longer needed to be sewn back onto the Santa jacket. He rubbed the smooth button and put it back in his pocket.

Peter returned to his spot in front of the living room window and then side-stepped toward the corner, so he wasn't facing the grey-haired ladies on the couch so directly.

A raspy voice startled him. "I guess you're the man of the house now."

A hunched-over old man in a shabby black and grey checkered suit stood uncomfortably close. Peter nodded at the man, who he didn't recognize. He must've just arrived. The man scanned the room as if he was looking for something, then pointedly turned his tanned face to Peter and trained his strange yellowy-brown eyes on him. The old man suddenly stood tall and straight as if he remembered that he could, and his suit released a strange odour—a mixture of musty attic, sweet outdoors, and rusting metal. Then he stretched his mouth into a smile so wide that it seemed to almost reach his ears. Peter took a step backwards.

"You must take good care of your mother," the old man said.

With her long, chestnut-coloured hair tied in a neat ponytail, Mom floated from guest to guest, holding a tray of assorted sandwiches in one hand and a pot of tea in the other. Peter knew that if she didn't keep busy, she'd fall apart.

He cringed when he saw her getting closer to her older twin sisters, who stood at a snobby distance from the rest of the guests.

Peter's aunts Bea and Agnes were successful real estate agents—business partners at ABC Realty, which stands for Agnes and Beatrice Connors Realty. Their unusually long and skinny necks defied the laws of physics by supporting their heads with their dark hair coiled into big, heavy buns on top. Peter secretly called them the Bobbleheads. When his aunts were children, they were the stars of their ballet class and aspired to dance for the National Ballet of Canada. But when they grew to six feet tall at the age of fourteen, they gave away their pointe shoes without sentiment. As usual, today they wore black suits and stood so close to each other that they looked like one giant black-bodied bug with two heads and eight skinny limbs.

Aunt Bea was a chain-smoker and Aunt Agnes had an odd habit of tilting her head back and inhaling deeply, sucking in Aunt Bea's exhaled smoke. Peter suspected this was an arrangement the miserly pair came up with to support their habit. As Aunt Bea nattered on, Aunt Agnes used her bobblehead to nod in agreement.

When Mom—in her short-sleeved, calf-length black dress—made her way to her sisters, she spoke in a firm but hushed tone. "I don't want you to smoke in my house."

"*Your* house?" snapped Aunt Bea. She exhaled a big cloud of smoke above her younger sister's head. Aunt Agnes flared her nostrils and inhaled until her chest could rise no more.

Mom looked tiny next to her towering sisters. When her left shoulder started twitching, Peter walked hastily over to the corner where the three were standing.

"Dad left the house and his paltry savings to all three of us." Aunt Bea said. "I guess you weren't the king's favourite daughter after all." She tittered and nudged Aunt Agnes, who took a sudden interest in her shoes.

"We want our share. We have to sell the house, sis," Aunt Bea hissed.

Sell the house?

Mom put down the tray of sandwiches and the pot of tea next to a snow globe on a nearby side table. "I need some more time… I'm going to buy your shares of the house."

Aunt Bea's dark eyes widened. "And, how are you going to do that with no savings and no job for…how many years?" She pointed to Peter with her cigarette. "Since he was born."

Peter had never worried about or given any thought to Mom's financial situation—until that moment.

"You can't even manage to leave the house for something as simple as grocery shopping without having an anxiety attack." Aunt Bea swept the air in front of her with her long, skinny arm, like a bug with its antenna, and the ash from the tip of her cigarette dropped to the floor. Peter smouldered, knowing everything Aunt Bea did was deliberate. She was marking the house as hers by disrespecting Mom in words and action.

Aunt Bea clicked her tongue. "We're holding the reception here instead of a spacious funeral hall because you can't handle being out of the house for a couple of hours." Aunt Bea nudged her twin again. Looking away, Aunt Agnes picked up the snow globe on the side table and shook it. The glittering, plastic snowflakes descended on the charming cottage and the colourfully-dressed mummers.

Aunt Bea's cheeks hollowed as she took a puff of her cigarette. "Tell us, Lil. What is your plan to get us our money?"

When Mom stood there looking lost, Peter spoke up. "Don't worry, Aunt Bea, Mom will come up with a plan." But he had a sinking feeling it was unlikely.

Before his aunt could continue to badger them, Peter took Mom's arm to lead her away and almost ran into the old man in the checkered suit. Was he standing close, listening all this time? Finding their corner too crowded, Peter's aunts moved away, puffing and inhaling.

"Albert Doyle, at your service." The man bowed his head of thick, coarse, grey hair. This action again stirred the strange mix of odours, now muddled with the smell of burning tobacco.

Mom shook his hand. "Thank you for coming, Mr. Doyle. I'm Lily."

She always advised Peter to respectfully address new senior acquaintances with the honorific and their last name. Most people would then ask to be called by their first name. Mr. Doyle did not.

"I know who you are, my dear. I was friends with your dad and mom. In fact, I'm responsible for them getting married."

"Oh, yes! Mom mentioned several times that a university colleague introduced her to Dad. She spoke highly of you."

"Did she, now?" Mr. Doyle made another impossibly wide smile. He pointed at Peter before reaching into his jacket pocket. "John sent me this photo of you and him."

Peter took it and examined the two figures—slightly blurred because the image looked to be zoomed in from far away—at the fishing pond, unaware of the camera. Showing it to Mom, he said, "You must've taken this photo."

She looked puzzled. "I don't recall." She suddenly remembered her hostess duties. "Would you like sandwiches and tea, Mr. Doyle? I also have coffee."

He sniffed the air. "Mmm...ham and cheese. Unfortunately, my dear, I must leave on a trip. There's a bottle of mead I've been after, and an opportunity has presented itself. But may I visit you another time?"

"Of course, any time."

Peter and Mom walked the guest to the front door. At the opened door, Mr. Doyle grabbed one of Peter's hands. He flinched, but Mr. Doyle held on and leaned in. "I'm so sorry you lost your grandpa."

And at that moment, there was something kind and caring in his expression that reminded Peter a great deal of his grandpa, who he missed so much. Mr. Doyle released the hand and turned to leave.

As Peter watched him cross the road, he realized he still had the photo in his hand. "You forgot your photo!"

Mr. Doyle waved. "Keep it for me. I'll be back."

5

Monsters' Dance

FOR FIVE DAYS AFTER THE FUNERAL, PETER stayed cooped up in the house reading. His favourite books were the ones where the hero journeyed to strange, faraway lands, adventure awaiting him at every turn. To him, books were more than entertainment, more than a way to pass time. Books were lifelines that kept him from drowning in the deep hurt he endured every miserable time he saw his mom slip into one of her trances, staring at the blue chair. Now, he needed a book to keep his nose above the sea of pain he felt for losing Grandpa.

On his overflowing bookshelf, *Cautionary Tales for Young Children* caught his eye. The hardcover picture book split open to the story that Grandpa had often read to him when he was a little kid. On one side, the illustration showed a wolf blowing down a straw house, and on the facing page, the same wolf was blowing down a house made of timber. He could hear Grandpa saying, "Big *bad* wolf," and see him wrinkling his nose. Many fairy tales gave wolves an unfair rap. In this tale, for instance, the message wasn't that the wolf was bad, but that working diligently and not taking shortcuts was good. As Peter saw it, the wolf had a meaningful role in the story; he was like a building inspector, giving out pass or fail grades and making sure the houses were to code, which was especially important in a windy place like Newfoundland.

Peter returned the book to its place next to the *I Spy* and other "find it" books.

Then he reached for *Puddicombe's Mythical and Fantastic Creatures Reference*, a thick, handsome book he had received from Mom for his birthday last year. She always gave him the perfect gift; the gift he wanted the most but didn't know it until he unwrapped it. *Puddicombe's* listed magical creatures found in literature. A full-page drawing of each creature was accompanied by a description of the creature's powers, weaknesses, where it could be found, and what it ate (in gripping, grisly detail).

The creatures Peter found most frightening were not the hideous ones with multiple heads and sinewy, scaly tails. He was most disturbed by the ones that were able to change into human form, because a creature like that didn't need to sneak up on you. The monster in human skin could come boldly up to you and befriend you. Then he'd unzip his human skin and the beast would emerge, as you realized too late that you had been deceived.

Once, the monsters had come to Peter's house.

It was the day after Christmas, the year he had started kindergarten. He woke up from his sleep wanting a cup of water. In pyjamas and fuzzy slippers, he walked into the kitchen just as someone banged on the back door.

Voices boomed in chorus: "Any mummers 'lowed in?"

As he was not supposed to be up at such a late hour, no one had told Peter about mummering, the Newfoundland Christmas tradition of friends in disguises going from door to door. Once allowed inside, the mummers spoke with distorted voices and moved in ungainly manners to conceal their identities. It was the job of the host to guess their identities and provide refreshments.

Grandpa, who was in the room setting out a bottle of rum, glasses, and warm tea biscuits Mom had baked, opened the door.

Cold wind and snow slithered in. Peter could not believe his eyes.

Costumed people with disguised faces marched into the kitchen. On their heads, the mummers wore cloth sacks with holes cut out to reveal their blackened eyes; ghostly veils that showed glimpses of painted, menacing faces underneath; and frightening store-bought masks with permanent wicked smiles. Under long coats, ill-fitting dresses, or tattered outfits—many turned inside out—they had padded their bodies with pillows, placing them strategically to look humpbacked or fat-bellied. Some even changed their postures, bending over, swaying side to side. It was a nightmare with no possibility of awakening.

Peter wondered why Grandpa was letting the monsters into the house.

Something lumbered at the end of the monster parade, and a beast even stranger than the mummers came into his kitchen. A crude wooden horse head led to a body made of rough burlap hide and two human legs sticking out from underneath.

When they were all inside, one of the mummers came up to the hobby horse and spoke in an ingressive voice, sucking in the air while speaking to disguise their voice. It made the other mummers and Grandpa roar with laughter.

With its all-white, protruding eyeballs, the hobby horse spotted Peter. A gloved hand reached out from underneath the burlap and pulled a rope attached to the wooden horse head, moving the lower half of the hinged jaw and producing a creepy knocking sound. The horse galumphed toward Peter, all the while clap, clap, clapping his jaws and revealing dozens of crooked teeth made of nails. Peter wanted to run from the motley pack of monsters, but his legs would not cooperate.

When the horse lowered his head until it was inches away from his face, Peter swallowed and asked in a small voice, "Why do you have eyes like that?"

The horse replied, "The better to see you with."

Peter touched his baby teeth. "Why do you have teeth made of nails?"

"I'll show you." The horse stood tall again. Clap, clap, clapping faster, and the nail teeth sparked.

That was the last straw. Peter didn't realize he was screaming and crying until Mom rushed over, picked him up, and comforted him. A man dropped the stick holding

up the wooden horse head and threw off the burlap hide. It was Ben, the next-door neighbour, looking sheepish. "I'm sorry. I didn't mean to scare the little guy."

Snivelling in his mom's arms, Peter saw for the first time that Grandpa looked at him with disappointment. *I should have been braver*, he thought, and buried his small face in Mom's neck. Peter realized now it was the same look Grandpa gave whenever he refused to go hunting. The look that chipped at Peter's heart every time.

Mom carried him upstairs to his room and stayed with him. Downstairs, someone started to play an accordion. The muffled and distorted sounds of laughing, stomping, and dancing came up through the floorboards. A small night light on his bedside table rattled with every stomp. Imagine, a monster's ball in the kitchen of his house! Peter dreamed terrible dreams for many nights after.

Flipping through the pages of *Puddicombe's Mythical and Fantastic Creatures Reference*, he shuddered. Even now, Peter didn't like to think about the monsters that had walked into his house. He wondered if the mummers and their hobby horse should be included in the thick book.

Peter took out the red button from his pocket and rubbed it. Grandpa, the pillar of his family, was dead, and the Bobbleheads were determined to sell the house. Peter desperately needed a book to carry him away from his distressing reality, even if it were just for a couple of hours. He combed the bookcase for a hero.

6

Return of the Bobbleheads

A KNOCK ON HIS OPENED BEDROOM DOOR.

Peter looked up from his folktale book.

Mom rubbed her puffy eyes. "I can't put off going to the grocery store any longer. Would you come with me for moral support?"

Grandpa had run most of the errands for her, but now she'd have to leave the house for things like shopping for food. Besides some canned food, there wasn't much but a freezer full of caribou meat that no one wanted to eat. It reminded them too much of Grandpa.

In the truck, Peter wanted to ask Mom what was

going to happen to them and the house. But when he saw her white-knuckled hands clutching the steering wheel, he turned his head and looked out the window. In the quiet truck, his thoughts drifted to a past trip to the supermarket.

On that day, as he and Grandpa walked from the parking lot to the front entrance of the store, a young man with a scarf stylishly wrapped around his neck approached them holding out a clipboard. "Hello there. I'm part of an environmental group collecting signatures to bring wolves from Labrador to Newfoundland to restart the wolf population. Would you like to sign the petition?"

Peter braced himself, knowing Grandpa's position on wolves.

Grandpa snorted. "Young fella, are you from St. John's?"

"Yes, I am," the man responded with an easy grin.

"I guess you and your environmental buddies don't foresee any problems with putting savage meat-eaters next door to folks living in rural towns."

The man adjusted his silver-framed glasses. With a strained smile he tried to respond but Grandpa cut him off. "Tell me, do you have a petition to have the wolves move into your office building in the city? Because I'll gladly sign that!" Then Grandpa stormed into the store.

Peter couldn't just walk away from the bewildered man. "Er…Newfoundland wolves were a distinct sub-species different from any other wolves, including the Labrador wolves. So, no one can ever 'bring back'"—Peter made rabbit ears with his hands—"the Newfoundland wolves." After several seconds of uncomfortable silence, Peter offered to sign the petition.

The truck came to a jerky stop in the same supermarket parking lot, snapping Peter out of his reverie. He knew they wouldn't be in the store for long, thanks to the grocery master file created by Grandpa. The master file listed all the grocery items under the heading of aisle numbers. Once or twice a year, Grandpa went on lengthy hunting trips; so, on the rare occasion that Mom had to pick up the groceries, she was able to use the master file to pre-plan her grocery list by using the aisle numbers for maximum efficiency, ensuring she'd return to the house in the shortest time possible.

Wearing a pastel green sweater, Mom fluttered around like a butterfly in the fruit and vegetable section. She smelled, prodded, and squeezed, picking out the best produce. Peter followed her with the shopping cart to the meat aisle, where she grabbed packaged chicken with quick glances at the dated freshness stickers. By the time they reached the dairy section, she had abandoned all choosing protocols. She flung open the glass door and grabbed the nearest milk carton.

At the bakery aisle, she pitched two loaves of bread into the shopping cart.

"Mom, what did Mr. Doyle say he was looking for?"

"Who?" She started rolling the cart.

"Grandpa's friend, the one we'd never met before. You know, the one in the checkered suit."

She said, "Oh, yes, from the reception. I think he said a bottle of mead. Why do you ask?"

"No reason. Just came to mind. What's mead, anyway?"

"It's an alcoholic drink made from honey." She stopped and looked on her list. "Honey's on my list. Peter, aisle four. I'll meet you in aisle five." She practically sprinted away with the shopping cart.

He returned with a tub of honey to find Mom in aisle five bent over, rearranging the items on a shelf to reach in and search behind. She muttered in an agitated voice, "It's not here. They moved the bags of barley." She straightened and scanned the shelves. "Have they moved anything else?" Her left shoulder started twitching.

Turning her wide, tear-rimmed eyes on Peter, she clutched the collar of his jacket. A few shoppers stared. His face began to heat up. "Mom, I'll find out where the barley's gone, and you can keep going down the list."

"Alright. You do that." She tried to smooth out the scrunch marks she'd just made on his jacket. "Make sure you tell me the number of the new aisle so I can change it on the master sheet."

When he found the bags of barley, he mentally noted the new aisle number: seven. He moved through the remaining aisles with Mom, praying there were no more changes. Peter was relieved when they got in the truck to go home.

From down the street, they could recognize the car with its horrid colours of moldy green, bruise purple, and sallow yellow. In the driveway, Mom parked next to the vehicle with the ABC Realty logo. The front door of the house was ajar. The Bobbleheads had returned.

Peter and Mom placed the groceries on the kitchen counter.

"As you can see, this room is also a good size," Aunt Bea said from upstairs.

"Yes. This could be the master bedroom," said a male voice.

An unfamiliar female voice then added, "And the two other bedrooms are perfect for the kids. By the way, what an interesting iron bed. Does it come with the house?"

As Mom hurried upstairs with Peter following behind, Aunt Bea could be heard saying, "It can be arranged."

"This house is not for sale!" Mom burst into Grandpa's room, startling the aunts and their clients. Peter hung back in the hallway, surprised by Mom's determined stance. Perhaps she could stop the house from being sold, a flame of hope flickered delicately.

Aunt Bea faced her younger sister, spread her arms as if trying to shield the couple from a mad animal, and talked in a low voice over her shoulder. "This is what I warned you about. She's confused. It's not really her house." Clad in her black suit and crowned with a bulbous hair bun, Aunt Bea appeared monumental and immovable.

The couple peeked from behind Aunt Bea at the shaking woman in the pastel green sweater. Mom balled her fists and stood ramrod straight. "I have to ask all of you to leave."

Aunt Bea met Mom's rare moment of assertiveness with a lopsided smirk. Behind her dark eyes, she formulated a sentence designed to crush. "Agnes, take Mr. and Mrs. Park outside and show them the greenhouse."

Mom's backbone splintered and her body sagged at the reminder that her Garden of Eden would be sold with the house. *That was a low blow, even for Aunt Bea.*

Afraid that Mom might collapse, Peter tried to go to her, but Aunt Agnes temporarily blocked him as she led the couple toward the stairs. She lowered her eyes when she passed Peter.

Peter went to Mom and wrapped his arm around her, and she leaned into him like a plant stalk against its supporting bamboo stick.

"Can't you see that this house is not just a house to me?" Mom pleaded. "Think of your nephew. This is the one home he's ever known."

Aunt Bea looked at Peter, and her face softened for a moment. In a sober voice she said, "Dad left the house to all three of us, and I think it's his way of telling us that he loved his daughters equally. So, you see, we must sell the house and divide up the proceeds to honour his will."

"Please, Bea." Tears streamed down her cheeks.

"Don't cry, mom," Peter said, pushing away the loose hairs that were getting stuck to her wet face. Peter wanted to tell Aunt Bea to leave, but he was still holding onto the hope that family bonds would prove to be stronger than the lure of getting richer.

The practiced realtor carried on. "Summer is the best time to sell. No one thinks about moving after school has started and pfft..." she swatted the air, "forget about winter with Christmas and the holidays. And," she cupped a hand around her mouth like she was telling a secret, "next spring, housing prices are supposed to drop. A lot. The time to sell is right now."

Mom cried, gulping air.

Aunt Bea clapped her hands together and bent down to be at eye level with her sister. As if talking to a child, she over-enunciated and spoke in a high-pitched voice. "Don't you want top dollar? Your third will be bigger if we sell now." She strained to look kind and caring, but a gruesome smile was all that she could manage. "We aren't going to charge you the agent fee."

Peter knew then that Aunt Bea's sliver of empathy buried somewhere in her ice-cold heart was no match for her all-consuming greed, and she would not change her mind. He and Mom were on their own. "You don't want to keep your clients waiting," he said.

Aunt Bea stood back up to her full height and pulled down the front of her black suit jacket. "The For Sale sign is going up Monday." She climbed down the stairs with her black-hosed daddy-long-legs.

They had three days to find the money.

7

The Twin That Never Was

AFTER AUNT BEA AND AUNT AGNES DROVE OFF with their clients, Mom went to work in her greenhouse, the one place that could calm her down. While Peter finished putting the groceries away, he thought about why his mom had to brace herself every time she left the house, practically holding her breath—her confidence crumbling with every passing minute until she returned home. He knew the answer. Thinking about that answer raked his stomach.

He went out the kitchen door and walked the short distance to the round greenhouse. When Mom had run out of windowsill space for her numerous potted herbs and plants, Grandpa had built her the greenhouse. Up to now, it had withstood many harsh winters without so much as a scratch. Grandpa claimed it was his great carpentry skills, but gale-force wind, hail, and rain that had pounded the house seemed to bypass the greenhouse. Even on cloudy or foggy days, a stream of sunlight always managed to find its way inside the small conservatory. That was, until Grandpa left this world. Since then, the greenhouse had been continually brushed with same dull grey as the house.

Peter opened the door of the greenhouse and entered a lush and colourful world. The warm, humid air, fragrant with the scents of herbs and plants of all kinds, washed over him. Pots of all sizes, housing healthy and vibrant plants—some with flowers, some not—were hanging from the rafters and were neatly arranged on an oversized worktable shaped like a round horseshoe and followed the curve of the wall.

Mom, with her long, chestnut brown hair cascading down from under a floppy straw hat, lovingly hummed and talked to her plants. Only birds fluttering around her head and little forest animals by her feet could have made her look more like Mother Nature. Looking at her now, no one would guess that this nimble-fingered gardener was the shaking mess of a shopper who had lost her senses in aisle five.

Between Mom's magical green thumb and Grandpa's mystical understanding of the weather, Peter seemed less than ordinary. He must've been asleep the day special

talents were handed out. Well, unless effortlessly finding
every single item in *I Spy* books counted. And that'd be a
pretty boring talent.

"Did you put the groceries away already?" Mom said.

"Yup."

"My poor rosemary, you need a trim." She fussed over

the plant and examined it so close to her face that she could have kissed it. "Pass me the mini shears, please."

All the gardening tools were hung on the pegboard beside the door. Peter took the smallest of the shears and placed it near her on the table.

He took a deep breath, starting the conversation he'd wanted to have with her earlier in the truck. "You don't have Grandpa to do stuff for you anymore."

"No, I don't."

"So, you'll have to take care of things yourself."

She took the shears and started trimming the rosemary plant. "You're growing up fast. You'll help me."

Definitely not what he wanted to hear.

Peter flicked the waxy green leaves of one of the hanging plants. "The Bobbleheads are coming back on Monday. What are you gonna do?"

Mom wrinkled her forehead. "I don't know. I don't want to think about that now. And don't call them that."

He suppressed an urge to rip off the green leaves. "When are you going to think about it, then? When the moving truck backs into the driveway?"

"I can't lose the house. I'll have to find a job." She continued to trim the rosemary, looking at it from all sides.

"Between now and Monday?" He threw out his arms. "It's the weekend."

"I'll apply in stores. Stores are open on weekends. Maybe a plant store."

Even if, by some miracle, Mom did get a job this weekend, Peter didn't believe that she could leave the house eight hours a day, five days a week, when he had just seen that she couldn't keep it together for half an hour at the grocery store. Nor would his money-grubbing aunts wait for the years that it would take Mom to pay back the two-thirds value of the house.

Losing the house seemed inevitable. A surge of anger pointed at Grandpa for making the decision to change his will, and another pointed at the dad he had no memory of for abandoning him all those years ago. But the sole person he could take out his frustrations on was sitting across from him in the sinking boat.

"It's all because of *him* you're this way. He's not even real."

Mom put down the potted rosemary close to the edge of the table and looked him straight in the face. "He exists."

Ever since Peter could remember, there were times he missed his mom even when she was right there with him in the same room. She'd go into a kind of a trance. As a small boy, he'd circle her, clutching a toy in his hands, waiting for her to snap out of it. He had assumed that this happened with all moms.

When he was older, he realized that Mom was not like other moms. On one of their fishing trips, Peter pestered Grandpa until he reluctantly told him the disturbing story of Peter's birth.

Mom, who hadn't liked doctors or hospitals ever since her own mother's untimely passing, had insisted on a home delivery. When she had gone into labour two weeks earlier than expected, she had had her trusted midwife by her side, but not her husband, who had been working offshore and hadn't been able to secure a flight back in time. After giving birth, she had fallen asleep, exhausted, then woken up convinced she had given birth to twins. Mrs. Kelly, the kindly midwife, had looked at her bewildered when Mom had asked where the second baby was.

With no evidence that his wife had given birth to twins, Peter's father, Phillip Hart, hadn't been able to understand or cope with her deep grief and had left his family before Peter turned one. Grandpa had worn an expression of disgust when he used the word "deserted." And Mom had come back to her childhood home, a broken woman with a baby in tow. Soon after, "Connors-Hart" had been shortened to "Connors."

Peter wasn't sure what to think about the supposed disappearance of his twin. But now, more than ever, he wanted Mom to confess that she was mistaken, that it was all a silly make-believe she had indulged in, and that she was ready to be a regular grown-up who could go out into the world and hold down a job. In his heart, he knew that wasn't going to happen. His bottled-up resentment frothed. *Why was I not enough? Why did she have to invent another child?* After all these years, she still held on to the fantasy scenario, crossing over in a trance to spend time with *him* instead of Peter.

"If he exists, where is he? How can you just lose him?"

Her shoulder twitched up and down, the shears clenched in her hand.

His pitch rose. "I think you made him up, so you'd have an excuse for not having responsibilities, like getting a job. Now, we're going to lose our home! Why didn't Grandpa do something, anything, to make you snap out of it?"

As he whirled around to leave, Peter was too close to the table and accidentally knocked the pot of rosemary off the worktable, sending it crashing to the floor.

When Mom saw her rosemary plant half-buried under dark soil and ceramic shards, her face turned as white as one of her delicate orchids. Her eyes welled up, and the corners of her mouth quivered. She was going to cry, and he had caused it, just like her miserable sisters had earlier. He was no better. Ashamed, Peter ran out of the greenhouse.

Up in his room, he paced back and forth. Afraid and frustrated with their predicament, he had gotten carried away. He should've tried to help his mother come up with a solution, but every time he thought about the house, he wanted to hide under a blanket like a little kid. *But I am a kid; she's the adult.* He picked up his pillow and whipped it at the wall. *She's supposed to take care of me, not the other way around.*

Peter flopped down on his bed, his hands behind his head.

Someone had said at the funeral reception that he was now the man of the house, but he didn't feel like one. More importantly, he didn't want to be one. He bitterly wanted Grandpa back.

8
Unwelcome Houseguest

FOR THE REST OF THE AFTERNOON, PETER avoided Mom, wanting to apologize but not knowing how to start. In his room, he dived headlong into a book. He tasted delectable fruits, entered magnificent buildings, and conferred with kings. Strangers and strange-looking beasts became his allies, and they fought and won battles against terrifying enemies who outnumbered them greatly. Peter lived and breathed the stories. He thought that reading must be a gateway into wondrous lands that existed somewhere far away.

As evening approached, the wind picked up and the sky darkened. The pleasing smell of Mom's cooking wafted into Peter's room. Soon, he'd have to sit with her at the dining table. The apology couldn't wait any longer. He closed his book.

As he made his way downstairs, someone knocked at the front door. Peter yelled, "I'll get it!"

When he opened the door, there stood the Mr. Doyle he'd met at the funeral reception. His face was swollen, like he'd been in a fight. Instead of the checkered suit, Mr. Doyle wore a tunic-like shirt and trousers made from an animal leather of some kind. Peter was struck with an impulse to close the door, but before he could act, Mr. Doyle placed his foot on the threshold.

"Hello, Peter. May I come in?"

Mr. Doyle smelled slightly different than he had at the reception: earthy, sweet, and metallic. Peter stood blocking the doorway.

"Yes, of course you may come in." Mom came to the door, wiping her hands on her apron. She gently pushed Peter out of the way, giving him a questioning look.

"Hello, Lily. I was passing near here when it seemed to me that we're about to have one of those unannounced storms."

Mom peered up at the fast-moving clouds. "I think you're right, Mr. Doyle. We're about to have supper. Please join us."

Inside the door, Mr. Doyle took off his sturdy moccasin boots, made from the same smooth hide as his clothes. The foyer light revealed inflamed lumps on his forehead and cheeks.

"What happened to your face?" Peter said.

Mr. Doyle's hand searched for the bumps. He said, "Oh, bee stings," as if he had forgotten about them, which Peter thought was highly unlikely because they looked so painfully taut. Peter narrowed his eyes. *They must have been some bees.*

Mom gasped, "Oh, your arms!"

On Mr. Doyle's lower arms, which stuck out from his tunic sleeves, his coarse hair was matted with blood that oozed from deep gashes.

Mom hurried to her greenhouse and pounded out two kinds of herbal medications with her mortar and pestle. By the time Mr. Doyle sat down at the square dining table, white paste covered every one of his bee stings, and a gooey yellow ointment covered the cuts on his arms.

He sighed. "Lily, your salves feel heavenly. Very soothing."

Mom carried in two plates, each with a scrumptiously-browned chicken leg with the thigh attached, tofu and vegetable stir-fry (Grandma Helen's recipe), and mashed potatoes—mixed with sweet potatoes and grated Parmesan cheese, just the way Peter liked it.

"Thanks, mom," Peter said sheepishly. She gave him a wink.

Using a knife and fork, Mr. Doyle cut the first slice of chicken and placed it in his mouth. He closed his eyes. "Delicious."

Peter suspiciously regarded the old man, who was sitting in Grandpa's chair. The torrential sideways rain that had begun shortly after Mr. Doyle's unexpected arrival showed no sign of letting up. It wouldn't be safe to drive, or even walk, in such a downpour. Knowing Mom would feel obliged to offer Mr. Doyle a room overnight, Peter couldn't enjoy his supper and picked at his food.

Mr. Doyle cut and ate another piece of chicken. "We can always count on a good storm in Newfoundland. My aching joints tell me this one will be raging all night." As if to underscore his words, the long branches of a tree slapped the siding of the house.

Please, Mom, don't ask him to sleep in our house, he begged in his head.

"It's quite a distance to your house from the bus depot. And there's no sidewalk for the most part." Mr. Doyle ate another piece of chicken.

The wind curled around the house. *Please, please, don't say it!*

Mr. Doyle picked up his chicken leg and started to pull the remaining meat off the bone with his teeth. "The long walk drained me. Tripped and fell. That's how I got the cuts on my arms."

Mom opened her mouth to speak.

"May I have another chicken leg?" Peter blurted out.

She looked at his plate. "You've hardly touched the one you have."

The dinner guest moaned and rubbed the elbow of his arm holding up the chicken leg, now picked clean.

"Mr. Doyle, I insist you spend the night. I believe you'll find Dad's room comfortable."

There it was.

"After supper, I'd love to hear more about how you introduced Mom to Dad," she said.

"I accept your kind offer." He cracked the chicken bone with his thick yellowish teeth. "The marrow is the best part."

When Mom brought a teapot to the table after supper, Peter went upstairs. Not that he wasn't interested in the stories, but he was irritated that another old man was in Grandpa's chair and would sleep in Grandpa's bed. He played a computer game, not caring whether he won or lost, then read for a while, trying to block out the sound of laughter from downstairs. When his eyes got tired, he lied in his bed and listened to Mr. Doyle retire to Grandpa's room.

Since that tragic morning, he had gone into Grandpa's room only once—to get the red button from the pocket of the Santa jacket. He had held his breath the entire time, wanting to preserve everything in that room, including the air. Would the room still smell like Grandpa tomorrow? Would objects in the room be moved or rearranged? Grandpa liked to have his things organized in a certain way. On his desk, he liked his writing papers neatly stacked and the tin pencil holder right next to the stack, almost touching but not quite. Peter kicked at the quilt. Mr. Doyle was contaminating the Grandpa-ness of the room.

9

Golden Proposition

THE SANDPAPER SOUNDS OF DRAWERS SLIDING in and out from the next room awoke Peter from an uneasy sleep. Day was breaking behind the thin curtains.

He tiptoed to Grandpa's room and opened the door as quietly as he could.

In the dim room, the hunched over body with the long arms rummaging through the desk drawers cut a menacing figure. Patches of white herbal paste were still painted on his face and his coarse, uncombed hair aimed in different directions. Peter frowned when he noticed that Mr. Doyle was wearing Grandpa's pyjamas.

The door creaked.

Mr. Doyle looked up, startled.

"What are you doing?" Peter demanded from the doorway.

Mr. Doyle motioned as if he was writing in the air. "I'm looking for a piece of paper to write a thank you note to your mother."

Peter turned on the ceiling light and pointed to a stack of paper on top of the desk. "Right in front of you." It was obvious Mr. Doyle had just made up the pretext of looking for a sheet of paper. He had lied, as he had lied about the bee stings.

Mr. Doyle forced a strained chuckle. "You caught me. What I'm really looking for is a large metal button with two holes. Have you seen it?"

Peter crossed his arms and leaned against the door-frame. "I don't believe you're looking for a button either."

"Well, it looks like a button, but it's much more than a button." Luminous eyes trained on Peter. "I have something important to tell you."

Peter's scalp tingled, and he looked down the hallway where his open bedroom door urged him to come back.

"Don't leave, Peter. I can help you save the house."

The hallway faded. "How do you know about the house?"

"I have good hearing."

At the funeral reception, as Peter had pulled Mom away from his aunts, they'd almost bumped into Mr. Doyle, he was standing so near.

The shiny draw of keeping his house eclipsed Peter's distrust of the dubious houseguest. He crossed the threshold and sat on the edge of Grandpa's bed.

After Mr. Doyle turned the desk chair around, he sat down with his hands folded on his lap. Now facing Peter, he seemed unsure what to say. "You'll have to go on a journey…an adventure, really, to a place called Lore Isle, inhabited by storybook-type characters." He appeared apologetic. "I know it must sound like rubbish, but I assure you the magical land exists."

Well, that proved it. The old man wasn't dangerous; he was as nutty as Mom's Christmas fruitcake. Peter stirred to leave.

"Gold," Mr. Doyle said quickly. "If you help me find what I'm looking for, there'll be enough gold coins for you to pay for the house."

The gold coins made Peter think of a hidden pirate's chest that could be only found with the right map. Perhaps Mr. Doyle had such a map or was searching for it. Peter saw himself pouring a glittering mound of gold coins into the hands of his miserable aunts as their eyes bugged out in astonishment. He slammed the door in their open-mouthed faces. *Good riddance, Bobbleheads!*

Yes, gold would do. "But a storybook world... It's not possible."

"Isn't it, Peter? When you read your books, don't you often say to yourself, 'this story feels so real, it must exist somewhere?'"

That was true.

Peter shook his head. "The chance of this Lore Isle existing is one in a billion. A gazillion."

"Well, that gives you a better chance of keeping your house than if you do nothing."

That was true, too.

Mr. Doyle leaned forward. "You have two choices. You can stay here and wait for your aunts to sell the house and kick you and your mother out." He held up his pointing finger. "Or, you can come with me, and I can give you more than a fighting chance to hold on to your home." His eyes glistened. "Poor Lily. You must look after her. She has endured so much heartache."

How much did Mr. Doyle know? Was he referring to the imaginary twin or his dad deserting them or Grandpa's death? Perhaps all three.

For the second time, the caring expression on the old man reminded Peter a great deal of Grandpa.

At that moment, Peter was tempted to say "yes," but what did he know about Mr. Doyle? Almost nothing. He had met the old man for the first time only days ago when he showed up at the funeral reception. Mom remembered that Grandma Helen mentioned him as an old college friend, but Mr. Doyle had not been part of Grandpa's life as far as Peter could remember. Last night, he had showed up at the house uninvited, wearing a strange outfit, sporting savage wounds, and lying about how he got them. Then he used Mom's kindness to spend the night so he could rummage through Grandpa's belongings.

Yet, Peter wanted to believe saving his house was possible. He asked, "Do you have some kind of proof that Lore Isle exists?"

From under his shirt, Mr. Doyle pulled out the leather string he was wearing around his neck and revealed a large iron button. On it was a relief carving of a raven with its wings spread. The leather strand was strung through one of the two small rectangles in the center, which looked like door openings. "This button allows me to cross into Lore Isle. There are two in existence. Your grandpa had the other one."

Peter had seen a button like it before. On the day of the funeral, Peter had gone into Grandpa's closet to search the pockets of the Santa jacket for the red button. He'd seen a metal button on a leather string hanging on the coat hanger underneath the jacket. It must still be hanging there.

Peter's head buzzed in an excited confusion. "Are you saying Grandpa's been to Lore Isle?"

"Yes." Mr. Doyle paused for a moment to let the word sink in. "I think John wanted you to go to Lore Isle to help me."

"Did he tell you that?" Peter asked eagerly.

"No. But, why didn't he leave the house solely to your mother?"

Peter shook his head. "That makes no sense. Why would he want me to go to Lore Isle to get the gold to pay for the house when he could've just left the house to us?"

"John was a mysterious man," Mr. Doyle said.

Mysterious and stubborn and loving. Peter missed him.

"I am not going to sugar-coat. Your journey may be dangerous at times, but I know my way around Lore Isle. And," he put a hand across his chest, "I give you my word that I will guard you with my life." Peter must have looked doubtful because Mr. Doyle added, "In case you're wondering how much protection an old man can provide, I have talents you'll find surprising.

"You must decide now. We need to leave this morning."

"This morning?"

"There is an event happening today in Lore Isle that I cannot miss. It's a necessary visit to get you your reward."

It was soon, but then again, Peter didn't have much time himself as his aunts were coming back in a couple of days with the For Sale sign.

He wouldn't get another opportunity like this. In a way, Mr. Doyle was the hero he'd been hoping for. A grown-up who had the answer to his mega problem. All Peter had to do was follow him, do what he said, and collect his reward. Besides, his whole body tingled with a cautious thrill at the thought of going to a faraway magical land. He was about to jump into one of his storybooks. Plus, it was a place Grandpa had visited. *That's a good omen.*

"I'll go with you, Mr. Doyle, but how long will this trip take? Mom will worry."

Mr. Doyle smiled. "Time in Newfoundland can be slowed down if you have the right friends. You'll be back before Lily has finished tending the herbs in the greenhouse."

Peter thought about his argument with Mom the day before. He still hadn't apologized. Hadn't had the chance since Mr. Doyle arrived. Coming back with the gold would make up for the ugly things he'd said—he hoped.

Mr. Doyle clapped his hands together. "Now, we need to find your grandpa's button so you can go through the portal. But where could it be?"

Peter said, "I know where it is," and walked toward Grandpa's closet.

Peter chased the last bite of his omelette with a glass of milk. Mr. Doyle, now wearing his leather outfit, wiped his mouth on the napkin. "Lily, thank you very much for your kind hospitality. Now that the weather has cleared up, I'll be on my way.

"Please, take all the time you need. I'll be in the greenhouse if you'd like a lift to the bus depot."

Peter followed Mr. Doyle to the upstairs hallway, touching the button that had belonged to Grandpa and now hung around his neck. He hoped it would give him the courage to not back out of going to Lore Isle.

"Change out of your pyjamas. Wear sturdy shoes and bring a jacket. You must not bring anything else." Mr. Doyle pointed a finger at Peter and said firmly, "Absolutely nothing." He waited until Peter nodded, then said, "I'll meet you on the path to the pond."

In his room, Peter changed into a pair of jeans and put on a pair of socks. Then he went to Grandpa's room and opened the closet for the second time this morning. From a hanger, he pulled off a plaid shirt. The sleeves were short on him. Grandpa and Mom were small and elegant like many of the Connorses, while Peter had started a growth spurt and showed signs of being tall and awkward like his aunts.

On his way down the stairs, his throat tightened. He went to the kitchen to get a drink of water. From the window over the sink, he saw Mom at the side of the greenhouse, trying to mend a splintered frame from last night's storm. It was the first time the greenhouse had been damaged. She wore a look of determination as she persevered in her repair work, and her workmanship showed that—well…she was great with plants. He wanted to tell her that everything'd be okay, that he'd soon return with enough gold coins to pay for the house. But he knew if he told her, she'd never allow him to go on this journey to an unknown place. Then where would they be?

He spoke aloud, knowing she could not hear him. "I'm sorry, Mom, for the things I said in the greenhouse. I'll be back with gold soon. Then you won't have to worry about the house anymore."

From the front hall closet, he picked out a waterproof jacket with a hood and put on a comfortable pair of ankle-high hiking boots. He slipped out the front door.

It was a beautiful morning, the kind of morning so fresh and blue that one forgave the weather gods of Newfoundland not only for the last storm but all the ones before.

He walked along the edge of the path, avoiding puddles formed from last night's downpour. Without his grandpa beside him, the walk to the fishing pond was long and lonely. The smell of Grandpa's shirt gave him some comfort.

Near the end of the path, Peter caught up to Mr. Doyle. When they reached the pond, Mr. Doyle said, "I rarely slow down time in Newfoundland when I go to Lore Isle, but you will be missed if you don't return quickly."

He looked up into the sky and shouted, "Raven!" A black bird came into view. "We're going to Lore Isle. Please do your temporal magic."

The bird began circling lower and lower. On its last pass, the raven dropped a feather.

They watched the big black feather drift down, arcing from side to side. It alighted on the water then sank like a rock. Mr. Doyle waved, and the bird cawed.

"The raven's magic slows down time in Newfoundland, while time in Lore Isle passes normally," Mr. Doyle explained. "You go first, Peter."

Peter looked around. "Go where?"

"To Lore Isle, of course. Fall into your reflection in the water," Mr. Doyle said, like it was common knowledge.

"What? The water's cold," he huffed, then looked toward the path back home.

Mr. Doyle said in a kinder tone, "You won't feel anything."

Peter hesitated. "Should I close my eyes?"

"If you want."

If he became soaking wet, the tale of Lore Isle just a cruel hoax, Peter wasn't far from home. He closed his eyes and fell forward. As Mr. Doyle had promised, he did not feel the slap of the cold water, but he felt a sensation like he was getting a pat-down. When he opened his eyes, he was still standing by the pond, dry.

Mr. Doyle frowned. "It didn't work. Empty out your pockets."

Peter fished around his jeans pocket and pulled out the big red button from Grandpa's Santa jacket, which he'd brought as a lucky charm.

"I told you," Mr. Doyle said, "you must not bring anything with you except the clothes you're wearing and the crossing button around your neck. The pond will *not* let you through."

Peter rubbed the red button one more time then placed it on the ground. On his second try, Peter again didn't feel the water, but he had the peculiar feeling that he was perfectly upside down in the water. When he opened his eyes, he was once again standing by the pond, looking at his reflection.

"I swear I don't have anything else in my pocket."

"I know, Peter. We are here."

10

Four Horsemen

THE NEW LANDSCAPE CAME INTO SHARP FOCUS as if it was being created right before Peter's eyes. Unfamiliar green shrubs around the pond were resplendent with budding silver flowers. The syrupy fragrance of the flowers—so unlike the scents in Mom's greenhouse— was so pungent, he could taste vanilla. The majestic trees behind the shrubs were much taller than the ones back home. He could not see glimpses of rooftops in the distance, as he could from his fishing pond. The wild green foliage seemed to go on and on. Only the pond itself was a duplicate.

Everything was dry; no recent storm had visited this part of Lore Isle. The radiant sun was halfway down. They had left Newfoundland on an early morning in August and arrived late in the afternoon on a spring day in Lore Isle. There was a slight chill in the air, and Peter was glad to be wearing his jacket.

With his mouth agape, Peter didn't know where to look. He ended up doing a slow 360-degree turn, trying to take in everything. A butterfly landed on his wrist. He raised his arm to examine the insect's striking copper and turquoise feathery wings. It fluttered away to join its family dancing above the sweet-scented flowers.

"No time to gawk." From a branch of a tree, Mr. Doyle took off a rucksack that he must have left there earlier. "We have a long journey ahead of us."

Surprised by how briskly Mr. Doyle walked, Peter had to break into a run every so often to keep up with him.

Once out of the woods that surrounded the pond, they passed through a vast open area with scrubs, shrubs, and purple and yellow wildflowers. In a field not too far away, large, eye-catching royal-blue flowers bloomed. A great number of unusual, plump black and yellow birds buzzed around the flowers. Peter squinted to get a better look. The strange birds were, in fact, enormous bees gathering honey. There were several hovering above the worker bees, which were even bigger and had hard, silver shells that glinted in the sunlight.

"Are those humongous bees wearing armour?" Peter said, not quite believing his eyes.

Mr. Doyle, who was a few steps ahead, turned to look at the place Peter pointed to. He touched the faint pink scars on his arms and walked faster.

On the other side of the open ground, the wayfarers entered a great boreal forest and followed the barely-there path dappled with sunlight. Tall spears of conifer trees shot out from the plush carpet of bright green moss. Small animals scurried, late for their next appointments, while opalescent dragonflies glided by lazily on the soft breeze. Peter's heart thumped. He peered deep into the woods where there were more shadows than light, hoping to catch a glimpse of, perhaps, a house made with cake and candy, or a heavy-hearted huntsman walking with an alabaster-skinned beauty, or the end of a red cape.

"Where are we going?" Peter said.

Mr. Doyle slowed down to walk beside Peter. "We're going to a wedding."

The wedding must be the event Mr. Doyle said he could not miss. "Are my gold coins at this wedding?"

Mr. Doyle laughed affably. "Oh, I wish it were that easy. I'm looking for a mirror."

"Really? A mirror? Is that what I need to help you find?" Reflecting on the fairy tales he had read, Peter guessed it was not an ordinary mirror.

"It's part of it. I need it to locate my goddaughter."

"What?" Peter looked at him in surprise. "You have a goddaughter here in Lore Isle?"

"Yes. Ella lives with her mother, who is like a daughter to me, but she disappeared two weeks ago. Her mother and I have searched everywhere. We can't find any trace of her."

"How will the mirror help you find her?"

"The mirror is magic. If you ask it about a loved one, it will show you where they are. The mirror belongs to Enchantress Elora of Upland. As tradition dictates, she will gift the mirror to her son on his wedding day."

"So, you're going to ask the enchantress for it?"

Mr. Doyle shook his head. "She doesn't know me from Adam. She'd never let anyone besides her son touch something so valuable."

"Then how are you going to get something you're not even allowed to touch?" Getting the gold coins wasn't going to be as straightforward as following a map to a treasure chest. "The only way I can think of is to steal the mirror," Peter said, hoping Mr. Doyle had a better idea.

"No. Borrow it," Mr. Doyle replied. "I only need it for a moment so I can ask it where my goddaughter is."

"You'll be the only guest who takes a gift, rather than gives a gift."

"Oh, I'm not a guest. I wasn't invited to the wedding."

"What?" Peter's face began to heat up. "Then how are you going to get in?"

"I have a plan to get *both* of us in." Mr. Doyle picked up his pace and Peter had no choice but to follow. Peter wondered, with a knot in his stomach, what Mr. Doyle was not saying. All he could do was trust that Mr. Doyle's plan would be as rewarding as a treasure map.

The path began to descend, mimicking the sun, and they entered a valley with large hills on both sides. A cool breeze stirred, followed by a snowfall, which was peculiar for a spring day with a clear sky.

Snowflakes, large and magnificent, glittering in the light, descended unhurriedly as if in a snow globe. Peter stuck out his tongue to taste the cold, delicate fluffs. Mr. Doyle's eyes darted, resting on the crown of a hill to their right. He emitted a sound like a low snarl.

Peter saw what Mr. Doyle saw—four strange men on horseback watching them from the hilltop. When the horsemen started their steady descent towards them, Mr. Doyle urged Peter to continue on their path. As the riders came closer, Peter saw that they were wearing disguises. They all had masked their faces and wore bizarre clothes over misshapen bodies.

Awash with the terror he'd felt as a five-year-old, he whispered, "Mummers."

Something dark moved on the hill to the left. A pack of six black wolves ran toward them. Grandpa's story about a toddler being dragged away by wolves popped into Peter's head and he wanted to run away, but there was nowhere and no time to hide. The black beasts streaked by them; their heads came up to Peter's nose, their chests wide, bodies long. He didn't dare breathe until the end of the last stiff tail had brushed past.

The wolves raced toward the mummers and chased them back up the hill, and they all disappeared down the other side. It stopped snowing.

Peter's heart drummed wildly. "I could have touched them."

Mr. Doyle looked surprised. "They didn't frighten you?"

"They did! They were huge." Peter took a breath. "But I've always wanted to see wolves running in a forest." He looked in the direction the wolves went. "There aren't any wolves left in Newfoundland, you know."

"Yes, I know." Mr. Doyle considered Peter with the look of someone doing a complex math problem in their head.

"They chased the mummers and ignored us," Peter said, thinking. "I'm surprised there's mummering in Lore Isle. It's not close to Christmas."

"The mummers here are not people in costumes looking for a good time. In fact, they're not people at all."

"What are they, then?"

"Desperate." Mr. Doyle started walking again.

11

A Cursed Wedding

AS THE PAIR MOVED FURTHER ALONG THE path, they no longer stepped on grass wet with melted snow, as it had stopped snowing when the mummers left. They eventually came to the edge of an expansive fen filled with pitcher plants, an unusual-looking carnivorous flower that grew to be about a foot and a half tall. A neat, raised boardwalk unfolded before them, gently winding.

They walked up the steps and followed the long wooden walkway. Stairs led to a huge, circular deck where a majestic tent with multiple spires had been erected.

Through the translucent material, Peter saw the outline of workers bustling to finish the set-up for the wedding. Below, in the surrounding fen, a sea of pitcher plants rolled out on all sides. From this vantage point, he saw, to his surprise, the plants did not grow randomly. They were artistically arranged in intricate patterns worthy of a palace garden. Peter felt a pang of guilt that his mom wasn't here to enjoy the garden with him.

Mr. Doyle led Peter around the tent to the back, where the deck became a narrow boardwalk again. Ahead of them was another circular deck on which a large white service tent had been pitched.

Inside, a short man clad in black dabbed his red face with a handkerchief. His high-collared jacket with white epaulettes looked too warm and fancy for the work kitchen. In a shrill voice, he ordered around the numerous cooks and helpers.

Mr. Doyle walked right up to the high-strung supervisor. "Sir, we're here for the wedding. I've been hired as kitchen help, and my grandson as a waiter." Peter frowned. The lies rolled off Mr. Doyle's tongue too easily.

"You're late! Old man, put on an apron, and boy, go get your uniform."

At the back of the tent, Peter found a dozen young men changing into crisp white shirts, white suits, and polished white shoes. One of the young men pointed him to a clothes rack with the uniforms. After everyone had changed, each waiter was given a pair of white gloves and a black masquerade mask.

The supervisor came to inspect them and yelled at Peter for being the only one to not have cut his hair short, as per the job description. Then he shrilled, "Enter and exit through the back opening of the guest tent. Do not talk to the guests. Your job is to serve them."

Each waiter lined up and waited for his tray of hors d'oeuvres. Peter stood at the end of the line.

In the hustle and bustle, he spotted Mr. Doyle by the stone fireplace, turning rows of quails on a rotisserie. The smell of the browned birds made Peter's mouth water. He hadn't had anything to eat since the omelette at breakfast. Mr. Doyle wiped his greasy hands on his apron and slid over to him.

"As the gifts are opened one by one, it's the waiters' job to move the gifts to a table set up out of the way. Make sure you're the one to move the mirror after it is unwrapped and shown to the guests. Bring it to me. I will ask it my question, and then you'll put it back." He made a gesture with his opened hands as if to say, "simple as that." But Peter wasn't sure it'd be that easy.

By the time the waiters carried their trays out of the service tent and walked toward the guest tent, it was dusk. Peter gasped at the beautiful sight before him. Magical lights had been placed inside every pitcher plant. The burgundy flowers glittered like rubies and the green pitchers of the plant sparkled like emeralds. Bewitching music, tender and hypnotic, rolled in from somewhere out in the fen.

Once in the gossamer tent lit with chandeliers that dripped with crystals, Peter stopped in his tracks and gawked at the guests until the supervisor came up behind him and poked him hard in his back. He shyly approached a small circle of graceful elves dressed in silk tunics with embroidered leaf designs. With their long, silver-ringed fingers, they picked up stuffed dumplings shaped like butterflies from Peter's tray, never looking at him, and continued to converse with each other. When he offered the dumplings to princesses in beaded ball gowns, they waved him off with flicks of their hands and went back to showing off their new dancing shoes to each other. He was most impressed with the shape-shifters who showed off their special ability to change their form. Engaged in a friendly competition, each responded to the efforts of the last shape-shifter by becoming stranger and more beautiful. When one grew a frilled collar and morphed into an opalescent lizard man in Shakespearean pantaloons, the shape-shifter next to him turned in to a verdant tree. Then the leaves changed from copper to silver to gold. Then another took the spotlight by taking the contour of a whale and filling it with small stars, which formed the shapes of ships of various whimsical designs. Peter almost dropped his tray when he started clapping along with the guests.

As Peter continued his rounds, the guests treated him like a walking tray. No one looked at him or talked to him, not even a "thank you." When one dumpling remained, his stomach growled again. He chose the dimmest spot in the tent, turned his back to the guests, and popped the dumpling in his mouth. *Mmm.* Savoury, flaky, spicy, crunchy, sweet, melt-in-your-mouth scrumptious.

"Is it good?"

He spun around, still chewing, and faced his accuser, a girl who looked a couple of years older than him. She wore a simple pink gown. Her pointy ears poked out of her greenish-yellow hair.

"It's delicious," Peter mumbled.

"Are you supposed to be eating the food?" Her eyes, the colour of leaves in the shade, twinkled.

"No, but I'm so hungry. I haven't eaten since breakfast."

"Oh, that's terrible." Her expression changed from one of teasing to sympathy. "I'll tell you what: every time you have one thing left on your tray, come and find me. I'll cover you from view and you can eat it."

He smiled and hurried back to the service tent. The cook loaded his tray with puff pastries, stuffed with quail and herbs and shaped like birds. Mr. Doyle scrubbed pots in a big sink. He looked up and nodded at Peter.

In the guest tent, Peter zigzagged from one conversation cluster to another.

"I am afraid that Enchantress Elora will not be coming to the wedding." Peter's ears perked up. A floating queen bee (about two and a half feet tall) in a black and yellow gown of silk had spoken. Peter inserted himself into the circle by holding out the tray.

"What? Not come to her only son's wedding?" A bearded man in a pointy hat that had celestial symbols orbiting around it took a pastry.

"She's terribly jealous of the bride, my beautiful goddaughter, Sarracena," sniffed the queen bee, suspended in mid-air as her wings beat noiselessly.

"My dear Queen Meliss, is that the only reason?" asked a witch in a black gown so glossy it looked liquid.

The queen bee became flustered. "Why…what else? Of course, it is!"

"There have been rumours that Sarracena is not… right," said a squat man with an oversized velvet hat and rows upon rows of gold chains around his neck. The others in the circle nodded.

Peter blurted out, "The enchantress has to come. What about the mirror?"

The guests in the conversation cluster looked at him and frowned. They pushed him out by making the circle tighter.

When he had two puff pastries left on his tray, Peter looked for the girl in the pink dress. He found her by the busy dessert table; they moved to a quieter spot.

"One for you as well," Peter said.

"Thank you." She took a puff pastry. "My name is Penelope, what's yours?"

"Peter," he said, after swallowing a delicious bite. Mentally, he flipped through *Puddicombe's Mythical and Fantastic Creatures Reference*, but couldn't find a match. "If you don't mind me asking, what are you?"

She tilted her head and gave him a quizzical look. "I am a tree sprite, of course."

He waited for her to finish her mouthful. "Where are your wings?" In *Puddicombe's*, the sprites were shown to be much smaller with wings.

She wrinkled her forehead. "I don't have any."

Maybe Puddicombe's wasn't as accurate as I thought.

As it turned out, Penelope was a distant cousin of the groom, George, who was about to marry the Pitcher Plant Fairy Sarracena.

Peter looked around to make sure no one was near enough to hear him. "I heard Enchantress Elora is not coming to the wedding. Do you know anything about that?"

"Yes, it's not a secret that George and his mum fought about Sarracena. The enchantress doesn't think the fairy is suitable for George. I think she just doesn't want her only child to live here in the fen, so far from her home high in the upland."

"Can they live somewhere between the two places?" Laughter erupted from across the tent. A pair of satyrs with voices as melodic as pan flutes were delighting the princesses in beaded ball gowns.

"Fairies cannot leave their realm of responsibility and as solitary beings they enjoy living alone, but Sarracena is different. A fairy getting married is unheard of."

"Is there any chance that the enchantress might send her wedding gift, the mirror, with a servant?"

"I don't think so." Her eyes narrowed. "Why do you ask?"

"Ah, no reason." Peter pretended to have heard something interesting by turning his head toward a nearby group of dwarves, who each had handsome handlebar moustaches and were drinking from dainty teacups on saucers.

Casually, Penelope took hold of his arm. Sprite magic quivered up his arm and pressed on his heart and he had no choice but to tell the truth, the complete truth.

The words came tumbling out. "I need to borrow the mirror, just for a moment—I need it to help Mr. Doyle find his goddaughter. Then, I will be rewarded with gold coins and my mom can pay off her wicked sisters and we can keep our house—"

She let go his arm, and he had control over himself again. He rubbed his tingling arm, relieved to be able to stop talking. "That's some talent you have."

"It makes up for *not* having wings," she said. Peter laughed. "I wish I could help you, Peter. I sensed how important it is for you to get the gold for your mother. It's a noble goal."

Her understanding hit Peter in a soft place. If Penelope went to his school, they might have become close friends. *I have been lonely for a long time*, Peter realized.

Back at the service tent, Peter told Mr. Doyle the bad news about Enchantress Elora not coming to the wedding. The old man was crestfallen.

Worried that this could mean the end of the road for his gold reward, Peter suggested, "Could we sneak into the enchantress's house and find the mirror?"

Mr. Doyle leaned against the stone fireplace. "She lives in a palace, and I can't begin to guess where she keeps it." The supervisor yelled to Peter that his tray was ready. "You better go. Let me think about it."

With the dozen waiters constantly approaching with trays of food and drinks, the guests were full, and Peter never got down to one, or even two, hors d'oeuvres again.

It was time for the ceremony. The groom—with a bulbous nose and big, round ears—wore a dark blue suit emblazoned with the Upland coat of arms (a great tree that was both a conifer and a deciduous). He walked with his lovely fairy bride—who donned a pastel green gown and wore a circlet of white flowers in her ebony hair—to the bishop waiting at the dais. The couple in love couldn't take their eyes off each other.

After the romantic ceremony, Penelope played a beautiful, soft melody on her fiddle while the couple danced. The guests swayed to the enchanting music and dabbed their teary eyes with handkerchiefs.

Then came the gift opening, and many of the kitchen help, including Mr. Doyle, stood in the back to get glimpses of magical gifts they would not get to see in their ordinary lives.

A round table was brought in and all the gifts were placed on it. The guests oohed and aahed as remarkable items emerged from beautifully-wrapped boxes, such as a golden decanter that never ran out of delicious wine, a vase full of exquisite flowers that never withered, and panels of silk drapery that changed colour and pattern every day. The waiters took the opened gifts over to a long table set up out of the way. As Peter carried the gifts away, he examined each one with great interest.

A woman in a gold gown, whose face resembled the groom's, stormed in through the front opening of the tent. Under one arm she carried a box, in the other hand she brandished a long and crooked wand. The startled guests gave her a wide berth.

She stood by the gift table. "Good evening, everyone. Although I have no intention of partaking in the festivities, I came to give my son his gift as decreed by our family law."

Peter silently cheered.

The groom, George, inched toward her with an arm out-stretched as if he was approaching an animal with sharp teeth. "Thank you, mother." He took the gift box and handed it to his bride, who opened it. George held up the silver hand mirror and showed everyone the back engraved with the family coat of arms and the word *Upland* in fancy let-tering. The guests clapped. As the mirror was gently placed back in the box, Peter readied himself to take the box to the long table, then secretly take the mirror to Mr. Doyle.

Enchantress Elora raised her chin. "You're a fool, George. You know what she's capable of."

"Mother, please," George clasped his hands as if in prayer. "Not on our wedding day."

"She cannot change. It's who she is." Enchantress Elora flailed her arms in frustration, and the guests, afraid of the wand, ducked in waves.

"But she has! She has changed, for me."

The enchantress placed her hands on her hips and sneered, "Are you so sure her cage is empty?"

Sarracena paled.

George clenched his teeth and splotches of red flared across his face and down his neck.

Enchantress Elora's voice became soft and motherly. "It's not too late, my boy. Come back home with me."

"My home is here in the fen with my wife." He pointed dramatically at his bride, who looked like an oracle who has seen a terrible future.

The enchantress gave him a hard look, then raised her wand. "You leave me no choice."

George said, "Mother," in a way that sounded like a question and a pleading at the same time.

In a voice clear as a bell, Elora delivered her curse:

Forests, wetlands, and barrens make up Lore Isle
No longer welcome in Upland, where tall trees lean
No happily ever after, where plants have wet roots
Windswept bleak landscape, your honeymoon scene.

You have your senses, but not for each other
Sight and hearing separate groom and bride
Live out your lives in the barrens alone and lonely
To this enchanted curse, you must abide

From her wand, she shot George with a golden beam that hissed and sizzled. He disappeared in an explosion of shockwaves. And even before the gasp of "No, Mother!" had completely faded, Elora had turned with the quickness of a gunslinger and shot Sarracena with a beam.

Nothing happened.

The horrified guests held their breaths.

Enchantress Elora stared at the fairy bride in disbelief, then tossed her head back and laughed uncontrollably. She tapped her head with the wand. "I should've realized that even *I* could not expel a fairy from her realm." She wiped her eyes. "However, it makes no difference because either way, you'll never see each other again."

To the bewildered bride and the guests, Elora explained that she had cursed the newlyweds so that they were invisible to each other. She intended for both to wander around the rocky barrens of Lore Isle, among the twisted trees and thorny brambles, unable to see or hear each other and unable to leave. "But I was only able to banish my son."

Peter was relieved George wasn't dead.

Wearing a cruel smirk, Enchantress Elora added, "This all worked out better than I imagined, really. Sarracena, now you'll spend the rest of your life racking your pretty head trying to figure out how to rescue your groom, whilst knowing in your heart of hearts that it's impossible." She made a mock sad face. "I mean, how do you find someone you can't see and release him from a place he is bound to?"

Sarracena's head tilted down at the opened box in her hands, and Peter knew what she was thinking. The magic mirror would show her where George was.

The enchantress raised her hand, and the silver mirror leapt up from the box and sailed into her hand. Holding tight to the mirror, she threw her arms in the air. The tent, along with the hanging chandeliers, blew upward in a great gust and disappeared. *The lady sure likes theatrics.* The guests stood like statues in the sober night air on the now-open deck, afraid to make a sound. The jewel-like pitcher plants in the fen quietly blinked their emerald and ruby lights, waiting to see what would happen next.

"This mirror was a gift for my son, and now I have no son." The enchantress threw the mirror, and it sailed up and up like it wanted to join the stars. She pointed her wand at the mirror. Peter pulled his hair. The trigger-happy spellcaster was going to destroy it. He thought about knocking her down and catching the mirror.

Swish!

A bird as long as a small car swooped in and took the shiny mirror in its beak and flew away. The enchantress, like everyone else, stared open-mouthed after the colossal creature.

Enchantress Elora tapped the wand on her palm as she glided over to the decadent dessert table. After popping a petit four in her mouth, she left, with her golden gown sweeping behind her.

The guests murmured, not knowing how to comfort the sobbing bride. The floating queen bee fluttered her delicate wings and flew to her. Sarracena looked up with her tear-soaked face and said, "Meliss, what am I to do now?"

"My dear godchild, thank goodness you have not opened my gift yet." Just two remained unopened on the table. She motioned for Peter to take away her gift, the tall, thin, yellow box. He took it and stood near, not wanting to miss anything.

Queen Meliss said, "I will not give you the gift of mead from my queendom, Sarracena. Instead, I will give you my most prized possession." Out of thin air, a leather belt with dragonfly embroidery appeared.

"This belt will release the wearer from any place they are held captive by a spell or a curse. My dear, I don't know how you plan to find George since you can't see him and you cannot leave your realm, but if you can get the belt to him, he will be liberated from the barrens."

Clutching the belt to her chest, Sarracena kissed the tiny cheek of her godmother.

Penelope, the tree sprite, stepped forward and picked up the one remaining unopened gift, a wooden box the size of a small loaf of bread. "Sarracena, I will also not give you the wedding gift I brought. Instead, I will undo some of Enchantress Elora's curse. If you and George hold each other's hands, you will be able to see and hear each other again."

A shape-shifter who had returned to his resting form of an average-looking man grumbled, "How can they hold each other's hands if they can't see each other?"

Penelope said, "I am not nearly as powerful as the enchantress. This is all I can do."

Sarracena took Penelope's hand. "Thank you. I believe I will see him again."

12

A Spritenapping

THE GIFT OPENING WAS SUPPOSED TO BE followed by dancing, but the groom's disappearance put a damper on the merrymaking and the party disintegrated like tissue paper in water.

Peter went back to the service tent absentmindedly carrying Queen Meliss's original gift. The other waiters were already changing back into their clothes.

Mr. Doyle said, "What's in the box?"

Peter looked down. "Oh, geez. It's Queen Meliss's gift. I'd better take it back."

Before he could protest, Mr. Doyle took the yellow box and pulled out an elegant bottle with a long neck covered in gold bees. "What irony," he mused. He quickly looked around before hiding it in his rucksack. "Go get changed."

When Peter had changed back into his own clothes, he found Mr. Doyle again.

Mr. Doyle slung the rucksack over his shoulder. "Time to leave."

As they passed the main deck, now without a tent, Peter looked for Penelope. He wanted to say goodbye, but he didn't see her anywhere.

Once off the boardwalk, they entered the forest, where they followed a path with moonlit pebbles as white as seashells.

"What do we do now?" Peter said. "Do you have another plan?"

"Nope. Same plan. Get the mirror, find my goddaughter."

"How?" Peter couldn't hide his worry. "The mirror is gone. Who knows where it is by now?"

"I've seen that magpie before. I know where it lives. But..." The old man sighed, pushing back his stringy hair. "Botheration. It's not easy to get there. We need to see a certain blacksmith."

"How far do we have to go?" Peter was getting cranky. He had woken up early, walked for hours, and worked for hours. He and Mr. Doyle smelled like sweat and the food at the wedding, especially the meat. Peter looked behind them to see if a hungry animal was following them.

"It's too late to see the smith tonight. Come, my cabin is not far from here."

It couldn't be close enough for Peter, who longed for a shower and a comfy bed to fall into.

The trees thinned out as Mr. Doyle and Peter walked on the ridge of a cove by the ocean. It was at least a twenty-foot drop to the beach and the dark, frothy waves.

"Your aunts, Bea and Agnes, are they very close?"

"Yes." *Odd that he would bring up the Bobbleheads out of the blue.*

"More than regular siblings, because they're twins?" he said eagerly, as if being a twin was a splendid thing.

Peter shrugged. "I guess so."

"Have you noticed any interesting twin behaviours?"

"Like what?" Peter didn't want to think about the Bobbleheads, but Mr. Doyle seemed keen to discuss them.

"Like, finishing each other's sentences, knowing what the other one is thinking, or sensing where the other one is when they're physically apart?"

"To tell you the truth, I don't see them much. They're always working."

"I see," Mr. Doyle said in a disappointed voice.

"Why do you ask?"

"No reason. Just making conversation."

Mr. Doyle suddenly crouched, pulling Peter down with him. "What are they doing here?"

Peter peered over to see what had alarmed Mr. Doyle.

The moon, much bigger and brighter than the one back in Newfoundland, illuminated a ship with a single square sail near the shore.

"Who are they?"

"Mummers."

From the ship, what looked like colourful laundry blew toward the shore, as quiet as a gentle wind.

On his hands and knees, Mr. Doyle crawled closer to the edge and looked down. Peter followed.

A girl in a pink dress was walking alone on the beach with a wooden box in one hand and a fiddle case in the other. "Penelope!" Peter said. Mr. Doyle frowned and put a finger to his lips.

It began to snow on the beach. The colourful clothes landed near Penelope and filled up with solid figures. They were the same four mummers Peter had seen on horseback earlier. The tall figures surrounded the poor girl, who hugged the gift box she had brought for the bride and groom.

The ocean breeze carried up her voice. "What do you want?" she demanded. Her regal head was held high, but her voice trembled.

The inhaled voice of the mummer was much more difficult to hear. "We want to take the lovely lady on a boat ride. We'll return you to shore shortly."

Penelope tucked the wooden box under the arm carrying the fiddle case and stepped up to the mummer who had spoken. She touched the sleeve of his green coat, worn inside out. "Are you telling the truth?"

The mummer could not lie while the hand of a sprite was on him. He blurted out, "We're kidnapping you. You'll never see your family again."

Penelope calmly took hold of her wooden box again and, with the agility of a doe, she turned and made a break for it—but two of the mummers grabbed her. "Let go of me!" She kicked the skinny leg of one of the mummers holding her, and he yelped in pain.

Peter wanted to help her, but his deep fear of the mummers froze him in place. All he could do was beg Mr. Doyle to do something, and Mr. Doyle replied, "We can't help her right now. We're outnumbered."

The fourth mummer, who was slim and wore a white jacket, said, "Let her go. The girl's frightened."

The mummer in the green coat snatched Penelope's fiddle and wooden box and snarled, "I am the leader and I've made up my mind!"

Penelope screamed, petrified, and the trees in the distance shuddered. The mummer wearing some kind of an animal mask covered Penelope's mouth with his gloved hand and lifted her up. Together, the mummers transformed into colourful clothes again, and billowed and floated toward the ship like a patchwork parachute.

Peter stood up and yelled, "Penelope!"

The ship sailed away on the black ocean.

"No!" Peter stabbed at the black spot the ship had dissolved into. "Where did they take her?" *And why? Was she kidnapped for ransom? Was her life in danger?*

"I have many contacts in Lore Isle. I'll find out where they've taken her." Mr. Doyle patted him on the back. "Come now. Let's get to the cabin."

Tired from a long day and emotionally drained from witnessing the abduction, Peter trudged on.

Mr. Doyle's cabin was small and rustic, facing a small clearing. Trees grew almost right up to the back. Inside, a stone hearth stood in the far-left corner. A kitchen counter ran along the back wall, and there was a water pump over the sink. A table, three chairs, and a worn hooked rug occupied the rest of the room. Off to one side, there were two small bedrooms.

In his cot, Peter, exhausted and yawning, could not stop worrying about the whereabouts of Penelope. His new friend, the one who understood him.

13

Pumpkin

THE NEXT MORNING, IT WAS TIME TO GO SEE A certain blacksmith—the only person, according to Mr. Doyle, who could help them get to the mirror.

Walking east from the cabin, Peter and Mr. Doyle met a well-trodden traveller's road. More than two hours later, high on a hill, Peter glimpsed a village. Handsome brick and timber buildings with steep clay tile roofs lined cobblestone streets. Barns and stables rested on the soft hills that surrounded the village. Peter could hear children playing and dogs barking. A stiff breeze carried the smell of smoke and hot metal up the hill.

Mr. Doyle pointed to two small buildings set apart from the rest of the village. "The blacksmith's house and the smithy."

A sign that read "Smith and Farrier" hung outside. Inside the wide doorway, the smith—an older, short block of a man wearing a leather apron—rhythmically hammered a piece of iron on an anvil. His wiry orange hair matched his thick brows and full beard. With a distinct underbite, his face reminded Peter of a bulldog. The smith stopped working when he saw the pair standing near the doorway.

Mr. Doyle bowed. "Sir, we're in need of your unparalleled skill with iron."

"What do you want made?" asked the smith in a flat tone.

"A pair of cleats that can cross the iceberg bridge."

The smith looked Mr. Doyle up and down with a flinty gaze. "How much gold are you offering?

"Not gold but—"

The smith cursed, took the iron rod, and stuck the glowing end in the large tub of water beside him. The water hissed and released a wall of steam.

Mr. Doyle entered the work area, waving away the steam. "Sir, we can pay with this." From his rucksack, he took out the bottle of mead, which was protected in a large, thick piece of cloth. He unwrapped it with the grand gestures of a magician, then rolled the bottle a little this way and that so the gold-leaf bees on the bottle caught the light.

The smith went back to work, but he was distracted, once completely missing the long piece of metal he was hammering. "How'd you come by that?"

"I have my ways," Mr. Doyle said in a humorous drawl to try to win him over.

The smith's bulldog expression didn't change. "I bet you do. I've seen you around." He reached for another piece of iron rod heating up in the coal pit behind him, placed it on the anvil, and began pounding again.

"Sir, I'm in dire need of the cleats. I can get you any kind of game you'd like. As much as you want. I am an excellent hunter."

"I'm not making anything for you. You're friendly with them wolves. And I don't think that's right."

Mr. Doyle's body stiffened.

The blacksmith gestured toward Peter with his hammer. "Your skinny arms don't look like they're made for striking metal, but I need an apprentice for a pair of gates I'm working on. If you work for me for a month, I'll make *you* a pair of cleats." He licked his dry lips. "And I'll take the bottle of mead, of course."

"A month!" Peter said.

Mr. Doyle motioned for him to quiet down. "Sir, we don't have a month. We need the cleats as soon as possible."

In a loud voice, the smith replied, "Well, I am not going to make anything until I finish the gates. With an apprentice, I could finish them in about two weeks. Then it'll take me another two weeks to build the cleats."

Mr. Doyle deflated like someone had punched him in the stomach. The smith said, "Cheer up, old boy. I'd have wanted years of apprenticeship if you didn't have the mead. That's my final offer. Now, take it or leave it, I've got a lot of work to do."

Mr. Doyle said, "Agreed."

Peter's heart sank. He knew with the dropped raven's feather, time was barely crawling in Newfoundland, but that didn't mean he wanted a prolonged trip in Lore Isle. The longest time he'd been away from home had been a four-day school trip to Saint-Pierre and Miquelon. He couldn't imagine being away from his mom for a month.

The smith laid out his conditions. "The boy works sun-up 'til sundown, seven days a week. The sleeping cot is over there in the corner. The privy and pump for washing are at the back of the shop. He'll get three breaks for his meals, but I'll not provide food for a growing boy who could eat everything in sight."

Mr. Doyle placed the mead on a clean table near the cot. He walked Peter away from the shop so they could talk in private.

Peter held his hair off his forehead. *What have I got myself into?*

"You heard the bigot," Mr. Doyle said. "He won't make the cleats for me. You'll have to cross the iceberg bridge to get the mirror from the magpie's nest. Thank goodness I have you."

Peter lifted a foot to show Mr. Doyle the sole of his shoes. "My hiking boots have pretty good grip. Maybe I don't need cleats."

"The bridge is smooth as glass and hard as diamond. Without the special cleats, you will slide right into the ocean faster than a rolling marble."

Peter couldn't picture what this iceberg bridge might look like. Often in late May, he and Grandpa became iceberg hunters. They'd listen to the news to find out where the icebergs were spotted and track down the best shore to view them. None of the windswept ice sculptures had remotely resembled a bridge.

Staring off into the distance, Mr. Doyle sighed. "Keep well, Ella. I *will* find you."

A month would feel longer for Mr. Doyle, who was obviously torn up with worry about his goddaughter. "A month will go by quickly," Peter said, even though he didn't believe his own words.

Mr. Doyle nodded. "I'll bring you your meals, starting with your supper tonight." He gave Peter a gentle push toward the shop. "Go see what the smith wants you to do."

The new apprentice entered the smithy.

"You have a name, lad?"

"Peter. My name is Peter, Mr....Blacksmith." Wanting to address him with a title and last name as Mom had taught him, Mr. Blacksmith was the best he could come up with.

"Mr. Blacksmith? My name isn't Blacksmith. Call me Pumpkin."

Peter almost smiled. Pumpkin was a round, short man with lots of orange hair. The name suited him.

For the rest of the afternoon and into the evening, Pumpkin made Peter swing the sledgehammer against the hot iron. Pumpkin used one hand to hold the iron on the anvil with a pair of tongs while the other hand tapped with a small hammer to indicate the spot where the metal was to be struck.

Later, not far from the shop at the base of a small U-shaped ridge, protected on three sides from any wind that might whip up, Mr. Doyle had set up a cooking station—a rotisserie spit for a wild turkey. When it was cooked, he called Peter over.

The smith snarled, "Don't take too long," and went inside his house to make supper for himself.

Peter could barely raise his arms to bring the meat to his mouth. "Oh, my arms and back ache. I don't know if I can do this for a whole month."

"It's only your first day. You'll get stronger." Mr. Doyle looked worried that Peter was considering giving up. "There's so much at stake."

"I know. Mom and the house are always on my mind. I have to keep working."

"That's right." Mr. Doyle sounded reassured. With Pumpkin's refusal to make Mr. Doyle the cleats, he needed

Peter to complete the apprenticeship and earn the cleats to find his goddaughter.

"You'll give me the gold coins as soon as Ella is found?"

"I don't have any gold," Mr. Doyle said matter-of-factly.

Peter's entire body tensed up. "What do you mean?"

"You and Ella will help me find what I've been looking for, for a very long time. An egg."

"An egg?"

"Yes. The egg and the gold coins are together."

Peter's stomach felt funny. "Why didn't you tell me before that there were so many things standing between us and the gold?"

"Just steps to one goal, really. You need to work hard for the next month to get the cleats. Just focus on that." Mr. Doyle kept eating, ripping the meat off with his teeth.

Peter didn't like the way the details kept changing. In Grandpa's room, Mr. Doyle had made it sound so simple: step one, help me find what I'm looking for. Step two, be rewarded with gold coins. Now, the steps were: help me find a mirror, then my goddaughter, then an egg. By the way, your gold coins are with the egg, so you have no choice but to keep going with all the steps that keep adding up.

Peter was tired. But he imagined a jewel-encrusted egg the size of a football sitting on a mound of gold coins. Such an egg must have once been owned by a king.

Not long after Peter had finished his supper, Pumpkin bellowed from the door of the smithy, "Are you coming back to work or are the hens going to chit-chat all night?"

14

Storyteller

IN THE FOLLOWING WEEK, PETER SPENT MANY hours striking iron. His other responsibilities included keeping the shop and the tools clean, building fire in the stone forge, operating the bellows to blast air into the forge to make the fire hotter, and cleaning out the spent coals. Pumpkin taught Peter to form basic shapes with the iron, while the gifted smith made his signature ornate bends, delicate but strong. Once used to the gruelling routine, Peter's body no longer ached, and he discovered that he enjoyed working with his hands.

Peter's favourite duty was to hold the reins of the horses as they were getting re-shoed. His gentle coos calmed the nervous horses, which allowed Pumpkin to work quickly and efficiently. Pumpkin called him "the horse whisperer."

Many of the customers were old farmers from nearby villages. "You got yourself an apprentice, Pumpkin," they would comment when they saw Peter. When they finished negotiating the price for the job, the farmer and the smith would try to convince the other that their own occupation was more taxing by bragging about the many body parts that ailed them.

As soon as a customer had left, Pumpkin would become quiet, focused on his work, and would only speak to Peter when he checked on the apprentice's progress. He'd nod and mumble, "Good work," before walking away. The last time he added, "I think you'd make a fine black-smith and farrier one day." Peter was glad to finally know he was good at some things even though the skills were not likely to be useful when he returned to Newfoundland.

At times, Peter was so focused on his work he didn't realize it was mealtime until the smell of cooked meat wafted into the shop. Mr. Doyle spent his days searching for his goddaughter and hunting. He looked weary preparing supper but always greeted Peter cheerfully.

Of course, there were no supermarkets in Lore Isle, and Peter was grateful to the hunter. He felt guilty that he appreciated Mr. Doyle's hunting skills when he hadn't appreciated Grandpa's. "You're a mighty ungrateful lad," Grandpa had said when Peter refused to eat the caribou stew, their last meal together.

But it wasn't fair to compare the two hunters. The game Mr. Doyle caught was more than food; it was currency for bartering with the villagers. He traded for all kinds of food, including baked goods and goat milk for breakfast, and leafy and root vegetables for suppers. The list expanded to include homemade soaps, an extra shirt, pants, underwear, and socks when Mr. Doyle began to wrinkle his sensitive sniffer every time he came near the sweat- and grime-layered clothes Peter wore. Even though Mr. Doyle hunted daily for their food, his clothing made of hide was always clean.

One afternoon, as they ate their midday meal, Mr. Doyle said, "I know where your friend Penelope is."

Peter sprang forward. "Where?"

Mr. Doyle motioned for Peter to lean back and calm down. "One of my contacts told me that a large area around the house the four mummers share has been cleared of trees. Tree sprites draw their magic from trees. I'll bet the mummers have enchanted their house to keep her trapped inside, powerless."

"Where is this house? Can we check it out?"

Deep furrows appeared on Mr. Doyle's brow. "We can't just saunter into the mummers' house without a plan. They're dangerous and have magic of their own. Besides, the smith is not going to give you a day off. Work hard for the cleats. One rescue at a time."

There wasn't much food left on his plate, but Peter didn't want to finish it.

"Oh now, look here. I brought you a special treat: a piece of chocolate cake, the baker's specialty."

Peter shook his head.

"A tale to cheer you up?" Mr. Doyle, a natural story-teller, often held Peter spellbound at mealtimes when he recounted tales from Lore Isle. Mr. Doyle had a deep, soothing voice.

This story begins after many days of fruitless searching for my goddaughter. All of Lore Isle was buzzing about the upcoming wedding for the reclusive fairy and the enchantress's son. When I learned about their family custom of handing down of the magic mirror, I hatched a plan to attend the wedding as a guest. I needed a special wedding gift. The Queendom of Bees was famous for producing marvellous mead. I set out to get a bottle.

Peter wanted to keep pouting but couldn't help himself from getting drawn into the story.

Queen Meliss's castle is the most beautiful structure in Lore Isle. It's entirely made of amber, which reminds the bees of honey. They exclusively used hexagons, the shape of honeycomb, to build the towers and turrets.

Through a loosely guarded back door, I found my way inside the castle. The interior was as beautiful as it was intricate. I made my way into the underground mead cellar. In the centre of the hexagon-shaped room, I saw one bottle of the coveted golden mead on a pedestal. The queen's mead-makers produce one precious bottle at a time. I purloined the elegant bottle and put it in my rucksack.

Peter interrupted. "Isn't 'purloin' just a fancy way of saying 'steal'?"

Mr. Doyle pretended to be offended and lightly tapped him on the head. Peter grinned.

I made my way back upstairs. With all the honey-comb-shaped hallways, I got confused. I must have taken a wrong turn somewhere, because when I opened the door I thought would lead outside, I found myself in Queen Meliss's chamber. In the middle of the room in an amber tub, the old girl was having a pollen bath!

Peter laughed out loud.

Mr. Doyle continued. "I covered my eyes and said, "Pardon me, royal highness. I'll just *bee* on my way." Peter groaned at the pun.

I turned to make a swift exit, but the queen's ladies-in-waiting started shrieking for help. Knights stormed the chamber. They told me to empty my rucksack. I took out the mead, and the queen and her ladies gasped as if I had could have committed no worse crime.

I carefully set it on a nearby side table, and profusely apologized, bowing repeatedly, but that didn't appease her royal jellyness. She started screaming, "Sever his head! Sever his head!"

Well, I didn't like the sound of that. I burst out of the room. The knights, armoured down to the stingers, chased me out of the castle. I ran for my life, covering my head with my arms while the knights stung me with their armoured stingers and retractable harpoons 'til I was clear of the queendom.

"You see, I was telling the truth at your house when I told you I had been stung by bees." He rubbed the faded scars on his arms.

Peter remembered the huge armour-plated bees from the first day in Lore Isle and winced, thinking about how long their mechanical stingers must be.

"After my botched attempt to steal the mead, I had no choice but to change the plan and go to the wedding as hired help, not a guest."

"I think you'd have stuck out like a sore thumb as a guest, anyway." Peter broke the large piece of cake in half and offered some to Mr. Doyle.

As he accepted it, he said, "You're probably right."

"Did you know Queen Meliss was the bride's god-mother?" Peter took a bite of his dessert.

"I had no idea. I almost ran into her after the gift opening. I covered my face with an empty tray just in time and hurried back to the service tent. The bottle I gave to Pumpkin to make us the cleats is the same bottle I tried to steal."

"Serendipity," Peter said.

Mr. Doyle chuckled. "Oh! Now who's using fancy words?"

Peter grinned. "What happens once I get the cleats? Where does the magpie live?"

Mr. Doyle provided no new details and repeated that the iceberg bridge was impossible to cross without the iceberg cleats.

So continued the apprenticeship. In quiet moments, Peter often thought of Mom. He missed her. Even though he knew time in Newfoundland was as slow as watching a plant grow, he was anxious to return with the gold. He wondered if Mom, moving in super slow motion, was thinking about him or the fake twin.

Green foliage flourished and filled in the negative spaces; summer was on its way in Lore Isle. One evening, rain drizzled down after supper was cooked. Peter and Mr. Doyle carried their tin plates into the shop and ate at the table.

With a mouthful of deer meat, Peter said, "There aren't any deer in Newfoundland."

"Do you like it?"

"Yeah. Kinda like caribou but gamier. You must be an excellent hunter to be able to catch game every day."

Mr. Doyle beamed, all teeth. "I do alright."

"Do you hunt caribou as well?"

"Yes. I usually go with friends for big animals."

"The last meal I had with Grandpa was caribou stew." Peter moved around the green beans on his plate with his fork. "We had a fight about hunting, and I refused to eat it. I wonder what he'd think if he knew I was in Lore Isle eating game every day."

"I think John would get a kick out of it." He pointed at Peter's plate with his fork. "Eat your vegetables."

Peter smiled and ate the green beans. "Did you ever hunt with Grandpa?"

Mr. Doyle almost choked on his bite and laughed as if that was a strange notion. "No, we never hunted together. We had different hunting styles."

How different could they be? "Did you guys ever come to Lore Isle together?"

Mr. Doyle put down his fork. "As you know, John and I became friends when we were young men. Several years into our friendship, I noticed he had a crossing button.

He had no idea what it was for. I brought him here on his first trip."

"Did he come here often?" Peter liked thinking about Grandpa in Lore Isle. It made him feel like they were still sharing something together.

"I doubt he came back." With two fingers, Mr. Doyle tapped on the table in synch with his next three words, "The truth is…John and I didn't agree on some things, things that were important to us, and regrettably, we parted ways after his first visit."

"Oh…but you liked him well enough to come to his funeral reception."

Mr. Doyle half smiled and Peter took that to mean, despite their differences, he considered Grandpa a friend.

Peter looked over at the partially finished iron gates, which made him think of something that had been bothering him. "I've never seen Pumpkin work on or give any thought to the cleats."

Mr. Doyle waved away the concern. "Not to worry. The smith has an excellent reputation for keeping his word." Then he produced a small cloth sack filled with wild berries, two tea biscuits, dried fish, and cheese. "Here's your breakfast and lunch for tomorrow. I won't see you 'til suppertime."

Peter looked at Mr. Doyle in worry. "Where are you going?" Mr. Doyle had become his protector and provider as well as the stand-in for his family.

"I'm going to meet up with Ella's mom, Nan. We're going to do another search for her. Go further out." He sighed, as if already defeated.

"Does Nan live far from here?" Peter hoped the answer was no.

Once again pretending not to have heard the question, Mr. Doyle gathered the plates and utensils. "Listen to me carefully. We're being watched. They'll know that I've left you alone and will seize the opportunity to come and see you."

"Who? Who's watching us?" In the dark corners of the smithy, the imagined bogeys opened their eyes.

"The mummers."

The bogeys flew, their flapping wings matching Peter's quickened heartbeat. "You mean the kidnappers?" With their talons, the bogeys drained his courage. Peter didn't want to face his childhood monsters without Mr. Doyle.

"Don't be afraid. I've asked my contacts here to keep an eye on you."

Peter didn't feel comforted by this. "Why are the mummers watching us? What do they want?"

"They want what I want—what's inside the egg."

What does that mean? Before Peter could ask, Mr. Doyle stood up and swiftly exited, leaving Peter alone with his imaginary bogeys.

15

The Mummers' Offer

PETER'S EYES KEPT DARTING TO THE NEARBY wooded hills that lay beyond the wide open doors. He hammered the iron on the wrong spot for the third time.

"What's up with you this morning?" Pumpkin yelled.

A cool breeze slithered into the smithy. Outside, big, delicate laces of snow floated down, and Peter shivered knowing what, or who, came next. From the slow whirl of white flakes, four mummers emerged on horses. They dismounted, their seven-foot-tall frames towering above, and led their leggy horses toward the smithy.

The smith stepped out and greeted them like regular customers.

The mummer in a long green velvet coat—worn inside out to display the tattered green satin lining—stepped forward. He had unusual proportions: narrow shoulders, huge hips and thighs where he must have stuffed his pants with pillows. He spoke to the smith in an inhaling speech, "Our horses need new shoes, and all hinges need to be checked." The white sheet worn over his head clung to some parts of his face as if wet and traced the contours of deeply pitted pockmarks. From the two cut-outs, cold, unblinking eyes stared at Peter.

"As you wish, Green Coat." Pumpkin called for his apprentice to take off the old horseshoes, before hurrying off to prepare his materials.

When Peter took the rein of the first horse, he was astonished to see that the horse, snorting and breathing, was made of smooth and fine-grained wood. A thick brown mane grew from the back of its wooden neck; its long tail swished. The other three horses were also wooden. They looked like carousel horses carved by a virtuoso sculptor that came alive and escaped before they could be painted in garish colours.

The four riders stood at a short distance and stared at Peter as he removed the worn horseshoes.

"Are they coming, Tree Bark?" Green Coat said.

Tree Bark had a mask made with bark that wound all the way around his head, cylindrical like a tree trunk. Bright eyes peered out from the tree knots. Chicken legs with claws dangled from where his ears should be. His purple shirt stretched taut over his stuffed chest and stomach. He had impossibly thin legs and mismatched boots.

Tree Bark said, "No," without looking around.

A mummer who wore a mask made from a skinned goat head with the horns still intact kicked Tree Bark with his heel.

"Ow!" howled Tree Bark. "Why d'you do that for, Goat Face?"

"Your fidgeting is annoying." The mummer wore the rest of the goatskin over his shoulders and down his humped back like a cape. He had placed a pillow on his back, underneath the burlap shirt, to give himself a hump. By far the oddest thing about this mummer was his backwards feet! It was unsettling to see the toes of his boots pointed backwards, yet he stepped perfectly, as balanced as anyone whose feet were on the right way.

The smith returned with the horseshoes. "I see that you have a new mummer in the group."

"Yes," said Green Coat. "This is Red Jacket."

Curiously, the fourth mummer wore a white fleece jacket, not a red one as his name suggested. He was slim, the only one who hadn't stuffed his clothes. Red Jacket's unusual mask covered his entire head and seemed to be fashioned from fish bones.

A horse became spooked when the smith approached with the new iron shoes. It tossed its head and whinnied, revealing teeth made from crooked nails. Peter didn't want to get close to it, but when he saw that the horse was distressed like his mother at the grocery store, he gently pulled down the tall horse's head and cooed, "It's going to be okay." This didn't have the desired effect, and the horse stepped backward, looking to escape.

"You can't use your regular charm, horse whisperer."

Pumpkin said, irritated by the delay. "You're not speaking its language. Talk like a mummer."

Peter tried again in an ingressive voice, inhaling his words. "You're okay. It won't hurt." The horse stopped moving his head, stood still, and blinked calmly. When it was their turn, Peter also soothed the other horses by speaking to them while inhaling.

Green Coat repeatedly asked Tree Bark, "Are they coming?" and Tree Bark always replied, "No," without looking around.

The smith checked the iron hardware on the joints of the horses. He inspected the metal parts of the bridle, paying special attention to the bit. Then he grabbed an indented handle at the side of the horse and lifted. The curved door on the side of the horse opened up. Peter couldn't believe his eyes. The horses were hollow! There was nothing inside the cavity. He guessed the hollow horses were lighter and faster than other horses. The smith raised and lowered the door, listening for squeaks that signalled rusted hinges.

When the smith finished replacing and oiling all the metal parts as needed, Red Jacket pulled out a small leather pouch and counted four gold pieces for the smith.

"Thank you, mummers." Pumpkin bowed. Peter gathered the tools and oil bottles in a wooden box.

Green Jacket said, "Smith, we need a word with your apprentice."

Pumpkin hesitated for a moment, but took the box from Peter and returned to the smithy.

The four mummers crowded around Peter. Red Jacket jingled the coins in the pouch.

A sickening knot formed in Peter's stomach. Their masks weren't masks. The masks were their faces. The fish bones grew out of Red Jacket's greyish skin. Goat Face really did have the face of a goat, with no edge to where the goat face ended and the human skin began. Green Coat was not wearing a sheet, his snow-white skin was loose and puckered in some parts, and cratered and marred where the skin was taut. The rough, cracked bark of Tree Bark's skin continued down his neck and disappeared under his purple shirt. Upon careful examination, Peter didn't see any pillows or towels sticking out from the four mummers' clothes, and he had thought they had stuffed their clothes. Their bodies were truly hard and lumpy.

Suddenly, Goat Face reached for the button around Peter's neck.

"Ow!" Goat Face screamed in pain and took his hand away. A big hole had burned through his glove, and the palm of his hand was blistered.

Peter reached up for his button. The metal felt cool, as it always did. He wrapped his hand around it and held it tightly. *Did Goat Face know what the button was for?*

Green Coat snatched the coin pouch from Red Jacket and pushed Goat Face aside. He scooped out a handful of coins and slowly dropped them back into the leather pouch. "All these coins are yours if you go back home now. We'll gladly escort you back to the pond."

So, they do know about the pond. Peter's mind travelled to the pond on the Newfoundland side and down the wooded path to the house with his mom. He wanted to go home, but Penelope's screams as she was carried off over the ocean, black as indelible ink, rang in his ear. He

had to see her again and make sure she was alright. "I will take the coins and go home when you release Penelope."

Green Coat said, as innocent as a choirboy, "Who is Penelope?"

"The tree sprite you kidnapped over a week ago. I saw you all that night."

Green Coat scratched his face then pretended he

remembered her name. "Oh, her. Well, she's free to go whenever she likes, but she wants to stay with us and be our housekeeper."

Inflamed by Green Coat's assumption he was that gullible, Peter repeated Mr. Doyle's guess. "You got rid of the trees and put a spell on the house so she can't leave."

Tree Bark took the bait and said proudly, "We had to. All sprites are real good fiddlers, and we likes to dance every night." *As if that justified a kidnapping.*

Green Coat slapped the side of Tree Bark's head. "Shut your trap, you fool."

Peter had confirmed Mr. Doyle's suspicions.

"Free her immediately!" Peter commanded, but he knew the loathsome foursome looking down on him must be thinking, *Or what?*

Red Jacket said, "If you take the coins and allow us to give you a ride to the pond, we will release her the moment we get home." The thin mummer was calm, different from the other three who buzzed with the impatience of an evil fairy tale stepmother desperate to get rid of the children before their father returned home. "All your problems will be solved," Red Jacket added.

All my problems, but not Mr. Doyle's. Even if he was positive Penelope would be released, Peter couldn't abandon the old man now.

Red Jacket must have sensed his conflict. "Would you like to hold the gold in your hands and think about it? Take all the time you need."

Well, there's no harm in that. Peter held out his hand, eager to feel the heavy coins.

Tree Bark, still staring at Peter, shouted, "They's coming! They's coming!"

Pumpkin appeared at the door of the smithy. Peter noticed an approaching rumbling sound.

A dozen wolves charged out of the forest, snarling and baring their teeth. Pumpkin swore out loud, rushed over, and pulled Peter into the smithy. Grunting with exertion, Pumpkin began rolling the big, heavy door shut.

The mummers hurried onto their horses. Peter saw that Tree Bark also had eyes in the back of his head; that's why Green Coat kept asking him "Are they coming?" Tree Bark had used the eyes in the back of his head to continually scan the forest for wolves.

Before that surprise could wear off, Peter got an even bigger shock. As Red Jacket turned his horse around, his white fleece jacket flapped open, revealing a red lining made from a waterproof material. Red Jacket was wearing Grandpa's Santa jacket, inside out.

Pumpkin slammed the door shut. Peter stood dumbfounded in the dark.

16

Open Pumpkin Carriage

WHEN MR. DOYLE RETURNED AT SUPPERTIME, Peter ran out to him and breathlessly reported the mummers' offer of gold coins.

Mr. Doyle seemed to be in a disagreeable mood. "You have no patience. Why would you even contemplate taking their gold? The gold meant for you is with the egg!"

Peter fell silent. *Why is he getting so upset?* he wondered. *I didn't take the gold.*

Mr. Doyle's amber eyes flashed as he thumped his fist into a calloused palm. "We made a deal! Yet, you considered letting the mummers give you a ride to the pond.

How can I trust you now?" He turned away like he couldn't bear to look at Peter anymore.

Mr. Doyle had never yelled at him like that before.

Peter replayed Mr. Doyle's last words. "Hey, wait a minute. I didn't tell you the mummers offered me a ride to the pond."

"The wolves told me. They have excellent hearing," he muttered, poking the fire with a stick.

Peter stepped around the fire to face Mr. Doyle. "The wolves understood what the mummers said and were able to tell you?"

Mr. Doyle sat down on a rock and turned a plump bird on the spit roast. He did not make eye contact. "Yes."

Peter dug his hands deep into the pockets of his jeans. "So," he pieced together what Mr. Doyle was reluctantly admitting, "the wolves were the contacts looking out for me while you were gone?"

"Right."

"Let me get this straight: you can communicate with the wolves. You can understand them, and they can understand you?"

"Yes." Mr. Doyle kept looking at the fire.

Peter was getting tired of one-word answers. His hands flew out of his pockets. "How? How's that possible?"

"Let's just say...I have an ear for foreign languages."

Another off-the-cuff response. Peter was about to raise his voice to get some real answers when Mr. Doyle buried his face in his hands.

"We still couldn't find any trace of Ella." The old man was hunched over, his bristly hair matted down with sweat from walking all day in the sun, and his hide clothes hung loose like he was dehydrated.

"I'm sorry, Mr. Doyle. I should have asked about the search first." Peter wanted to hug Mr. Doyle as Grandpa had hugged Peter when he had a bad day.

Mr. Doyle grabbed Peter's hand and pulled him down so Peter was sitting. "Do you have any sense, any gut feeling of where Ella is?" The fire danced in his eyes, and he looked as mad as a hatter.

I've pushed him over the edge by going on about the mummers' offer of gold, Peter thought. He squeezed Mr. Doyle's hand. "You can trust me to get the mirror."

Mr. Doyle patted the top of Peter's hand before he let it go.

Peter didn't tell him about one of the mummers wearing Grandpa's Santa jacket. It was just a coincidence. Red rain jackets were sold in stores all over; there might be a similar red jacket or two even in Lore Isle. Although the seven-foot-tall Red Jacket had the same proportions as Grandpa, Peter couldn't bring himself to think that the mummer with the fish bone face could somehow be him. Grandpa was dead, he told himself. No matter how much he wished it to be otherwise.

Tense, Pumpkin continued to work on the ornate gates. Over time, the metal transformed into an exquisite piece of art. The climbing metal vines with spiralling tendrils and hanging berries looked real, as if living vines at the peak of their beauty had been dipped in liquid metal.

Late one evening, Peter helped the smith brush off the oxidation scales with a wire brush and polish the gates with beeswax to prevent rusting. These were the final steps to complete the gates. When they finished, the smith uncorked the bottle of mead Mr. Doyle had given him and poured himself a large cup. "Delicious," he said, while admiring his handiwork.

In the warm shop, Pumpkin shivered. He poured himself another cup of the strong brew.

Hoping the smith would soon start working on his cleats, Peter went to the forge to fill it with coal for tomorrow.

Thud.

He turned around and saw Pumpkin splayed out on the ground.

Peter dropped his shovel and rushed over to help the drunken man back up on the stool.

"Lad, do you know who the gates are for?" he slurred.

"No."

"It's for Racem—one of the fairies. He is the fairy of the wild berries. Fairy, berry. Hey, that rhymes!" The smith giggled and then started to cry. "I really dread it when I get a commission from a fairy."

"'Cause they won't pay?"

"Not that," Pumpkin said. "In fact, they pay very well. They'll never try to swindle you."

"Then why?"

"Fairies have tempers like the Lore Isle weather. You never know when they'll turn. One minute you're talking to a fairy and he is so witty and charming, you relax, forgetting that they're solitary creatures who want you to leave as soon as possible. Then you say something innocent, which, for some reason, offends him and, *bam*! He curses you."

Pumpkin almost slipped off the stool in his excitement. Peter quickly propped him back up and said, "And that's bad."

"Ha! That's an understatement if there ever was one. My boy, when a fairy curses a human, a mere mortal, it cannot be undone. Even if the fairy himself is sorry for having cursed you, he cannot take it back. And tomorrow I deliver the gates to Racem, the most volatile of all the fairies."

"You don't have anything to worry about." Peter walked up to the gate for a closer look. "I've never seen anything so amazing."

By chance, he noticed a built-in lock. The small, round lock was easy to miss in the gate's busy design. On either side of the keyhole was a miniature scaly lizard that looked real, like they could crawl away if they chose.

"Did you make a key for the lock as well?"

"No. The key and lock are dwarfmade. My lizard design over it is a concealer."

"Is there something special about locks made by dwarves?" Peter closed one eye and peered through the keyhole.

"Come here. I'm gonna to tell you a secret about them."

Intrigued, Peter sat on the stool beside the smith and leaned in. The alcoholic vapours from Pumpkin's breath stung his eyes.

Speaking slowly in slurred words, the smith said, "When I make a delivery to a fairy, he always asks if I've made only one key—the one I just gave him. And I say yes because it's the truth, and the fairies know when you're lying. But I'm afraid I'll say something by mistake and be locked up forever behind the gates I laboured on with my own hands..."

When Pumpkin stared at his palms with his twisted eyes and didn't move, Peter nudged him.

"Wha?"

"You were telling me a secret about the locks."

"Oh, yes. Dwarfmade locks can be opened with a key *and* a code. The lock comes already set up and is delivered through the post. The dwarves are discreet and know the words I want to use for opening my locks are 'Open Pumpkin Carriage.'" The smith giggled. "I'm thinking, even if I's in a bad way, I'd still remember them words. As soon as the lock clicked open, I'd run the heck out of the fairy's realm. The fairies cannot leave their land, you know."

Peter remembered poor Sarracena, unable to leave her realm of the pitcher plants to look for her groom.

When Pumpkin garbled his words so much that Peter couldn't understand him, Peter helped the rubber-legged smith to his house. They entered the front door, which opened to a cozy kitchen with black and white checkered linoleum tiles. It was a small place, and Peter found the bedroom easily. As soon as Peter laid Pumpkin down on his bed and removed his shoes, the smith belched and started snoring.

Something glittered in a dull, iron bowl on top of the dresser.

Peter peered in and saw the gold coins the smith had received as payment. It must have taken him many years of hard work to earn so many. *Pumpkin couldn't possibly spend all those coins, he lived so modestly.* Peter grabbed a handful. *Pumpkin wouldn't even notice…unless he had counted them.* Could he rob his boss? He liked the smith. Pumpkin was not warm and fuzzy, but he was always straightforward with Peter and not stingy with praise for a job well done. Peter put the coins back and returned to the shop.

17

The Guardian of the Egg

THE NEXT MORNING, THE SMITH SHUFFLED into the shop cradling his head. He gave no indication that he remembered the conversation from the night before. After breakfast, Mr. Doyle stayed to help load up the horse cart, one gate at a time. Peter was amazed by how strong Mr. Doyle was when he lifted and carried the heavy gates. As Pumpkin finished tying the gates down in the cart, Peter gave the two muscular (real) horses a carrot each, and they nickered.

With doleful eyes and a downturned mouth, the hungover smith grabbed the reins and started to drive away.

Peter jogged several steps beside the cart and said, "Good luck, Pumpkin. Leave the fairy realm as soon as you can." Pumpkin raised two fingers to his head in a salute.

Outside the shop hung a sign that said, "Smith away today."

Peter was left with a half-day's work. Bent over the worktable, he cleaned the tools, thinking about what Pumpkin had said about the volatile temperament of fairies. Since fairies were easily offended, he hoped the smith spoke as little as possible. But then again, being quiet could be misconstrued as being unfriendly. At least he has the secret magic words: "open pumpkin carriage"—unless he gets turned into a toad or a bat and can't speak. Then who'd make the iceberg cleats? Now Peter was really worried.

When Mr. Doyle arrived at lunchtime, he had no game with him. "We're going fishing!" He held up two rods and a bucket of worms. Peter's face broke into a wide grin.

They cut through the main street of the village, which was lined with charming stores. The shoppers and strollers wore practical and streamlined versions of what Peter would call medieval clothes: calf-length dresses, tunics, and leggings were trendy here. Muted pastel colours mixed with bold patterns made the clothes look modern.

Mr. Doyle elbowed Peter. "I get your breakfasts from this baker."

A stocky man wearing a baker's cap and frilly white apron stood in the doorway of a store with a big chimney.

He looked up from reading and waved. The baker looked to be thirty years old or so.

"What are you reading there, Hans?" Mr. Doyle said as they approached him.

"Lies an' truth," he said, waving a newspaper. The two men laughed. "You must be Peter." Hans slipped the folded newspaper under an arm and offered a hand. They shook. "Whoa! Strong grip, my young friend."

"What did you expect from a blacksmith's apprentice?" Mr. Doyle looked proudly at Peter.

Hans turned to Mr. Doyle. "Any good news on Ella?" Mr. Doyle shook his head.

Hans's smile drooped. "We're both missing a loved one. I haven't seen my sister Greta for years. Since she went to the other side."

"What do you mean by 'the other side'?" Peter asked. Hans glanced at Mr. Doyle and, reading something in his face, did not answer.

"Hold on a minute, b'ys," Hans said and disappeared inside the bakery. He came back out with a loaf of bread and a bottle of cider. "These will go well with all the fish you'll be catching."

The glazed bread was studded with partridgeberries, cloudberries, and walnuts. Peter's mouth watered looking at it.

Peter and Mr. Doyle thanked the baker and walked on. Not far beyond the town, they arrived at a pretty pond rimmed by a beach of blue and green pebbles.

"What kinds of fish live in this pond?" Peter asked.

"Perch, catfish, sunfish, eels, bass, flounder, trout—you name it.

After he hooked a worm, Peter eagerly cast his line with a small metal sinker.

It wasn't long before the fish started biting. They caught all kinds of fish—some so strange, neither one could say what they were. "I'd bet Grandpa would know." Peter's eyes welled up, and he looked away to wipe them.

Mr. Doyle said, "No one knew more about fish and fishing than John," and rested a hand on Peter's back for a moment.

They released the fish they didn't like the look of and cleaned the ones they wanted, skewered them, and cooked them over an open fire, as Peter had done many times with Grandpa.

Thrilled to be out of the dark shop, Peter suggested they have fish again for supper. So, they spent the afternoon talking. Filled with nostalgia, Peter once accidentally called Mr. Doyle "Grandpa." He turned beet red and was grateful that Mr. Doyle pretended not to have heard him.

"This is the best day I've had in a long time."

"For me, too." Mr. Doyle passed him the bottle of apple cider.

Peter poured some into his tin cup. "The only thing that could make the day more perfect is one of your stories."

Mr. Doyle beamed. "I'll tell you a story from Newfoundland. It's a true story and just as fantastic as any Lore Isle tales."

Peter gave an enthusiastic thumbs-up.

"A long time ago in Newfoundland, there lived a loving couple," Mr. Doyle began.

As the years rolled along, and the husband and wife grew older, their happiness turned to anguish because no child had been born to them.

One beautiful autumn afternoon, the wife, in a sad reverie, went for a walk. When the trees cast long shadows, she came to a tall and narrow cabin. It was empty except for an exquisite tree growing from the dirt floor up to the ceiling. The tree bore large, red-speckled fruit, the likes of which she'd never seen before. She ate the fruit, wiping the sweet juice on her sleeves.

After she had had her fill, she heard a curious whimper. She followed the sound outside to the edge of the nearby woods. There, she saw a wolf sitting with its hind leg caught in a hunter's trap.

Frightened, she turned to run when the wolf said, "Wait!"

She couldn't believe her ears. She turned and stared at the wolf.

"I can smell on your breath the juice of the forbidden fruit from the tree of life. There will be consequences."

"I didn't know the fruits were forbidden," the wife protested. "How can I make up for my wrongdoing?"

"You can start by releasing me from this trap."

The wife found a sturdy stick, jammed it between the teeth of the clamp, and, with great effort, pried it open. The wolf stood, looming over the woman, and motioned with his head for her to follow him back to the cabin.

He told her to climb the tree, look for a small nest, and retrieve the egg in it. The wife carefully climbed and when she had almost reached the ceiling, she spotted a nest spun out of gold. In it, she found an ordinary-looking egg, then descended the tree.

The wolf spoke in a deep voice, "The egg is your reward for saving my life. Take it home and open it. A child that is both man and wolf will come forth from the egg, and this child will have to perform a difficult task."

The wolf told her to take the large metal button hanging from his neck. She was afraid to reach so close to the wolf's long jaws but obeyed.

"When the child grows up and he sees wolves being hunted toward extinction, he must place two young wolves in the magic egg he was born from and keep them safe," the wolf said.

The woman ran home with the egg and excitedly told her husband. She placed the egg on their bed and opened it neatly in half. A bright and shimmering golden dust fluttered out and came together to form a solid shape. The shape became a healthy baby boy. The couple hugged and cried tears of joy. They named him Noah, and the new parents chose to forget all about the wolf business.

One day, two-year-old Noah was playing around his mother's laundry basket. As she reached up to secure a sheet on the washing line with a clothespin, she heard her son sneeze. She turned to him, saying, "Bless you," and was shocked to see a wolf cub with soft brown fur wearing her son's clothes. When the wolf cub sneezed, her son returned. What the wolf in the forest had told her was true: her son was man and wolf.

As Noah grew older, these accidental transformations happened less often. When he could completely control his gift, his parents begged him not to turn into a wolf, for there was a government bounty on wolf skin.

Noah had a big heart and loved all forest creatures. He was always on the lookout for any living thing in need of help. He freed animals from snares and traps, and tended to their wounds. No creatures were too small for saving. Drowning ants were rescued from pockets of rainwater and relocated onto dry leaves; slow-moving snails were picked up from footpaths and placed on moss-covered logs.

Most of all, he was fascinated by the wolves. He didn't go near their dens, but admired them from afar. He understood their language. With his acute sense of hearing, he eavesdropped on them, laughing when a wolf played a trick on another and crying with them when one died.

By the time Noah was fourteen years old, the wolves were being hunted at an alarming rate and he knew it was a matter of time before the wolves were wiped out. Every day he puzzled over how he could save them.

One morning, Noah's mother's delicious porridge was bubbling in a pot. Noah went to the cupboard and reached for a large bowl at the back and in the bowl he found an egg and a large iron button with a raven design on a leather string.

He said to his parents sitting at the table, "What are these?" They looked at each other as if to say, *it has caught up to us.*

Noah's mother reluctantly told him everything that had happened on that extraordinary autumn evening fourteen years ago. His mother thought Noah would be angry, but he was thrilled he had been chosen to save the Newfoundland wolves. Setting out on his journey, he tied the button around his neck, placed the egg in his pocket, and carried a sack in which his mom had packed an oatcake and a canteen of water.

Not knowing which way to go, he let his intuition guide him through the forest.

After about an hour of brisk walking, he heard a frail caw. Down by his feet was an injured raven. "Poor feathered friend." Noah gave the bird a piece of his oatcake and some water. As he set the broken wing, the button on the string around his neck dangled in front of the raven's beak. The bird cocked his head when he saw the button.

Something rustled in the leaves.

The jittery raven awkwardly flew up to the highest branch it could manage. From between the trees, an ancient wolf emerged followed by six more—the last remaining Newfoundland wolves. The old wolf said, "Open the egg, Noah, and place it between the two adolescents."

The chosen male and female wolves stepped forward. When Noah placed the opened egg between them, the young wolves yawned and fell into a deep slumber. They began to glow, transformed into floating golden dust, which poured into the egg, and the egg snapped shut.

"You're our one hope, Noah, Guardian of the Egg," said the old wolf in a tired voice. "Take it to Lore Isle. Only someone with wolf blood can harm the egg, and we know you will protect it."

Noah's head swam with excitement. "How do I get to Lore Isle?"

"Go through the pond. You have the button," the old wolf replied.

Gunshots rang out and the wolves ran. With a heavy heart, Noah knew the grim destiny that awaited them.

The raven alighted on Noah's shoulder, nodded his head, then flew ahead low. Noah followed. They arrived at an ordinary pond surrounded by trees.

"I don't know how long I'm supposed to stay in Lore Isle. My parents will worry," Noah said.

The raven nodded. With his beak, the raven plucked one of his feathers and dropped it into the pond.

Holding on to the egg, Noah fell into his reflection. Raven rested beside the sack, helped himself to more of the oatcake, and waited for Noah's return.

Noah reappeared looking a little older.

He told the raven that he had lived two years as a wolf with the black wolves of Lore Isle, who were eager to help him protect the egg. But with no one ever coming for the egg and the egg not seeming to be in any danger, he thought it did not merit such a scrupulous safeguard. He had become lax with his duties as guardian, and the egg had gone missing. He had lost the egg! It was not his intention, Noah explained to Raven. But the intention was meaningless. Only the outcome mattered.

"Noah in the story was my Sunday school teacher," Mr. Doyle said. "I loved him like he was my own grandfather. He often returned to Lore Isle to look for the egg, but he never found it. On his deathbed, he made me promise that I'd keep looking for it. I was glad to carry his torch."

Mr. Doyle sighed deeply. "But I've not had better luck. Here I am, an old man myself and still searching—but," he said with determination, "I can't let Noah down."

Whoa. Peter was not disappointed that the egg wasn't football-sized and encrusted with jewels. The fact that two Newfoundland wolves still existed was sky-full-of-shooting-stars awesome. And who knew that a lycanthrope, a magical being that could live both as a man and wolf, had lived in Newfoundland of all places? This was one of the best days ever.

The two fishers walked back with their catch. When they came by the bakery, they went inside and gave a couple of the fish to a pretty woman with sky-blue hair.

When they left the store, Peter asked, "Was that the baker's wife?"

"No," Mr. Doyle laughed. "That was the same baker, Hans. He's a shape-shifter."

"Really?" Peter looked back toward the bakery.

"Shape-shifters have regular jobs, too."

Shape-shifting could be a formidable power in the wrong hands, Peter thought.

They walked back to the smithy just in time to see Pumpkin ride up with a big smile on his face. Peter was glad to see the smith had not been turned into a toad or a bat. He ran up to the cart holding a couple of fish he had brought back for the smith.

18

Whale Mine

THE SMITH, IN A GOOD MOOD, MADE DRAWINGS for the iceberg cleats. He measured Peter's feet from all angles, recorded his height and weight, and studied his gait and posture.

After he completed the drawings, he said, "These cleats will be for you only. No one else will be able to wear them."

"Alright."

His eyes drilled into Peter's. "Lad, are you sure you want the cleats?"

"Of course I do."

Pumpkin grunted. "Heat up the forge."

The cleats were difficult to make. For two weeks and two days, Pumpkin worked on them every chance he had. The bottoms of the cleats were lined with long, sharp iron spikes—all slightly different shapes, heights, and textures. Each shoe had six pairs of ingenious curved hinges, and six intricate clockwork clasps that, with a touch, fastened over Peter's boots.

Peering through a magnifying glass attached to a headband, the smith performed an endless amount of fine tuning. Like an operating room nurse, Peter was ready with an array of tools (many designed by the smith himself) to hand to the metal surgeon as he called out for them. More and more, Peter could anticipate the tool Pumpkin would need next and passed it to him before he asked for it.

On the last night of the apprenticeship, as Peter swept, Pumpkin sharpened the cleats and made final adjustments.

"Lad, I know where you're going tomorrow. There's just one reason for wanting the cleats."

Peter stopped sweeping. "You know I'm going to look for a mirror?"

Deep grooves formed on his forehead. "Bunkum! You're after the gold in the leprechauns' Whale Mine."

Peter perked up. "What mine? There's gold in the mine?"

Pumpkin pointed his tool at Peter. "Don't play games with me."

"Honest, I'm not. I need the cleats to find a mirror for Mr. Doyle."

Pumpkin's face darkened with worry as it had the night before the delivery of the gates. "I don't trust your Mr. Doyle. He's friendly with them wolves." Pumpkin's unblinking eye, magnified by the lens attached to the headband, looked serious. "Are you two kinfolk? Are you family?"

"No." Peter capped the top of the broom handle with both hands.

"Have you known him for long?"

"About a month."

"That's not a long time." Pumpkin picked up a new tool.

"But we've become good friends," Peter said, feeling defensive, and started sweeping again.

"I hope you know what you're doing, cause I heard the leprechauns have some kind of a nasty pet."

"He wouldn't send me into danger," Peter said confidently, but somewhere in his head there was a warning bell going off.

"Why doesn't he go into the mine himself?" Pumpkin's tone said *checkmate*.

Peter turned and faced Pumpkin squarely. "He wanted to, but you refused to make him the cleats."

"Oh, right... Not one of my best decisions," Pumpkin grumbled. Then he opened one of his desk drawers and motioned for Peter to come over. "I have a gift to make it up to you. A family heirloom." He held out a small candle in a simple iron holder and said, "Light!"

The dimly lit shop filled with bright light as the candle illuminated. The smith blew it out like an ordinary candle. He placed it in Peter's hand. "It's a dark place you're going to tomorrow."

The next the morning, Mr. Doyle came to fetch Peter for the last time. He brought the rucksack for the cleats and dried fish, bread, cheese, and two water canteens for their journey.

Pumpkin shook Peter's hand. "I'm gonna miss having an exceptionally fine apprentice."

Peter was touched. "Thanks for everything, Pumpkin."

From the big front pocket of his leather apron, the smith took out a handful of gold coins. "Will these be enough, so you won't have to go to that godforsaken place?"

Gold to go back home with! Peter felt he could float back to Newfoundland.

Thrilled, Peter reached out to accept, when Mr. Doyle slapped his hands down and said, "No thank you." Peter crashed to earth. "We'll be on our way." Mr. Doyle seized Peter by the arm and pulled him away.

"Good luck, Peter!" Pumpkin yelled as he dropped the coins back into his front pocket.

As the village fell behind them, the travellers entered a forest with a sharp scent similar to spruce.

With the cleats in the rucksack on his back and his jacket in his hand, Peter traipsed beside Mr. Doyle. "Pumpkin said we must be headed to the Whale Mine." He kicked a stone.

"Did he now? Well, he's right."

"He also said there are gold coins in the mine."

"Sure are," Mr. Doyle said, continuing to look forward.

"I suppose those aren't for me either."

"Nope, they're not."

Peter stopped walking and threw down his jacket. "Is there something special about the gold coins with the egg? Gold is gold. The mummers wanted to give me gold, and your wolves chased them away. Pumpkin offered me gold, and you turned him down. Why? What's going on?"

Mr. Doyle faced him. "You help me find the egg and you get the gold found with it. That's the deal."

"Why couldn't I take Pumpkin's gold and still help you find the egg?" Peter's outstretched hands said, *isn't that reasonable?*

"Because you wouldn't be motivated to get to the end if you already had the prize in your hand." Mr. Doyle jabbed a finger on Peter's palm.

"I see," Peter said bitterly. "In other words, you're going to make sure I don't get what I want until you get what you want. That's so unfair!"

Mr. Doyle looked tired. "You have to trust me."

Peter snorted. "Even though you don't trust me." He snatched up his jacket, knowing he had no other choice but to keep following Mr. Doyle's plan. He had to believe that, in the end, both would be holding what they wanted.

They walked a long way, not speaking until they came to a steep cliff's edge. Peter looked straight down and saw it was a long drop to the jutting rocks below. A blue-green wave came in with a deafening roar, hurled itself against the purplish jagged rocks, and changed into white foam before receding, making room for the next wave to do the same. Peter was mesmerized by the relentless rhythm until Mr. Doyle tapped him on the shoulder and pointed to something far out in the murky sky.

A gust of wind shredded the mist to reveal an island shaped like a whale, suspended high above the ocean. Peter gasped. That was extraordinary enough, but what was equally astonishing was that a bridge carved from an iceberg stretched from the edge of Lore Isle to the floating island. The long bridge arced gracefully. It was smooth on top and wide enough for three people to walk side by side. Mammoth support columns stretched down into the ocean and were cut like crystals. They sparkled with all the colours of the rainbow even when the palest light touched it.

Gawking at the architectural marvel, Peter contemplated the walk across the polished ice. "That's going to be a long walk."

"The cleats will not fail you," Mr. Doyle said, and then added in a sober tone, "But be mindful of every step."

The rocks and sparse patches of green plant growth covered the floating Whale Island like barnacles and algae.

"What do I do once I cross the bridge?"

"At the tail of the island, there is a door for the miners. Go through the door and look for the magpie's nest."

"Where do you suppose it is?"

"It must be underneath that hole." Mr. Doyle pointed to the head of the Whale Island. "Where the blowhole would be on a whale, I've seen the magpie fly in and out. Somewhere in its nest of stolen treasure is the mirror."

"So, I'm robbing the robber." Peter felt uneasy about crossing the long bridge, and going into a massive, dark mine alone. But he wanted to find the mirror and find Mr. Doyle's goddaughter so they could get on with the business of finding the egg and the gold.

"The leprechauns work at night and sleep during the day. They do not have a good sense of hearing or smell. But under their feet they have growths, long and sharp as nails, that allow them to walk on the iceberg bridge without slipping. They're the only creatures in Lore Isle to have them."

Mr. Doyle's description of the leprechauns did not match the information in Peter's *Puddicombe* reference book, which described them as little gold-loving men in green clothing, kind of cute when they got angry, jumping up and down. Leprechaun *miners*—that was different.

"As long as you don't touch their gold, you'll be fine."

Peter rolled his eyes. *Figures he'd throw that in.* "Pumpkin said they have a pet."

Mr. Doyle frowned. "He's a chatty one, isn't he? I'm surprised he got any work done. I've heard they look after a two-headed insect."

"A bug for a pet?"

"The leprechauns are not the brightest creatures in Lore Isle."

Hearing about a two-headed bug reminded Peter that his insectoid aunts were coming back armed with a For Sale sign. He needed to return to the house with the gold before they did.

19

Fool's Gold

WHERE THE ICEBERG BRIDGE MET THE LAND, Peter placed the cleats on the ground. He stepped into them and touched one of the open clasps. All the curved hinges on the sides folded upwards as if sitting up. As the interlocking parts of the clasps reached for each other, the intricate clockwork parts spun this way and that, then the clasps closed and locked on their own. Mr. Doyle marvelled at the smith's ingenious design. "I wish I could go with you."

Me too, thought Peter.

Taking a thick cloth out from inside the rucksack, Mr. Doyle instructed him to wrap the mirror carefully. "I almost forgot." He put the cloth back in, then pulled out a big ball of string. "This will guide you."

"Is it magical?" Peter asked hopefully.

"It glows in the dark. Tie it to the handle of the mine door and unravel it as you go down, so you can easily find your way out again."

With the rucksack on his back, Peter walked across the iceberg bridge. On the surface, smooth as glass, he could see the reflection of his face and of the fast-moving clouds in the sky. Past the reflections, he could see through the ice to the rough ocean far below.

After the initial tentative steps, Peter began to loosen up. The cleats dug into the ice, gripping with every step as he walked sure-footed. Cold wind whipped up and he wrapped his jacket tightly around himself.

A pod of whales swam far below, and Peter waved and talked to them, pretending they had come to keep him company. He wondered, if he had his skates, if he could have skated all the way across. He imagined he was handling a puck with a hockey stick and jumped side to side, almost running. By this point, he was more than halfway across, and he was too relaxed for his situation.

At the right moment (or the wrong moment), a powerful gust shoved his back violently like a giant bully and knocked him flat on his stomach. Peter was caught completely off guard. With no part of the metal cleats in the ice, the wind swept him forward, and he slid and turned like a curling rock. The wind screamed, or was he hearing himself?

Peter wanted to stand up and dig the cleats into the ice before he came to the edge. The ice was so slippery, he couldn't even get on his hands and knees. He was beyond panicking. The edge was coming up fast now. The ocean roared, demanding a sacrifice for the water god. *I am going to slide over the edge and plummet into the freezing ocean wearing deadweight heavy metal cleats!* He rolled onto his

back and kept on sliding. With bent knees, he smashed his feet down. His right cleat stuck, and he came to an immediate stop. He slowly sat up and saw he was so close to the edge, his left foot was dangling off the bridge.

With wobbly legs, he stepped away from the edge, then bent over with his hands on his knees. He took deep breaths, as his pounding heart threatened to burst through his chest. *That was too, too close*. The small figure that was Mr. Doyle was yelling unintelligible words. Peter wasn't sure how aware Mr. Doyle was of what just happened, watching from the edge of the bridge, but Peter waved to show that he was okay.

No more daydreaming! he told himself. *Be mindful of every step.* Yearning to feel land under his feet rather than ice, Peter walked on.

When he reached the Whale Island, Peter touched the first clasp of one of the cleats, and all twelve clasps unfastened, the hinges opening on their own. He stepped out of the cleats, and his uncaged feet felt light. Worried that the sharp points of the spikes would damage the mirror once in the rucksack, he looked around for a landmark to leave the cleats by, because he'd need them for the re-crossing.

He decided on a clover-covered mound, hoping at least one of the clovers had four leaves.

When Peter opened the door by the whale's tail, he was greeted by a stinky animal smell. Inside, he took out the string and tied it to the door handle.

Even with burning torches placed on every column, a damp dimness permeated the mine. When his eyes adjusted to the dark, he could see that the whole island was once a solid rock filled with iron veins. The numerous support columns that remained after the removal of the iron made the expansive mine look like a maze.

Not sure where to go, Peter decided to walk down in as straight a line as possible, unravelling the ball of string that, true to Mr. Doyle's words, glowed in the dark.

As he descended deeper into the mine, he heard snoring. He couldn't tell if the leprechauns were sleeping in chambers far away and he was hearing echoes, or if they were snoring just beyond the dark gloom, where no light reached.

When the ball of string had unravelled to a small flat thing, up ahead Peter saw a shaft of light coming down from the ceiling. *The blowhole.* After side-stepping a couple of thick columns, he saw a resplendent tree bathed in sunlight. Instead of fruit, it bore glittering gold coins. An enormous nest crowned the treetop.

The coins—bigger and thicker than the mummers' and Pumpkin's—made soft tinkling sounds like wind chimes caught in a lazy breeze. Peter climbed the tree's long, graceful branches and pushed himself over the prickly wall of the nest. Not wanting to accidentally damage the mirror, he carefully rummaged through the bird's collection. All he touched were pretty and colourful, often shiny, but worthless: paper, shells, feathers, frayed cloths, tin cups, broken copper cookware, and fragments of glazed tiles.

Then, he saw a silver handle sticking out of the weave of the nest. He snapped some of the entwined twigs and gently pulled out the rest of the object—a large silver hand mirror. He turned it over. Engraved on the back was a coat of arms depicting a great tree and the word "Upland" in fancy script.

He had found it in this heap of clutter! It shouldn't have surprised him because he was good at finding things. He had yet to come across a hidden-object book or game he found challenging.

I'm not ordinary after all, Peter realized. He was special like Grandpa and Mom. He was an adventurer who found treasures, which was way better than "merely" understanding the weather or nature. Maybe a book would be written about him: *The Adventures of Sir Peter the Finder.*

As he took out the thick flannel cloth from his rucksack, he remembered what the mirror could do. Peter looked at his reflection and said, "Show me Mom."

The mirror became cloudy white then cleared to show Mom repairing the greenhouse. She seemed so still, frozen in mid-motion, swinging a hammer. Newfoundland time had almost come to a standstill, thanks to the raven feather. The image of Mom became smaller and smaller as the mirror showed Peter the entire greenhouse, then his house beside it, then some of his neighbourhood. He kissed her tiny sad face before wrapping the mirror in the cloth and placing it in the rucksack.

As he climbed down the tree, having just seen his mom, the temptation to grab the gold coins was overwhelming. Twice he had been denied gold. Now, it was just him and the gold-bearing tree—no wolves or Mr. Doyle to stop him from taking a few gold pieces. There were so many coins, thousands of them! It wasn't like he was taking hard-earned coins from Pumpkin's bowl. The tree just grew them. Heck, he was already a thief with the mirror in his rucksack.

Mr. Doyle had only warned him against taking the gold coins because he was worried Peter wouldn't continue to help him. Peter knew he was fully committed, but what if, for whatever reason, he couldn't get to the egg and the gold? No gold meant no house. Mr. Doyle never needed to know that he had some gold coins in his pocket.

The leprechauns have poor hearing, Mr. Doyle had said. Plucking a few softly clinking coins surely wouldn't wake them. *I will take just twenty. Maybe more. How many will pay for the house? How many can I jam into my pockets?* He wrapped each hand around as many coins as he could hold and jumped down from the lowest branch.

An ear-piercing alarm!

With clenched fists holding the coins, Peter covered his ears, desperately trying to muffle the painful sound drilling into them. Several creatures lumbered into the sunlit area. Peter froze.

The so-called leprechauns were not wearing green and they were not cute. As tall as grown men and about twice as wide, they had huge, hairless heads; flat foreheads; and wide, twisted mouths. They had no necks to speak of—their wide shoulders extended into long, sinewy arms and hairy-knuckled hands that reached below their knees. Their torsos were long, their powerful legs short. They and their coveralls were coated in grey iron dust. *Puddicombe's Mythical and Fantastic Creatures Reference* needed serious updating.

The leprechauns looked at Peter with their tiny, deep-set red eyes, lit with fury at being woken up. Some yawned, revealing chipped yellow teeth. They looked at the tree, then back at Peter. It took a moment for the sleepyheads to figure out what had happened. Then, the beastly miners lunged forward.

Peter fled. The screaming alarm utterly confused his sense of direction. Aimlessly, he ran, unable to find the way out of the vast labyrinth. The glowing string was nowhere in sight.

Before long, he was surrounded by a mob of angry leprechauns and their noisy exhaled breath, which smelled like lumpy milk. Two of them forced his hands open and took the gold coins. Another took Peter's rucksack, before swatting him with a meaty hand. Sprawled on the ground, Peter gagged from the revolting odour of their shoeless feet.

20

the Leprechauns' Pet

WITH HIS ANKLES ROPED, PETER HUNG UPSIDE down from a pulley system. His wrists were bound at the front. The blood rushed down to his head, making his ears thrum. At least the alarm had been turned off. A couple of leprechauns in the crowd below fought over the mirror they had discovered in his rucksack.

"Stop! That's mine!" Peter yelled.

The mirror slipped from the sausage fingers of the winner. When it landed on the ground, the oval glass cracked, and one half popped out of the mirror frame.

"No!" Peter felt like he had split his mom's heart open. He had failed her. It was all over. His body went limp like a neglected plant.

Six feet from the ground, his head dangled over a black hole bigger than a sewer medallion. From the hole, two long arching sticks similar to fishing rods appeared. What followed the sticks made Peter's heart stop. For they were not sticks at all, but the antennas of an enormous bug. A second head without antennas squeezed out. The two heads—black and shiny, as if they were wet—shared one body that partially emerged from the hole. The lithe feelers of the first head reached up for Peter. He squirmed like bait on a fishing hook. The wiggly, sticky hairs on the feelers travelled all over his face.

"Gross!" He wiped the trail of slime on his sleeve. The bug had just tasted him.

The two-headed monstrosity rubbed its feelers together and screeched a high-pitched noise of approval. Peter shuddered to think how much more of the bug was still below the surface of the hole. A leprechaun brought out a rusty knife and started sawing the thick rope.

"No, no, no! Don't cut the rope, Mr. Leprechaun!" He needed to haggle for his life. What could he offer? He remembered Mr. Doyle bargaining with Pumpkin. "I have a friend who is an excellent hunter. He can get you any kind of game you'd like. As much as you want."

Either the leprechaun didn't understand Peter or he didn't care to negotiate. With a satisfied snort, he cut through the rope. Peter had enough sense to twist his body in such a way that he landed at the edge of the hole and not on the bug. A lightning bolt of pain went through his side. Pawing at the ground with his tied hands, he wriggled toward the broken mirror. When he felt the knot loosen a bit, he extended his arms as far as he could and grabbed the big shard that had fallen out of the mirror frame. A large claw grabbed his boot. The leprechauns gathered in a big circle and grunted with excitement.

Towed by the bug, Peter disappeared feet first into the hole. The leprechauns cheered, stomping their clawed feet on the ground, stirring up clouds of iron dust.

Holding the smooth, curved part of the glass, Peter used the broken side to saw the rope that bound his wrists. When the light high above disappeared and it became pitch black, he grazed his hand and wrist with the shard, and he had to stop.

Once down in the chamber, the bug released his foot. Peter sat up and scooched back a bit, then stopped, not knowing where the bug was. The dank air and the heaviness of the leaden black stifled him. He went back to sawing the rope, now that he was not being dragged. The rope had loosened a bit more and it was getting easier.

The bug produced a shrill noise. Peter heard and sensed the movements of tiny feet. Something licked the blood on his hands and took a nibble as he cut the last of the rope and freed his hands. Rubbery things climbed and squirmed on his legs. He brushed off the crawling critters and sawed away at the ropes wrapped around his ankles. He was able to work assuredly in the dark, knowing his thick boots were protecting his feet and ankles.

When he cut through the rope, he remembered the gift from Pumpkin and prayed it had not fallen out of his pocket while he hung upside down. It certainly was a dark place he'd ended up in, as the smith had forewarned. Peter gingerly put down the mirror shard beside him, sure he'd need it again.

By a stroke of luck, he had put the candle in a jacket pocket that was buttoned. He pulled out the candle and yelled, "Light!"—and immediately wished he hadn't.

White, roly-poly larvae the size of dinner rolls covered his legs, crawling over each other in a race to the cuts on his hands, now smeared with blood. The big black bug with two heads was backed against the wall of the enclosed chamber, wildly flailing its many legs, greatly pained by the bright candlelight. The bug was ginormous—only about a third of its body had been out of the hole when it had started dragging him. The fat tubular things were its babies. Peter was baby food.

Peter jumped up and shook his legs, all the while screaming his head off. In his panic, he dropped the candle, which rolled away somewhere but didn't go out. He noticed heaps of skulls and bones from what appeared to be large rodents strewn about. He swallowed the next tidal wave of a scream, picked up the mirror shard, and started his long, steep climb back up the tunnel. The hungry babies mewled.

He had climbed about halfway when, down below, the candle went out and the tunnel became darker. With dread, he heard an approaching scuttling noise. Long feelers brushed his back, and a claw grabbed a boot and started to drag him back down. Peter turned and slashed and stabbed repeatedly with the shard, and the insect emitted harsh cries. With all his strength, Peter made one last jab and left the shard impaled in the bug. It released his foot. Unencumbered from the shard, he climbed freely until he was out of the hole.

There were no leprechauns around. They must have gone back to bed. Peter's rucksack and the piece of cloth were on the ground next to the broken mirror. With his sore hands, he picked up the mirror frame—now with almost half of the glass missing.

"Show me my mom."

Peter's dirty and bruised face continued to stare back at him, and he fell to his knees.

Squish. Squish. Squish.

Even before he spun his head around, Peter knew what he'd see. The bug emerged from the hole. The mirror shard was protruding from the crown of the head with the antennae, and Peter's despair turned into adrenaline. He knew what he had to do.

The bug was more than halfway out and standing straight up now. Peter ran toward it, and, using the insect's hairy legs and ridged underbelly as steps, he climbed up the side of the bug without the clawed limb. This side led to the head without the antenna. From the top of the unadorned head, he leapt to the other, reaching out for an appendage. With his boots firmly planted in the bug ooze seeping from the lacerations he had caused, Peter yanked out the mirror shard.

The bug tossed its head and shrieked. Peter windmilled his arms, balancing like a beginner surfer. Peter thought he saw the wound in the insect's head closing, healing itself. The bug started to bend and twist, snapping at him with the claw. When the bug's head swung remotely close to the ground, Peter let go of the antenna and jumped. Sticky bug goo pulled at his shoes, and he ended up sort of falling off the head.

Peter snatched the dusty cloth and wrapped the shard in one half and the broken mirror in the other, and placed them in his rucksack.

He started running.

He passed pillar after pillar, with no trace of the glowing yarn. *Which way is out?*

After some minutes, Peter's feet clomped, and he

panted and wheezed. The adrenaline had worn off. Before long, the sound of leprechauns in hot pursuit reverberated throughout the mine.

Somehow, Peter ended up back at the golden tree. He reached for a branch. At his touch, it snapped off, landing at his feet bare and black—as if burnt. It was the branch he had taken the coins from. He grabbed a healthy branch and started climbing. The noise of the screaming leprechauns rang unbearably loud in his ears. Frightened and exhausted, Peter pushed himself over the wall of the nest and flopped down. As far as he could tell, the leprechauns were not able to climb after him; perhaps they were too heavy for the branches. But it was only a matter of time until the dullards figured out a way. Maybe one had already gone to the storeroom to get a ladder.

Trying to catch his breath, Peter looked straight up at the bright hole high above him. There was no ladder tall enough to escape through the Whale Island's blowhole.

Something eclipsed the bright circle, then swooped down. A car-sized shadow crossed the nest.

Peter froze.

A black and white bird with green and violet wings and tail feathers dropped a few shiny objects into the nest. Slowly, slowly, Peter sat up, wanting to slide into the shadows.

A twig snapped under his leg.

The magpie cocked its head toward the sound. With an indignant caw, it rushed toward the intruder. It tried to knock Peter out of the nest, first with its beak, then with its feet. The giant bird kicked him closer and closer to the edge until he was hugging the ridge of the wall for dear life. One more kick and he'd be delivered to the leprechauns below, who would do a better job of tying him up and then he wouldn't have a fighting chance against the bug.

When the magpie came at him with another kick, Peter lunged and wrapped himself around the bird's leg. It flapped wildly, circling the tree and flying lower and lower, trying to cope with the added weight. With all the jerky motions, Peter started to lose his grip and slipped down to the bird's ankle (if birds have ankles). With their long arms raised, the leprechauns started jumping, trying to grab his dangling legs. A tip of a finger brushed his toe and Peter yanked his knees up, and begged the magpie to fly higher.

The magpie regained its balance and flapped its powerful wings.

Swoosh.

It flew straight up and out of the blowhole and into the sunlight. With a flick of its leg, the magpie dumped the stowaway on the ground and flew away.

Determined not to further damage the mirror in his rucksack, Peter landed on his front, painfully banging his knees before face-planting. His teeth cut through the inside of his bottom lip and he tasted the metallic tang of warm blood.

With no time to lose, Peter limped toward the iceberg bridge. He was sure, underneath him in the mine, the angry leprechauns were making their way outdoors. As he passed the door at the whale's tail, he heard the approaching thunderous footsteps and knew he was right.

At the edge of the bridge, Peter stepped into the cleats, keeping an eye on the door. He touched the first clasp, thankful to Pumpkin for making cleats that basically closed by themselves. The leprechauns spilled out of the door, blocking the sunlight from their eyes with their oversized hands.

Luckily, the wind had died down, and Peter ran the race of his life—making sure every step landed firmly. He had no time to be afraid of falling off the bridge.

The lumbering leprechauns hit their stride with their sure footing on the bridge.

Once on the other side, Peter abandoned his cleats and continued to run, yelling, "Mr. Doyle!" but there was no answer. He ran into the forest.

Soon, a savage clamour filled the air. Peter's head pounded, and the cuts on his hands throbbed painfully—but the fear of feeling hairy knuckles on his shoulders fuelled his legs to keep moving. When he looked back, the hair on the back of his neck stood up. About half a dozen leprechauns were so close he could see the streaks of dirt-soaked sweat on their faces.

Growling and barking sounds came from up ahead.

Dozens of Lore Isle black wolves led by a smaller grey wolf charged toward him. Peter curled up in a ball and crouched beside a fallen lichen-covered tree. As the grey wolf jumped over the tree trunk, something shone dully around its neck.

The leprechaun that met the grey wolf used its club-like arms to swat it and sent it sailing, smashing the pack leader against the side of a tree. Undeterred, the snarling black wolves leapt up and sank their teeth into the leprechauns, drawing gelatinous, greyish blood that could not have tasted good. The leprechauns kicked with the sharp growths on the bottom of their feet. The wolves howled in pain. Trembling in terror, Peter couldn't look anymore. He stood up and ran until he could no longer hear the battle noises.

21

the Beast Under "L"

TRIPPING OVER PROTRUDING TREE ROOTS, Peter wandered around the forest. He thought he should go back toward the iceberg bridge. After all, that was where Mr. Doyle must be looking for him. But he wasn't sure which direction that'd be, and he certainly didn't want to run into the leprechauns.

Grimacing with pain, Peter took off his rucksack and sat down. When he looked inside it, he found to his relief that his rushed wrapping job had protected the shards from breaking. Would it even work, once put back together?

His throat felt gritty like he had swallowed iron dust.

The grey wolf that led the black wolves to fight the leprechauns—he had seen that wolf before. But not in Lore Isle. *Then where?* Peter pictured his fishing rod pointing to a grey wolf before it slunk away into the shadows of the trees. *The fishing pond back home. How could that wolf be here in Lore Isle?* Yet, he was certain it was the same grey wolf.

Something metallic around the wolf's neck had caught his eyes when it jumped over him and the fallen tree. Peter fingered the button hanging from his own neck. Could a wolf manage to put on a button and fall into its reflection to cross into Lore Isle? Even if it could, Mr. Doyle had said there were only two buttons.

Blood drained from his face. *What if it wasn't a wolf when it crossed the portal?* Mr. Doyle, a stranger, had shown up at the funeral just days after he and Grandpa saw the grey wolf. He thought about Mr. Doyle's peculiar yellow eyes, his bristly grey hair, his hunched-over posture, his clothes made from animal hide, and the fact he could communicate with wolves. Peter mentally thumbed through *Puddicombe's Mythical and Fantastic Creatures Reference*. He stopped at "L."

"Lycanthrope," he whispered. A magical beast that could live as a man or a wolf. He clearly saw the illustration that came with that word: a tortured beast, half man, half wolf, standing on its hind legs in mid-transformation. With its torso twisted, it looked out at the reader with demonic red eyes, saliva dripping from its dagger-like teeth.

The story about Noah, Mr. Doyle's lycanthrope Sunday school teacher, was a preamble to a confession. Deep inside he'd known it then, but Peter couldn't reconcile that image of the monstrous creature in his reference book with his companion and guardian in Lore Isle.

Where was Mr. Doyle now? What if they couldn't find each other? Could Peter find the village where Pumpkin lived and ask for the gold coins and somehow retrace his steps to the pond? Wincing with pain, he stood up. *Which way?* He had run aimlessly. If he started walking in the wrong direction, he might starve to death miles away from the smithy.

A wall of tall, dense bushes nearby rustled. Peter held his breath. Had a leprechaun followed him?

Mr. Doyle half crawled out from between the bushes, holding on to his side.

A wave of relief washed over Peter. "You found me. I couldn't see you near the bridge."

"Oh, Peter, so glad to see you're okay." He slumped down. "Boy, I'm spent." There were bruises and gashes on his temple and blood seeping through his hide clothes, making dark circular spots. "Sorry to worry you. I went for a walk and got lost. And as I was coming back, I inadvertently ran into a clash between the wolves and the leprechauns. I'm lucky to have gotten away when I did."

Peter remained standing. "I don't believe you were lost." He was afraid to say what he knew, but the words spilled out. "You went to get the wolves to help you fight the leprechauns." Before Mr. Doyle could protest, Peter swallowed hard and said, "You're the grey wolf. The same one who watched me and Grandpa at the fishing pond."

Mr. Doyle's tanned face looked up open-mouthed as if he was going to deny it, but in the end he said, "You're a smart lad. You'd have figured it out sooner or later."

The words of confirmation boomed in Peter's ears, but sounded far away at the same time. His legs wobbled like jelly. He sat down before they gave out.

"You should have told me earlier," he reprimanded, trying to convince himself that he was not scared to be sitting within easy reach of a lycanthrope.

"You're right. I should have," Mr. Doyle said. "But when was the right time? I didn't want you to be afraid of me."

"Should I be afraid of you when, you know...when you change?" Peter checked Mr. Doyle to see if there were any signs that he was getting hairier.

"No, not at all. My mind is the same whether I'm a man or a wolf. When I'm in my wolf form, my body is stronger, more coordinated, more agile, and I feel fearless. But I would never harm you. You must know that by now." There was hurt in his voice.

Despite the explanation, Peter's legs continued to shake, even though he was sitting down. At the same time, he was awestruck that he was talking to a mythical creature, not just reading about one in his reference (although quite inaccurate) book. He wanted to know more. "I have so many questions."

"Ask them. I owe you that much." Mr. Doyle's mouth stretched into a wide smile, pleased that Peter was curious.

Peter didn't know which of the questions swirling in his head to ask first. He decided to start at the beginning. "Were you born in an egg like Noah?"

"No. I was born a human baby in Newfoundland to human parents."

"Your parents weren't lycanthropes?"

"No. Just ordinary humans." In a clear attempt to make Peter less afraid of him, Mr. Doyle added, "Just like yours."

Fascinating. "Do you have many lycanthropes in your family tree?

Mr. Doyle scratched the stubble under his chin. "As far as I know, my family has never had a lycanthrope before. Lycanthropes are very rare."

"Do you know of any other lycanthropes?" Peter pulled in his legs, which had stopped shaking, and sat cross-legged. "How many are there?"

"Let's see. I know of one born in Lore Isle; a middle-aged gent who lives on the far side of the island. A nice chap. Writes poetry."

"Poetry?" *Puddicombe's* didn't list any hobbies for the mythical creatures and Peter had never thought of them as having leisurely pursuits.

"Mostly haiku, some free verse. When he visits a nearby village, I can smell his scent. And I know of two others born in Newfoundland beside myself. My dear mentor, Noah, who you know about, and one other who, I believe, is quite a bit younger than myself."

Peter wondered if it could be someone he knew. He pointed to Mr. Doyle's outfit. "Your leather clothes. Do they have something to do with you being a lycanthrope?"

Mr. Doyle explained that the material of his clothes was hide from wolves that had died long ago. If he wore regular clothes, he'd have to take them off when he became a wolf and put them back on when he was a human, which was quite cumbersome. But the wolf hide just became a part of him when he changed into a wolf, giving him all the abilities of the hide's original owners. "And the hide has its own temperature control. It's comfortable in all seasons."

"I read in my mythical creature reference book," Peter said, "that lycanthropes must transform into a wolf when the moon is full. How does the moon affect you?"

Mr. Doyle made a face like that was a silly thing to say. "It doesn't. The moon is always full in Lore Isle so, by that reasoning, I should be a wolf all the time."

When I get home, Peter thought, *that reference book is going to the bottom shelf with the boxes of games with missing pieces.*

He couldn't think of any more questions and stared at Mr. Doyle with his mouth open. He had just interviewed a lycanthrope. *Un-bee-lee-va-ble!*

Seeing Peter also had open cuts and gashes, Mr. Doyle said, "We could use Lily's healing skills right about now." In the long silence that followed, Mr. Doyle glanced repeatedly at the rucksack. Finally, he said, "I see you still have the rucksack. Did you manage to get the mirror?"

"The frame is in good shape, but the glass is in two pieces." Peter said.

Mr. Doyle pulled a clump of grass next to him.

Peter added in a meek voice, "Do you think it'll still work once put back together?"

"I don't know," Mr. Doyle said through gritted teeth. "I knew the moment you took their gold. The alarm could be heard on this side of the bridge. My stomach rotted. I feared you would not make it out alive. All I could do was pace back and forth near the bridge and wait. For what? I didn't know."

Peter hung his head. He shouldn't have plucked any gold coins, but at the same time, he hadn't felt he'd had enough information to be completely deterred. "Did you know the leprechauns were built like rhinos on two legs?"

"I did," Mr. Doyle said.

"When they caught me, they tied me up so their pet…" Peter shivered. "Did you know about the size of their pet bug? Cause that was no ordinary bug."

With a raised finger, Mr. Doyle seemed ready with an explanation, but with a sigh, he just said, "Yes."

Peter described the encounter with the giant bug and its hungry babies. And the horror he saw when he lit the candle. "There were so many grubs," Peter said with disgust. "What's going to happen when they turn into proper insects?"

"It's been well over a decade since I've heard about them. It seems they do not grow up, and the two-headed insect must take care of them forever. Perhaps the bug is cursed."

"Why didn't you tell me what I would see in the mine?" Peter raised his voice.

"Because you were never supposed to see them!" Mr. Doyle also raised his voice. "With my repeated warnings, why would you even touch the gold coins? If you hadn't taken them, you'd have never woken the leprechauns nor met their dreadful pet." Mr. Doyle took a breath to contain his rising anger. "Once you had the mirror, you should have retraced your steps by following the glow-in-the dark yarn and you'd have come out of the mine without a scratch on you or the mirror."

Peter wrapped his arms around his bent knees and put his head down. "I made a mistake. A big one."

Mr. Doyle cooled down. "It seemed like an eternity after the alarm was triggered that I saw the magpie go in the blowhole. I didn't know why, but the sight gave me hope. And when I saw the bird come back out with you holding on to its foot, I knew you'd make it back across the bridge. That's when I went to get reinforcements."

Peter lifted his head. "The wolves. They saved my life. How'd they do against the leprechauns?" he asked quietly. "Are many hurt?"

Mr. Doyle's face twisted with anguish. "I am afraid so."

Peter's eye filled with tears. "It's all my fault."

"The wolves know what's at stake here."

"You mean they know what's in the egg?"

"Yes," Mr. Doyle said. "When Noah first came to Lore Isle, he asked the wolves for their help. These are not the same wolves, of course, but generation after generation, their dedication to finding the egg and returning their counterparts to Newfoundland has not wavered."

Peter wiped his eyes. "They're amazing." He had just seen the black wolves of Lore Isle fearlessly fight the leprechauns. And now he had learned the wolves were committed to this cause, even if meant putting themselves in danger.

"The egg itself is amazing too." Mr. Doyle gently massaged his knee. "It's a magic vessel that allows it and its contents to go through the pond undetected. That's how we'll get your gold across the portal as well—in the egg. Without it, we have no hope of taking the gold from Lore Isle to Newfoundland."

Peter slapped his forehead. He hadn't thought about how he'd take the gold coins through the pond, which wouldn't even let him pass with a single red button in his pocket. Gold without the magic egg would be pointless. He saw now that he needed to find the egg for himself as well as for Mr. Doyle.

"Do you have any idea who has the egg?" Peter said.

"I don't know who first stole the egg, but the best information I ever got led me to conclude that the mummers have it now."

Peter didn't like that he kept crossing paths with that gruesome foursome. "They are not like the Christmas mummers that came to my house nor like any storybook characters I've read about. What exactly are Lore Isle mummers?"

"They are spectres of people who have passed away in Newfoundland, but can't go on to where they're supposed to because they have unfinished business."

"So, these spectres are stuck here forever?"

Mr. Doyle massaged his knee again. "After some reflection on why they came to Lore Isle, most mummers find peace, even if they can't fully achieve their goals and move on. But there are others who are stubborn and stay indefinitely—unless they're killed."

"Spectres can be killed?"

"Well, it's more like forcing them to continue to their final destination. They're already dead."

There was something sad and haunting about souls who couldn't find peace even in death.

"Why do these undead mummers want the egg?"

"They lived in a time when everybody hated wolves," Mr. Doyle explained. "These mummers, especially, hated them because they were either hunters and saw the wolves as competition or they were farmers and saw them as a threat to their livestock. They don't know that the world Newfoundland belongs to has changed. People are becoming aware of the need for nature conservation and discovering it's not right to drive species to extinction. The Lore Isle mummers are stuck in the past. They are focused on the fact that they got rid of the wolves in Newfoundland, and if the wolves in the egg go back and repopulate, their accomplishment would be for nothing."

"Since they hate wolves, how d'you even know the egg still exists? The mummers could have destroyed it by now," Peter worried.

"Because the egg can only be harmed by someone with wolf blood."

Peter remembered the old wolf had told Noah the same thing. "Someone like you, a lycanthrope."

Mr. Doyle nodded. In a sober tone, he said, "Do you agree with me that restoring the Newfoundland wolves to their native land is the right thing to do?"

Peter pulled at the collar of Grandpa's shirt he wore and shrugged, as if trying to shake off a heavy load. Anxiety filled him, like the time he argued with Mom in the greenhouse. That time, he had pushed all the responsibility on her. This time he couldn't just run up to his room and close the door. Whether Mom would be able to continue to live in her home, her sanctuary, was up to him now. "Are you certain my gold is with the egg?"

"Yes, yes," Mr. Doyle huffed. "The mummers are superstitious. They always keep plenty of gold coins with objects for luck. Now, really think about what I'm asking. Do you believe in the quest to return the Newfoundland wolves? These wolves are unlike any other wolves in the world."

Peter thought of the wolf in the display case at the museum. Given that his great-great-grandpa was a champion wolf hunter, there was some chance that his ancestor had killed that wolf and handed the skin over to the government to collect his reward. Perhaps the wolf had recognized Peter as the descendent of a hunter who had killed so many wolves, and its outrage had shattered the glass. Peter had the opportunity to undo his ancestor's wrong of driving a species to extinction, by bringing back the wolves to Newfoundland.

"I believe it's right to bring back the wolves," Peter said in earnest. "I'd be proud of that accomplishment all of my life."

Mr. Doyle's face appeared re-energized, almost younger. "Will you give me your word that you will do all you can to return the two wolves in the egg to Newfoundland?"

"Yes."

Mr. Doyle laid his hand, heavy as a knight's sword, on Peter's shoulder, as if to seal a sacred oath. He stood up. "Let's head back to the cabin."

22

In the Mirror

IT WAS A SLOW AND PAINFUL WALK FOR THE TWO weary wayfarers. They quenched their thirst by drinking from a stream but remained famished. The provisions Mr. Doyle had brought had been left somewhere near the bridge when he went to get the wolves and were likely being enjoyed by forest creatures. Along the way, they passed a lone farmhouse with a thatched roof and leaded windows. Within a fence, dozens of speckled hens strutted around, bobbing their heads. The plump birds had black-and-white feathered bodies with crimson red combs and wattles, and long plumes of peacock-blue tail feathers. With no one around, Mr. Doyle wiped the back of his hand across his mouth and considered the fowls with the steady eyes of a predator. A farmer came around the corner with a bucket of feed.

Mr. Doyle waved and said, "Beautiful birds you have there."

The farmer said, "Thank you," and waved back, but he appeared unsure of Peter and Mr. Doyle, who must have looked quite dubious.

As the sky began to darken, they entered Mr. Doyle's cabin.

Mr. Doyle said, "I'm going to grab us some dinner." He sounded like Grandpa when he went to get takeout. "Are you ready?"

It took a moment for Peter to realize Mr. Doyle was asking for his permission to transform in front of him. Peter nodded coolly, but he did not want to see the live action version of the tortured beast transformation from *Puddicombe's*.

With his eyes bored on a spot on the wall, Mr. Doyle began. His hide clothes shrink-wrapped around his body. Long pinpoints of white light, densely packed, shot out all over the hide, outlining him like a ghostly porcupine, as he dropped down on all fours. The air in the room crackled as if charged with electricity. In the luminescence, Mr. Doyle's face protruded into a long snout. His mouth pulled back as if by wires, exposing teeth that lengthened and sharpened. Mr. Doyle twisted uncomfortably as his bones creaked and popped, extending and shortening to the right lengths, then snapping into place. The pinpoints of white light shortened, bristled, and turned into grey hair. The transformation was complete.

The grey wolf looked at him with amber eyes that seemed to say, "That wasn't so bad, was it?"

No, it wasn't. Mr. Doyle's metamorphosis was kind of beautiful.

The wolf padded out the front door.

The stars came out, and Mr. Doyle still hadn't come back. It couldn't be easy for a wolf so injured to hunt prey. With all that Peter had seen and learned that day jumbled up in his head, and his body sore and tired, he went to lie down for a moment on his cot and fell asleep.

He opened his bleary eyes when he heard the door open and close, followed by the crackling sounds of transformation.

Peter dragged his feet into the kitchen. In the dark room, the outline of a now-human Mr. Doyle stretched a long arm up and rubbed the back of his neck. "It gets harder as you get older."

A limp, plump bird with long tail plumes hung from his other hand. Too hurt to catch wild game, he had taken another tack. The farmer's instinct to be suspicious of the two passers-by had been spot on.

"I'll drop off game meat for the farmer when I can hunt again."

He carried the hen to the kitchen counter and started plucking. "Fire up the hearth, Peter."

The hungry diners filled themselves up with the stolen bird. Warmth and light from the hearth filled the cozy room.

"Your hide clothes are clean," Peter said.

"Yes." Mr. Doyle replied. "The transformation does that. But it doesn't help at all with the wounds."

On the walls, flickering dark shadows took the shapes of the black wolves that had saved Peter from the furious leprechauns. His guilty conscience was tormenting him.

"If I came back to Lore Isle years from now, would the wolves still be around?"

"Of course. The first moment Lore Isle came to be, the wolves did too. They will always be a part of the life cycle as long as Lore Isle exists."

Peter liked the explanation because that's how he saw the Newfoundland wolves. They were a part of Newfoundland like the trees, hills, and ocean. He imagined that if he didn't succeed in bringing them back, every time he walked in the forests of Newfoundland, he'd see white, wolf-like shapes, as if cut out from a picture, as a painful reminder of his failure.

"Why do you ask? Would you like to visit Lore Isle again?" Mr. Doyle asked.

With a knife and fork, Peter cut the breast meat. "I want to know that I could always come here to see wolves in case we can't make it happen for Newfoundland."

Mr. Doyle put down the drumstick he was gnawing on. "You have a special attachment to the wolves. I'm glad I brought you here. With your help, we will succeed. I've never felt so confident."

Peter was cheered that despite his mess-up in the mine, Mr. Doyle still believed Peter would be useful. Then, guilt as sharp as an arrowhead pierced him for having a dream that Grandpa would not have approved of.

"Did Grandpa know you were a lycanthrope?"

Mr. Doyle wiped his hands on a napkin. "About three years after meeting him, I brought John to Lore Isle and I told him…well, showed him I was a lycanthrope. I can still hear his ugly rant against wolves. It broke my heart."

Peter was as quiet as a priest hearing a confession.

"John must have been so shocked to discover the friend he thought of as a little brother was half wolf, half the thing he hated. I think he despised wolves more from that day on, because of me. Perhaps that was another reason I was reluctant to tell you I was a lycanthrope. Maybe you would hate me, too."

Peter said without delay, "But now you know how I feel about wolves. I admire them."

Mr. Doyle sighed. "I wish John did, too. I missed his friendship for a long time after."

I will miss Grandpa for the rest of my life, Peter realized then. He knew there were only two people in the world who truly loved him and since Grandpa had died, there was only Mom.

"Do you know why John hated wolves so much?" Mr. Doyle pulled off one of the large wings from the cooked bird.

This was a topic Peter had mulled over many times in his mind. "I think it had a lot to do with *his* grandpa, the bounty hunter. Grandpa told me that his grandpa passed down stories about wolves. In his tales, the wolves were always villains and killers, and that made Grandpa hate them.

"And of course, his grandpa taught him to hunt. He told Grandpa the wolves were his competition and would destroy his food source."

Mr. Doyle nodded. "But that's just not true."

"I know. In class, we learned that wolves weed out sick and old animals, allowing the strong to escape, so the prey populations are actually healthier than when there are no wolves." Peter drank from his mug.

"That's a good point. Did you tell that to John?"

"Yes, but he would always tell me, again, that he knew a little kid that a wolf tried to drag away."

Mr. Doyle rolled his eyes. "That doesn't sound right."

"The museum guide told my class there was no evidence that wolves attacked people."

"Despite John's efforts, you love wolves. Why do you think that is?"

"I was always interested in wolves, and after learning about them in school, I saw wolves as a vital part of the environment."

"I feel the same way." A smile stretched across Mr. Doyle's face like a rubber band. It was nice to talk about the wolves without someone getting upset.

Lying in his cot with a full belly, Peter was unable to find a side of his body that didn't have a tender bruise. He turned, unable to fall asleep. Muffled noises came from the kitchen. He went to his door and silently cracked it open. The dying fire in the hearth dimly illuminated Mr. Doyle, who was sitting at the table holding the mirror. He had cleaned the two pieces and fitted them back into the casing.

"Show me my goddaughter," he whispered.

Peter couldn't make out the moving image that played out in the mirror.

Hunched over, Mr. Doyle muttered crossly, "Foolish girl, so that's where you are. It's not going to be a simple rescue." Then his tone became tender, "but you are safe." He touched the mirror. "It will be your last night in the cage." Mr. Doyle sighed and rewrapped the mirror in the thick piece of cloth.

23

Realm of the Pitcher Plants

PETER AND MR. DOYLE TRAVELLED AWAY from the village and entered a forest to the south. Mr. Doyle, who walked with a limp, handed Peter the rucksack with the mirror and picked up a sturdy stick to use as a cane. It was a long, slow walk for the injured pair.

"I saw you looking at the mirror last night. You know where Ella is."

"Yes. She's a prisoner of Sarracena, the pitcher plant fairy."

"The bride." Peter remembered that Enchantress Elora cursed the groom, her own son, to the barrens. "The enchantress knew something dark about Sarracena and tried to warn George, but he wasn't having it."

Mr. Doyle groaned as he stepped over large rocks. His injured knee was hurting him. "George knew Sarracena had a secret, but would not acknowledge it to save face in front of the guests. And he was convinced that their love had changed her. Do you remember the enchantress asking George, 'Are you sure her cage is empty?' She knew Sarracena had a prisoner."

"Your goddaughter."

Mr. Doyle nodded.

"Why do you think she keeps prisoners?"

Mr. Doyle scratched his head as he puzzled it out. "When one fairy dies, another is born in a flower named the nativity fatum. With minimal help from their assigned godmothers, all fairies raise themselves in their realm, which they cannot leave. They don't mind at all that they are fated to live alone, as fairies are, by nature, solitary and scholarly creatures. In fact, they write many of the textbooks used at the University of Lore Isle. And no one dares to bother fairies at work because their curses are so powerful." Mr. Doyle shook his head in confusion. "So, when I heard that George, the son of an enchantress, was to wed a fairy, I was as surprised as everyone else. No realm fairy has ever wanted to get married."

"George and Sarracena seemed very much in love, though." Peter remembered how they had looked at each other at their wedding ceremony.

Mr. Doyle said, "Yes, I am sure they were, which makes it more difficult to figure out why she keeps prisoners. Maybe Ella can tell us."

"We have to get her out of the realm of the pitcher plants first. How are we going to do that?"

Mr. Doyle's creased forehead smoothed as he pointed to the rucksack. "It's lucky we have the mirror. I'm sure Sarracena would love to have it so she can find her groom in the barrens. We'll give her the mirror in exchange for Ella's release."

Peter was reassured.

The smell of damp moss in the shadows mingled with the sweet scent of blooming flowers in the beams of sunlight that broke through the canopy of trees. Birds hidden in the branches sang a sweet, harmonized melody. Frogs croaked rudely, complaining that the birds should keep the music down. Three lemon-chested birds, as pretty as their voices, appeared from the trees and flew past the travellers. Perhaps the slighted songbirds were searching for a more appreciative audience.

The trail often disappeared, but Mr. Doyle knew exactly where to go to pick up the path.

"Will the bride and groom have a happy ending?" Peter mused out loud, stepping over tree roots.

"There's a good chance. Sarracena will see in the mirror the exact location of her groom and send a hired servant with her godmother's gift—the magic dragonfly belt that will release him from the barrens. The servant will be able to see him. The newlyweds are only invisible to each other."

Peter said, "Yeah, but that's the problem. When he comes back, they still won't be able to see or hear each other."

"Didn't your friend Penelope, the tree sprite, take care of that?" Hearing Penelope's name, a torrent of worry filled Peter. After Ella, he must help Penelope. But how would he get her out of the mummers' house?

Mr. Doyle continued, "The servant will join their hands. When they touch, the curse will be broken."

A ladybug landed on Peter's sleeve—a sign of good luck. Yesterday, he was a thief; today, he'd been promoted to a fairy godmother of sorts, reuniting a fairy tale couple. Tomorrow, he'd find a way to rescue Penelope.

The treeline stopped and the ground became marshy. Peter gasped. Just up ahead, pitcher plants as tall as lamp-posts lined a raised boardwalk and filled the expansive fen. They were at the edge of the fairy's realm. Compared to the forest, it was too quiet.

"Is this the way we went to the wedding?" *It couldn't be.* On the path to the wedding, the pitcher plants had been the same size as the ones in Newfoundland.

"No. This is the way to Sarracena's home." Mr. Doyle's forehead glistened with sweat; his sallow face grimaced in pain. "Peter, I'm afraid you'll have to go the rest of the way alone. My leg has been getting stiffer with every step." Mr. Doyle rolled up a pant leg to expose a grossly swollen, purple and yellow knee that would not bend. "I don't want to hold you two back if you need to get out in a hurry."

Peter didn't like having to go into another unfamiliar place alone. It wasn't Mr. Doyle's fault that Pumpkin wouldn't make him the cleats or that he was too hurt to continue into the realm of the pitcher plant fairy, but Peter couldn't help feeling resentful. He came to Lore Isle with the understanding that Mr. Doyle was going to do the major lifting and he was just going to help. This whole trip was beginning to feel like his own quest. That irritated him like an itchy sweater he was dying to take off.

"Pumpkin said fairies are temperamental. She could just turn me into a toad and take the mirror," Peter said.

"Fairies are capable of many things, but cheating others out of a fair trade is not one of them."

Peter remembered the smith telling him that fairies would never try to swindle anyone. He looked up at the colossal flowers and shuddered, thinking about the corresponding size of the leafy pitchers that waited below the raised boardwalk.

Mr. Doyle followed Peter's gaze and said, "You must take great care not to leave the boardwalk. These pitcher plants have a taste for things much bigger than insects."

Great. More flesh-eaters.

Mr. Doyle put a hand on Peter's shoulder and made sure he was paying attention. "Once you step onto the boardwalk, you're in Sarracena's realm. The moment you return and step off, she cannot harm you." Unconsciously, his fingers dug into Peter's shoulder, and Peter knew Mr. Doyle was more apprehensive than yesterday when he had sent him into the mine with the leprechauns.

Mr. Doyle leaned heavily on his makeshift cane and said in a chipper voice, "I'll see you *both* back at the cabin!" He pulled his mouth wide, but his eyes—under worried brows—had no smile in them.

Peter walked up the steps to the boardwalk. His leg muscles and nerves were as taut as bowstrings.

24

Sarracena's Curse

THE STEMS OF THE PITCHER PLANTS CURVED down at the top like candy canes, and the burgundy flowers tracked Peter's movements from above. He hurried toward the blanket of mist up ahead.

Unfortunately, he didn't feel any safer in the mist. Even though he could no longer see the pitcher plants, he had the sinking feeling that the plants knew exactly where he was. When a sandpaper tongue licked his ear, he fought the urge to bolt. Falling into a supersized pitcher would be like falling into a well, with slippery walls that would prevent him from getting out. The carnivorous plant would then feast on his decomposing body. Petrified of slipping off the boardwalk and into a pitcher, Peter considered crawling.

To calm his jagged nerves, he focused on his end goal: gold for his mom. She'd be so happy to be able to live in Grandpa's house for as long as she wanted. And when he told her about his dangerous adventures and how brave he'd been, she will be proud of him. So proud that she'll forget all about the imagined twin. Finally, he will be enough. No more staring at the blue chair, no more trances, no more slipping into her dark fantasy world. In reality, always. Present with him, always.

And with that hope, he shuffled forward.

The mist had cleared by the time the narrow boardwalk came to an end at a grand circular deck. Peter was light-headed from looking down, straining to see the scarcely-visible boardwalk. On the far side of the deck, a winding staircase ribboned up to an upper deck. Amazingly, the stairs were the only structure supporting the second storey.

As soon as Peter noticed a big cage under the staircase, fine lime green dots floated up like dust disturbed in sunlight and enveloped the cage to hide the prisoner inside. He walked over and reluctantly stepped into the suspended powder. His nose tingled and his throat tickled from inhaling the stuff.

With his arms stretched out front, walking like a zombie, he found the metal bars of the cage. He strained to see inside and made out the blurry shape of a person sitting.

"Are you Ella?"

The blurry shape stood up. "How do you know my name?"

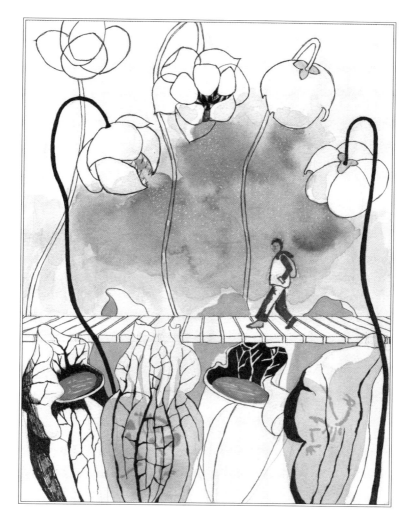

Somewhere from the upper deck, a voice bright as a bell rang down. "All visitors must come upstairs."

"Tell me your name," Ella said with urgency.

"It's Peter. I'll be back."

He walked out of the lime green haze and, with wobbly legs, climbed up the staircase. He saw a gazebo sitting at the far end of the upper deck. The granite structure, which was a pinky-tan colour with flecks of sparkling azure, had a domed roof.

At the edge of the deck, Peter gazed out on Sarracena's vast, wet empire. How could he be so high up when he had climbed only a single storey?

He entered the stone gazebo through an arched doorway. Oddly, it was much bigger on the inside. In the centre, Sarracena sat on an elaborate throne woven with the stems of the oversized pitcher plants and lined with their waxy burgundy petals. Flanking the throne was a bed and a wardrobe made of the same material. The curved wall was lined with bookshelves that held thousands of books.

Sarracena motioned with her long fingers for Peter to come closer. The floor, carpeted with soft, green moss, was spongy and pleasant to walk on. He looked up at the indigo ceiling decorated with moving stars—they were fireflies. The tall, narrow windows had curtains the colour of moonbeams, which were so shimmery and fine that they couldn't have been made by human hands.

When Peter came close to Sarracena, he locked on her amethyst eyes. Her flawless skin was the shade of pale gold. Her long ebony hair, crowned with a wreath of thorns, gently swayed even though there was no breeze. She wore her beautiful, pastel green wedding gown, lined with delicate red rubies that mimicked the veins on the pitcher of the carnivorous plant.

"Why have you come?" Sarracena said.

"I want to make a trade," Peter replied, blushing. He rummaged through the rucksack, thankful to have a reason to look away from her eyes, which seemed to see right through him.

Fumbling, Peter pulled out the cracked mirror from the bundle of cloth, then quickly flipped it over to reveal the Upland coat of arms engraved on the back.

Sarracena caught her breath, then stood up so fast that she startled him. "What do you want for it?"

"I—I want the release of your prisoner, Ella," Peter stuttered.

The fairy stepped back, reached for her throne, and wilted into it. "Ask for anything but that."

"Are you kidding me? Isn't there someone you want to see in the mirror?"

"Yes." Tears glittering like diamonds rolled down her cheeks. "More than anything. But I'm afraid to have the cage empty. I need assurance that I won't ever be alone."

Eager to give her a clear plan, Peter said, "You won't be alone. The mirror will show you where your groom is, and a servant can use your godmother's dragonfly belt to break him out of the barrens. Once the servant leads George to you and places your hand in George's, Penelope's undoing spell will kick in, and you two can live happily ever after." He almost added, "Ta-dah!"

Sarracena twitched once and regarded him with a steady gaze. "Well, my dear, you seem to know quite a bit about my story." She stood up and walked toward him. Her dress skimmed the floor as if she was gliding an inch off the floor, and the rubies winked like tiny Christmas lights.

"Stay with me forever, and I'll take care of you." Her singsong voice lulled him.

No more worries about money for the house, no burden of a quest. Living with Sarracena seemed like the ideal life.

"I want to have an ordinary life again. I'm tired," he confessed.

"Sapped, you might say." A chair appeared behind Peter. Sarracena gently pushed his chest with her long fingers, and he fell back into the chair, holding tight to the mirror.

Yes. He was sapped. Grandpa's death has been hard enough, but the altered will, the evil aunts, and Mom's condition left Peter with little choice but to follow Mr. Doyle and his promised gold coins. And in Lore Isle, the list of what he needed to accomplish kept growing—it now included the responsibility of the resurrection of the extinct Newfoundland wolf. "It's all too much!" Peter blurted out.

"I understand," Sarracena cooed with a motherly expression.

The fireflies floating around the indigo ceiling blinked their sympathetic lights. The gossamer drapes undulated in a gentle, warm breeze. Sarracena's dress grew tall and wide and multi-layered like a giant wedding cake. Delectable desserts appeared on every layer. He had seen similar, ornately decorated cakes and pastries at her wedding. His mouth flooded with saliva in anticipation. *Where to start?*

"Try them all. They're all for you," said the honeyed voice from above.

Peter picked up a petit four covered in smooth, pale blue icing and decorated with an exquisite lily of the valley made from green marzipan for the leaves and precious, pearled candy beads for the flowers.

He popped the entire creation into his mouth.

It tasted delicious...but stale. *Could these be the same desserts from the wedding?*

"Have another, my sweet."

Peter had another, and another. He couldn't stop eating them. Outside the windows, the sun, in slow motion, rose and began to come back down. Patiently, Sarracena watched him from above, smiling like an angel on top of a Christmas tree. Peter was sure the fairy was proud of him for eating so well.

An ostentatious gold goblet appeared in her hand. From a small packet, she sprinkled lime green powder into the drink. It fizzed. "A little fairy dust." She winked.

She opened her hand and the goblet floated down to him. The beads of sweat covering the metal vessel promised a cold drink. The dry pastries and cakes had made him thirsty.

Peter gulped down the refreshing liquid. Bright flashes of his life in Newfoundland burst in his head. He saw his grandpa with a fishing rod, Mom pruning a plant, the school bus pulling up to the museum, Ben and his dog Willow coming around the side of the house, his aunts puffing and inhaling. Then the memories began to fade like sun-bleached photographs 'til he even forgot his own name. Tension drained from his body as if he had put down a heavy object he had been holding.

"You may stay with me forever once you give me the mirror," said a fuzzy and gooey voice.

That's a fair trade. He held up the mirror like big toy rattle.

"Don't do it, Peter!" the girl in the cage cried out. Her voice resonated in Peter's head. He remembered his name.

"My, what good hearing you have, Ella!" Sarracena yelled down. She appeared colossal and malevolent.

Peter's skin burned like ice water had been poured over him. He jolted back to his senses. The full memory of Newfoundland came rushing back. Stiffly, he stood up and held the back of the chair with one hand so his sore legs wouldn't buckle under the onerous weight of what he must accomplish. "The mirror for the prisoner, please." He didn't dare look into Sarracena's face.

The chair disappeared, and Peter almost lost his balance. The desserts and goblet disappeared, too, and Sarracena's dress shrunk back to a normal size.

"The mirror is damaged. I'll have to make sure it works." Sarracena held out her hand. "You may wait downstairs."

"Can I trust you?" Peter stammered.

"You don't have a choice," she said through gritted teeth.

Peter hesitated, then placed the mirror in her outstretched hand.

The blinking fireflies on the ceiling made jagged patterns. A gust of wind blew through the gazebo and ruffled the bedding and opened the door of the wardrobe. Peter recognized the dragonfly belt hanging inside one of the doors.

With his empty rucksack, he turned to leave. At the arched doorway, Peter looked back. Sarracena sat at the edge of her bed trembling, holding the mirror face down, unable to bring herself to ask the question yet.

Outside the gazebo, Peter saw that the sun was moving toward the horizon. *How long was I in there?* He went down the stairs. *Why is it always more difficult to walk down the stairs than up when your leg muscles are stiff?*

Uncomfortably full from eating so many treats, Peter followed his distended belly to the cage. The lime green fog still surrounded the cage, and it was hard to see Ella. "Thanks for yelling out when you did," Peter said.

Ella stood opposite. "No problem. I knew she would give you the fairy dust drink to make you forget who you were."

Peter wished he could see the face of the prisoner who had saved him from becoming another prisoner. The feeling that things weren't going to go as planned gnawed at him, and he felt around the cage and shook its sturdy bars. In a low voice, he asked, "Do you know where she keeps the key?" hoping it was hanging somewhere nearby.

"She always has it with her," Ella said.

"Oh."

They stood facing each other in glum silence in the gloom of the fog.

Peter forced a bright voice. "I just gave Sarracena the magic mirror she needs to find her groom. Once she sees him, she'll let you out. Any minute now."

"No!" A wretched scream pealed down from the upper deck. There was the sound of glass shattering. "He's dead! My love is dead!"

The fog-obscured shape of Ella pushed her face between the bars. "Run, Peter. Run!"

Peter took a few fast steps to the boardwalk, spurred by the urgency in Ella's voice. Then he stopped, because the mirror—his only bargaining chip—was worthless, and he was leaving Mr. Doyle's goddaughter behind.

"Where are you, messenger of death?" screeched the fairy, who had nothing more to lose. Peter feared for his life.

He tried to sprint toward the thick mist, but with the injuries he had sustained in the mine, he scurried, halting every few steps, terrified of falling off the boardwalk into a pitcher-shaped belly. The mist enveloped him and made him invisible. However, the boardwalk was narrow enough that Sarracena needed only to run with her long arms open and she wouldn't miss him. It just came down to who was the faster runner. Peter knew who that'd be. The fancy cakes in his bloated belly did somersaults.

Then an odd thing happened.

Peter heard Ella's voice inside his head. She said, "I know the boardwalk. Let me guide you."

Peter instinctively relaxed. It was as if Ella had entered his body and taken over. All his aches stopped hurting. With confidence, he ran faster than he had ever run in his life, faster than he thought he was capable. He hugged the curves of the boardwalk, his arm and leg muscles flexed taut like he was running on all fours. The heads of the pitcher plants opened up to reveal razor-sharp teeth. They bent down and snapped at him. His deft manoeuvring avoided most of the chomps, but the serrated teeth once deeply grazed his cheek and twice his arms, although he felt no pain.

Within a fraction of the time it took to walk the other way, he came to the end of the boardwalk. He didn't bother with the stairs, but jumped off, shoulder-rolled onto the dirt path, and collapsed. Then without warning, his body went from feeling nothing to feeling everything. The pain from his injuries yesterday plus the new ones from the run erupted in unison.

Whimpering in agony, Peter raised himself to his knees, huffing and puffing, trying to draw more air into his lungs. His sweat-drenched shirt clung to his back.

Soon, the pitcher plant fairy glided to a stop at the end of the boardwalk. Peter sat down and scuttled backwards like a crab, even though he knew she couldn't step off the boardwalk as it marked the end of her territory.

Sarracena's silky tresses rose, waving and reshaping until they looked like the long, waxy stems of the pitcher plant, then winding and coiling like severed snakes. Her wreath of thorns had sprouted black flowers. On her

gown—no longer a pale apple green but poison green—
the blood-red ruby veins pulsated.

Her face was contorted with grief. "George is dead in
the barrens, and I have no one to curse but the messenger
who has shattered all my hopes."

"B...but you can't do anything to me now. I'm off the
boardwalk, I'm not in your realm."

Sarracena pressed her lips together in a bitter smile,
"My dear, I cursed you the moment I threw down the
mirror."

Pumpkin had said that a fairy curse on a human, a
mere mortal, could not be undone, not even by the fairy
who had cast the curse. Peter tried to swallow but his
throat was constricted.

"I know why you're here in Lore Isle. Gold, gold everywhere, but none to keep. You will *not* return to your land
with what you came searching for."

Her words hurt Peter more than all his wounds
combined.

25

Uncle Albert

PETER TOTTERED AWAY FROM THE BOARD-walk with his long and sombre shadow at his heel. He sat down on a rock, not to rest, but to think. *Since fairy curses are sure to come true, am I really going home with no gold? After all I've gone through?*

He touched the sticky wetness on his burning cheek. Without Ella's help, he couldn't have escaped. He tried to find Ella in his head again to see if he could talk to her, but only his own thoughts were there. He moaned. How could he go back and tell Mr. Doyle that he had left his goddaughter in the cage?

The cage!

When Peter had grabbed the bars and shook them, the vertical rods hadn't felt smooth, they had felt ornate—like the gates made by Pumpkin. Could he have built the cage for Sarracena? He had built the gates for another fairy. In his drunken stupor, the smith had told Peter that he used dwarfmade locks that could be opened with a code because he was afraid of being locked away by an ill-tempered fairy. That meant Peter also knew the code to open the locks on any ironwork made by Pumpkin.

With his sleeve, Peter wiped the film of cold perspiration on his forehead. Sarracena must be seething, dreaming up loads of curses to throw at the "messenger of death," if given the opportunity. He was scared to go back, but she might take out her anger on Ella, who had thwarted her attempt to capture the next prisoner. He had to go back for Ella and he had to go now. He adjusted the rucksack and hobbled back toward the realm of the Pitcher Plant Fairy.

Next to the boardwalk, the towering pitcher plants with slack goose necks tracked his movement. Some yawned, exposing rows of serrated teeth. One made a half-hearted attempt to bite him. Peter couldn't hear the voice that had helped him earlier and feared that Ella was hurt—or worse. Ceaselessly, he walked.

It was almost dark when the cage came into view and there was no lime green haze surrounding it to conceal the prisoner. Peter saw the outline of a figure hugging her knees. He breathed a sigh of relief.

Ella's eyes bugged out when she saw him. "Peter, is that you?" she whispered, standing up. She was as tall as him. Her face was tanned, and her uncombed hair was short and dark.

"I'm going to get you out. I promised Mr. Doyle."

"Mr. Doyle? You know Uncle Albert?"

Peter had a flashback to the funeral reception where the old man had bowed low and said, "Albert Doyle, at your service."

"Where's Sarracena?" he asked.

Ella tilted her head toward the upper deck. "She drank a lot of wine. Came downstairs for a while and paced back and forth, ranting and crying. I couldn't make out what she was saying, but the way she kept looking at me sent chills up my spine. It's been quiet up there for a while, though. I think she's sleeping."

Peter inspected the cage door, searching for the lock.

"Hey, I appreciate you coming back and I wish you could get me out, but I told you—Sarracena has the key."

The cage was crafted with beautiful butterflies, dragonflies, and pitcher plants, not the berries, vines, and tendrils on the gates for Racem. After scrutinizing the door for a few more seconds, Peter found the small round lock with the two-lizard design and knew without a doubt that it was Pumpkin's work.

"Open Pumpkin Carriage."

A soft click.

Peter opened the cage door. Wide-eyed, Ella slipped out. Without delay, she moved toward the boardwalk, but Peter didn't stir.

When she noticed that Peter was not behind her, Ella whispered, "Come on."

"I have to get something from Sarracena's room," Peter whispered back.

"You've got to be joking!" Her arms flapped in frustration.

Peter motioned for Ella to go on ahead. "I'll catch up to you." Peter moved to the staircase.

"I'm not leaving you. I'll come up with you," Ella said, and doubled back after him.

Peter turned and said, "No. Wait here. Please." The seriousness in his voice stopped Ella from following him any further.

Peter climbed up the stairs and crept into Sarracena's domed residence. It was darker than the moonlit outdoors. The luminescence from the fireflies on the ceiling showed the outline of the bed, chair, and wardrobe. There was something large and rotund on the bed, waiting like a hungry spider. It swelled and shrank as it breathed. The air held the odour of plant decay.

Peter wanted to turn around, but he knew he couldn't leave without it. After many careful tiptoes to the wardrobe, he reached for the handle. The door opened with a tattletale creak, and he snatched what was hanging on the inside of the door.

Tentacles rose up from the rotund shape on the bed. It spoke in Sarracena's voice: "Who's there?" Peter nearly jumped out of his skin.

All the fireflies fluttered down and illuminated the thief holding the dragonfly belt.

"Are you stealing from me?" said the giant octopus-like Sarracena. The singsong voice that had enticed Peter to stay was now a mournful tune.

"No. Kind of. Er...yes. Penelope, George's cousin, the one who undid some of the enchantress's curse at your wedding, she's trapped by a spell herself and she needs the belt."

"Ah, sweet Penelope devised a loophole in Elora's curse. She gave me hope." Her tentacles swayed like seaweeds in water.

The fireflies returned to the ceiling.

Peter clutched the belt in the dimly lit darkness. "We became friends at your wedding. The belt will allow her to go home."

"Everyone wants to go home," Sarracena said bitterly. "Fairies are fated to live in solitude, and it can't be changed. I was a fool to try but...I was so lonely." She choked back a sob. "Poor George." The black blob kept grasping for something in the air with its many limbs.

Peter's heart went out to her. "I'm sorry about your groom. I thought I was going to make you happy by giving you the mirror."

Sarracena wondered aloud, "Was it always George's fate to die or did he die because he fell in love with someone who was destined to be alone? I think the latter. Unlucky man." She gave a sad laugh.

Her despair filled the room like water seeping into the cabin of a boat, and Peter felt he was running out of air. "May I take the dragonfly belt?"

"You must really want it, to risk another unbreakable curse to come back for it."

"Penelope doesn't know it, but she's relying on me."

"You impress me, Peter. How old are you?"

"Thirteen."

Her tentacles curled softly like tendrils. "Thirteen is a beautiful and trying age for humans. Everything is changing. You're growing up fast whether you want to or not." Her voice was motherly, and Peter thought of Mom, who needed him the most.

"I am so tired." Her voice was tinny and far away. Her tentacles stopped waving. The black blob went back to just breathing, inhaling and exhaling, swelling and shrinking.

Peter put the belt in his rucksack and hurried to the door.

Ella was waiting for him at the bottom of the stairs.

"I think we should walk softly instead of running," Peter whispered. Ella nodded.

The sun had set. The moon behind the clouds gave the mist an eerie green glow. Ella took the lead, and Peter followed. They didn't speak a word the entire way, but listened for the fairy who might have changed her mind about the belt or noticed that her prisoner was gone. All was quiet in the fen. When they came out of the mist, they saw why: the bulbous heads of the pitcher plants bobbed up and down in peaceful slumber. Ella and Peter picked up their pace.

At the end of the boardwalk, Ella jumped down. "I can't believe it! I'm free!" She ran up the path whooping and performed a cartwheel and a front flip. "It feels so good to run and move!"

Peter, brimming with questions, caught up to her. "When I left you earlier, when Sarracena was coming for me, I could hear your voice. Did you hear me?"

Ella performed joyful jumping jacks. "No, I didn't hear you, but I could feel how afraid you were about falling off the boardwalk. I could see in my mind where you were and knew I could guide you."

"How'd you do that? How were you able to see where I was and feel what I was feeling?"

"I don't know. That's never happened before." She started to jump up and down like she had springs on the bottom of her shoes and *boing-boinged* down the path.

Peter, who had to take big steps to keep up with her, said, "I've never run so fast in my entire life. Not even close. It was like getting powered by the fastest animal on earth. I didn't even feel any pain from my injuries until I got off the boardwalk."

"Hmm." Ella stopped jumping and walked. "Somehow all your aches and pains were passed onto me because I felt them all, including the pitcher plant chomps. Really burned."

Peter touched the dried blood on his cheek.

"I liked the feeling of a full stomach, though. I was getting so homesick I lost my appetite." Ella rubbed her concave stomach. "How many cakes did you eat anyway?"

"Enough to make a house with," Peter said, ashamed.

"Anyway, I saw the end of the boardwalk, then suddenly I couldn't see where you were anymore. And all the hurting stopped."

"That's when all the pain came back to me. My entire body burned," Peter said.

The cloud covering the moon moved away, and moonlight lit the wooded path. Peter took long glances at Ella because her profile was familiar, somehow.

"How did you end up in her cage anyway?"

"I love adventures—going on excursions and seeing landscapes I've never seen before. Only a few have explored the realm of the pitcher plants, and I decided to follow the boardwalk and have a look around. Somewhere deep in her land, there is supposed to be a spectacular waterfall that flows upwards. Of course, I didn't get anywhere close to it."

"What about those carnivorous pitcher plants? Weren't you afraid?"

"I guess so, but I can run pretty fast."

Peter believed her because he felt like he had experienced how fast she could run.

Ella continued, "When I reached the end of the board-walk, where the mist clears, I was surprised to see the fairy standing there waiting for me. She took me upstairs, gave me cakes and the drink with the forgetting powder, and asked me to stay with her forever. And I said yes, and the next thing I know, I'm in a cage."

"Did she keep you as a prisoner for trespassing?"

"That's what I thought at the beginning, but she just wanted someone to talk to."

Peter was confused. "But aren't all fairies supposed to be solitary creatures who want to be left alone to study?"

"During the day, she read her books and wrote, but in the evenings, she wanted to hear about what I've seen outside of her realm and to tell me about her research on entomology—that's what scholars call the study of insects. A lot of it was beyond my knowledge level, but what I could understand was pretty interesting."

"She was lonely," Peter said, thinking about the black blob in Sarracena's bed. "I think she's an anomaly. She isn't like all the other fairies." *Just like I am not like all the other Connorses.*

"She sprinkled the forgetting powder in my food at every meal, and I was pretty content. But after I don't know how many weeks, it stopped working on me, and I asked, begged, and demanded to be released every day. She told me I would be free to go after she got married because she would always have company. But on her wedding day, she came back alone, and I wasn't released as promised."

Peter knew why that was.

Ella then asked, "What village are you from?"

"I'm not from anywhere in Lore Isle, I'm from Newfoundland."

"Oh!" She clapped her hands in excitement. "You're from the magical place the wolves in the egg are from."

"Yup. Your uncle brought me here. He promised me gold coins if I helped him find you and the egg. Since I got you out, I guess I'm halfway to my reward."

"Poor Uncle Albert." Ella placed her hands on the sides of her face. "My poor mom! They must be so worried about me. I suppose your family is worried about you coming to Lore Isle?"

"My mom doesn't know I'm here."

The moonlight coated the forest with a velvety soft glow. The path back to the cabin was long and impossible for Peter to see, but Ella guided them back without any trouble. Fiddlehead-shaped smoke rose out of the chimney and uncurled.

A figure came out of the door of the cabin, hollering and waving.

Ella shouted, "Uncle Albert!" and sprinted toward him.

Mr. Doyle hugged her so hard that Ella's feet came off the ground. "How I missed you."

He held her at arm's length and looked her up and down. "I think you've grown some more," he laughed.

"There's more white in your grey hair, and I think that's my fault," Ella said.

"Are you alright, my girl?" There was a catch in his voice.

She wiped under his eyes. "Don't cry, Uncle Albert. I'm safe." He hugged her again.

They stood with their arms around each other, waiting for Peter to catch up.

"Thank goodness. When you didn't return by suppertime, I thought something terrible had happened to you."

"Something terrible almost happened," Peter said.

Mr. Doyle motioned to the door. "Come inside and tell me all about it."

The warmth from the hearth and the aroma of soup welcomed back Peter. Grinning from ear to ear, Mr. Doyle carried over the pot and ladled the soup into bowls. In the broth, along with bits of the stolen hen, there were root vegetables from the cellar and foraged plant leaves and mushrooms.

Grabbing her spoon, Ella said, "I'm starved."

Noticing that Peter was barely eating, Mr. Doyle asked, "What's the matter, Peter? Aren't you hungry?"

Peter told Mr. Doyle what had happened in the realm of the pitcher plant fairy: eating the dozen cakes and pastries, getting chased by the fairy, recognizing Pumpkin's work, and remembering the words to open the cage.

"And you'll never guess what I have in the rucksack, Mr. Doyle."

"Your adventure has my head spinning. I can't begin to guess."

"The dragonfly belt." He pulled it out of the rucksack.

"Is that why you went back up?" Ella said with her mouth full.

Peter nodded. "It's a magic belt. I am going to give it to Penelope."

"Who's Penelope?" Ella said. Peter explained that she

was a tree sprite who was a prisoner of the mummers and was in need of rescuing.

Mr. Doyle didn't even glance at the belt, but continued to eat his soup. "So, when Peter was chased on the boardwalk, you shared some kind of a mental connection?"

"Yes," Ella said. "Just like Peter told you. I felt what he felt. Weird, huh?"

"Not completely," Mr. Doyle hesitated. "You are twins, after all."

Peter and Ella stared. Ella turned and studied Peter's features.

"That's impossible," Peter said to Mr. Doyle, his heart thumping.

"It's not impossible," Ella followed. "I was adopted."

"You were?" Peter examined Ella's face closely, noticing the familiar curve of her nose and angle of the jawline. They were the same height, too. His head reeled.

"Uncle Albert found me as a baby in the forest and brought me to my mom. Well, he's not really my uncle, but I call him 'uncle' and I love him like a grandpa." Ella smiled at Mr. Doyle. "He and Mom guessed someone from one of the villages couldn't take care of me and left me there."

"My mom said I have a twin, but he...or she"— Peter said "she" like there was a question mark after it—"disappeared."

"Disappeared?" Ella was shocked.

"Disappeared, went missing. I'm not sure. I thought Mom just made it up."

"What?" Ella scratched her forehead. "That's a strange thing to say. You think your mom would lie to you about something like that?"

The answer was no. Mom wouldn't lie about something so serious; in fact, she had never lied to him. Yet all these years, he had never believed her. But if there was a twin, that didn't necessarily mean it was Ella. Why would his twin be in Lore Isle?

Peter turned to Mr. Doyle. "How do you know Ella is my sister? How did she get to Lore Isle?" The answers couldn't come fast enough, yet a part of him was afraid of what he'd learn.

"Why didn't you tell me before that I had a brother, Uncle Albert? I'm surprised you'd keep such a big thing from me," Ella added.

A scratching sound came from the door. Mr. Doyle stood up and went to answer it. Peter turned from the table to see a black wolf enter the cabin.

Ella dropped her spoon onto the table and ran toward the wolf crying, "Mom!" Just before she reached her, Ella turned into a wolf herself. There was a crackle of electricity in the air. Her transition was fast and smooth, with a flash of pins of light and no glimpses of uncomfortable transitional moments like with Mr. Doyle.

Peter's jaw dropped. *My twin is a lycanthrope!* Ella must be the one Mr. Doyle had vaguely mentioned as the lycanthrope born after himself in Newfoundland.

Ella, like Mr. Doyle, was smaller than the Lore Isle wolves, but larger than the wolf in the glass case in the museum. She had thick, pale grey fur sprinkled with light brown. She was magnificent. The reunited mother and daughter tumbled and licked each other, knocking into the empty chair. Why hadn't he noticed before that Ella wore clothes made of wolf hide similar to Mr. Doyle's? Perhaps because the clothes looked more like dirty rags.

Ella moved and talked excitedly in wolf language, unable to contain herself, like a kid who had just returned from summer camp, telling her mom everything that had happened as fast as she could so as not to leave out a single detail. Peter wondered if Ella would tell her mother that she'd just found out she was a twin. Judging by the way the black wolf eyed his face, he guessed yes.

The young wolf changed back to her human form effortlessly. Her hide shirt, trousers, and moccasin boots now looked clean. The transformation had renewed and cleaned the hides.

"I told my mom about being captured by Sarracena and how you rescued me and that you came to Lore Isle to get gold coins. My mom said to tell you 'thank you.'"

The wolf mother came over to Peter. She lowered her huge head and pressed it to his hand. Not knowing what to do, he awkwardly patted her head.

"Peter, allow me to introduce you to Nan, Ella's adoptive mother," Mr. Doyle said. "All Lore Isle wolves understand human speech, just as El and I understand wolf speech even when we're in human form."

"You're welcome," Peter said to Nan.

Nan said something in wolf language. Mr. Doyle took Ella's empty bowl and filled it with soup for the second time. "Nan says her cub looks thin."

After she finished her second bowl, Ella suggested they all sit on the hooked floor rug so she could be close to her mom when Mr. Doyle told his story of how she came to Lore Isle.

26

Mr. Doyle's Story

SITTING CROSS-LEGGED ON THE RUG, PETER said, "Don't leave out anything."

"I won't. There are some things that even Nan doesn't know," Mr. Doyle said.

Nan lifted her head. Her yellow eyes flickered. Ella sat so close to Nan she seemed almost on top of her.

"Do you remember the story of Noah, my Sunday school teacher and the lycanthrope who was the guardian of the egg containing the last two Newfoundland wolves?" Peter and Ella nodded in synch.

"You also know that, unfortunately, he lost the egg. He devoted the rest of his life to finding it." They nodded again.

Shortly before he passed away, Noah told me that he had no desire to spend time in Lore Isle as a mummer. He gave me his button and said, "Albert, you are like a grandson to me. It is my last wish for you to find the egg and bring the wolves back to their forest in Newfoundland." And I gave him my word I would.

When I crossed into Lore Isle for the first time, I was in university. It was love at first sight. I introduced myself to the black wolves and they were very sad to hear of Noah's passing, but excited that another lycanthrope had come to take his place.

After months of following a few leads that turned out to be wild goose chases, I came back to St. John's and returned to my studies. My two favourite classes were Literature and Mythology, because a young lady who was smart and funny was in both classes. Helen and I had a great rapport and we made an effort to be in the same study groups.

Mr. Doyle's eyes were far away. *Helen was the name of my grandma*, Peter realized.

During the week, I was studious, but on the weekends and breaks, the outdoors beckoned to me. I explored the vast wilderness of Newfoundland, thinking about when I should go back to Lore Isle.

Hiking along a river, I met a fisher.

Here, Mr. Doyle looked at Peter. "It was your grandpa, John."

Peter sat up. He was about to learn more about Grandpa's life as a young man.

We liked each other right away, and he became an older brother to me. One day, I introduced him to my classmate Helen, who I had come to adore, but with whom I'd never had the nerve to share my feelings. Well, they fell in love, and a year after Helen graduated, they married.

Mr. Doyle chuckled wistfully.

Peter said, "I wish I got to know her. Mom misses her a lot."

"She died a couple of years before you were born." Mr. Doyle sighed deeply before continuing.

On one of our fishing trips, John accidentally knocked over his tackle box, and to my great surprise, I saw a portal button fall out. He explained that a poor old woman who couldn't pay for his finished carpentry work had given it to him as payment. He didn't know what it was, so he kept it in his tackle box.

I told John about the power of the button. He thought I was mad. I showed him my button and convinced him to go through the pond with me. Once in Lore Isle, I was overcome with guilt because I had not looked for the egg in a long while. I confided in John about my mission to bring back the Newfoundland wolf and asked him to help me.

Oh, no. The beginning of the end to their friendship. Peter was sad for both parties.

Well, if I was unsure about his feelings for wolves before then, he let me know it right between the eyes. Boy, we really got into it. When he said that he didn't want his homeland infested with the wolves his grandfather had exterminated, I became wild with anger. Without thinking, I transformed into a wolf and snarled at him.

"Hope you scared him good." Ella's eyes flared as she stroked Nan's fur.

"Hey, he was your grandpa, too," Peter said, but he knew she wouldn't feel any attachment for the grandpa she had never met.

Mr. Doyle snorted.

John wasn't frightened; he looked at me with disgust. Friends to enemies in an instant. John immediately returned to Newfoundland, and I focused all my efforts on finding the egg. There were some promising leads that took me on incredible adventures, but in the end, no egg. I began to feel depressed about having been bequeathed this impossible task.

I went back to Newfoundland. Not to the city, but to a picturesque outport town where I had always planned to live out my life. After a few years, I went to see Helen because I'd never said a proper goodbye to her. She was still an engaging conversationalist with an infectious laugh. And she had twin toddlers.

"The Bobbleheads," Peter mumbled under his breath.

She wanted to know why John and I were no longer friends. John had been sparse with the details. I told her everything–the buttons, Lore Isle, my powers. She was fascinated and begged me to show her Lore Isle. We made plans. In the dead of night, we met by the pond. She had John's button around her neck, and I called a raven to drop a feather so time would be slowed in Newfoundland. We crossed, and it was pure joy to see her like a kid, wide-eyed and all smiles. It was one of the best times of my life.

Helen returned in under a minute, Newfoundland time, raced home, and no one was the wiser.

"Did you see her again?" Peter asked.

"Just once more, when she told me she and John were expecting another child."

Helen was enjoying her life with the man she loved. I had long accepted that I was lucky to have someone as wonderful as her as a friend and carried on with my life. The years flew by. I was content in my town, and I returned to Lore Isle less and less. I was becoming an old man, and it occurred to me that I might never find the egg.

About fourteen years ago, I ran into an old university classmate, Dorothea Kelly. I learned that Helen had died. I was crushed with sadness. Dorothea told me where she was buried.

The name Dorothea Kelly sounded awfully familiar to Peter.

With a bouquet of lilies, Helen's favourite flowers, I went to the cemetery. I saw a young man with a young pregnant woman in front of a grave.

The wind carried their scent to me and I stopped dead in my tracks. She didn't smell like other human beings. I smelled two unborn babies, one human and one lycanthrope. I was gobsmacked.

The couple moved away, hand in hand, as it began to rain. I saw the grave they were standing by was Helen's. The young woman was Helen's third child.

"Mom," said Peter.

"Standing at Helen's grave with a head full of grey hair," Mr. Doyle said, "I was overcome by the realization that I was not likely to find the egg in my time on earth. And I had no heir to bequeath the task that I had promised Noah I would accomplish."

The scalp on Peter's head prickled. He was beginning to figure it out. By "heir," Mr. Doyle meant a young lycanthrope who would, by nature, be invested in finding the egg containing the wolves and be able to open the egg, once returned to Newfoundland.

"I thought, what would John do with a grandchild who was half wolf? Could he ever love or even accept a lycanthrope grandchild?"

Peter said, "Yes, Grandpa would have loved her," but Mr. Doyle did not hear him because he was back in the cemetery, his amber eyes bright and focused.

"I thought to myself, the magical being belonged in Lore Isle with me."

Peter's chest tightened. He could hardly breathe. A shadowy image of a grey shape with pointed ears leaning over a bassinet darkened his mind. "You didn't take Ella after she was born." His voice faltered. "Did you?"

Mr. Doyle lowered his head. "I had help: Dorothea Kelly, my university classmate. She was a midwife by profession. She had befriended your mother."

"Mrs. Kelly." Peter now remembered how he knew that name. "The midwife took the baby from the room." He blurted it out like a police inspector at the end of a whodunit story.

"Yes."

"How did she know which baby to take?" Ella asked softly.

"I told her to bring me the baby born with hair and teeth."

The room became silent.

"I was prepared. Earlier, I had slipped into John's house and 'borrowed' his crossing button for Ella to wear. The button was gone for a short time in Newfoundland."

Peter was speechless. He had anticipated a fantastic fairy tale about how Ella got to Lore Isle. But this was a cruel story authored by a lycanthrope who committed the ruthless abduction of a baby to make her the heir to his holy grail. *How selfish!*

Ella sat up. "Mom, you told me that Uncle Albert found me in the forest. Did you know I came from Newfoundland?"

Mr. Doyle answered for Nan. "I told Nan that I found you in the forest and thought you were abandoned by a human mother because you were a lycanthrope. I wanted to keep things simple for the both of you. I told her that she should name you Ella and to take good care of you, but I had no doubt she would."

Ella hugged Nan and buried her face in the thick fur around her neck. Nan gave Ella a lick on her ear.

Peter was bewildered that, after hearing the story of her abduction, all Ella cared about was whether Nan knew where she was born. And now, satisfied with the answer, she was cuddling with her wolf mom. She didn't seem to care about her original family, the three generations who were affected by the fallout.

Mr. Doyle slapped his thigh. "I was sure that two lycanthropes could find the egg, but—"

"I'm sorry, Uncle Albert. I haven't been much help," Ella's face became twisted as she bit her upper lip.

Mr. Doyle shook his head as if to say, "it's not your fault." "Though you had us very worried when you disappeared without a trace. After days of fruitless searching, your mother and I were becoming more frightened every minute. I knew we needed help." The old man tapped his head. "I thought about your twin aunts, Bea and Agnes, when they were toddlers. They were building a grand structure with their toy blocks. Neither spoke, but their hands moved non-stop. They never got in each other's way. They understood what the other was doing without words. Helen asked them if they'd like to play hide-and-seek outside since it was a nice day, and one of the girls replied that they didn't like hide-and-seek because they always knew where the other one was hiding."

"Is that when you thought of my twin?" Ella said.

"Yes. I wasn't sure if there would be any connection between you two, since you grew up separately, but I had no other options."

When Ella saw Peter's glowering face, she said, "It worked out great for me. Peter rescued me. Otherwise, I'd still be sitting in a cage." She beamed him a grateful smile. Nan made wolf noises in agreement, followed by more infuriating cuddling. *Why are they acting like everything has turned out fine for everyone involved?*

"You kidnapping Ella devastated my mom."

Mr. Doyle flinched when he heard the word "kidnap."

"My dad couldn't cope with her grief and left us. You broke up my family. You had no right to do that!" Peter yelled the last sentence and, startled, Ella sat upright. All eyes were on him.

"I am sorry, Peter. But to be able to bring an extinct wolf species back to life…" Mr. Doyle closed his eyes. "It's a dream worth some sacrifice."

So, you're not that sorry, Peter seethed. Mr. Doyle wasn't getting it. Lives were changed that night. Peter stood up, shaking all over. "You sacrificed *my* family for *your* dream." With those words, he walked out of the cabin, slamming the door after him.

27

Red Jacket and Green Coat

PETER FOUGHT BACK THE TEARS. HOW LAUGH-
able that he had thought of Mr. Doyle as a grandfather-like
figure, that he had been grateful to have someone who
cared for him. The person Peter thought was a saviour
was a betrayer who had started Peter's journey to Lore
Isle even before he was born.

A few minutes later, two wolves came out. The younger
wolf tried to go toward Peter, but Nan nudged her away
and they loped toward the forest.

Mr. Doyle came out and stood near. "I really am sorry. I'm an insensitive fool who gets carried away."

Peter's fingernails painfully dug into his palms. "I am done with you. Take me back to the pond."

"Please, Peter. Stay and help me find the egg," Mr. Doyle begged.

"You have your lycanthrope heir to help you find the egg," he shot back.

"Ella loves me and she tries, but her heart isn't in it. She doesn't know Newfoundland like us. She has no connection to the place. Of course, she will stand beside me and fight any fights to get the egg, but you dream of bringing the wolves back to their homeland."

Peter stared ahead, trying not to think about the slumbering wolves in the egg who had already waited a hundred years to restart their lives back in their homeland.

"And what about your friend, Penelope? You got the belt for her."

Peter snorted. "You're not interested in helping her. At supper, you didn't even look at the belt when I pulled it out of the rucksack."

Mr. Doyle grabbed Peter's arm. "Don't you want to go back with the gold coins? For your mother?" He was trying every angle.

"If you cared about Mom, you would not have taken her baby and put her through misery."

Mr. Doyle's grip slackened and his hand slipped away. "I can never make up for what I have done to Lily."

Peter's head swam. He needed to go home with gold, but he was angry, red-hot angry, and couldn't think of anything but hurting Mr. Doyle. "You've taken so much from my family. It's more important to me to make sure you don't get what you want than to get what I want."

"You don't mean that." There was alarm in Mr. Doyle's voice, and Peter enjoyed it.

"I do mean it. Take me back to the pond right now!" He would have said anything now to keep Mr. Doyle's amber eyes wild with panic. He rummaged through his mind furiously, looking for something to say. *Of course!* "Mummers, take me to the pond!" he shouted.

Mr. Doyle looked frantically all around. Snowflakes began to fall, not with grace as before, but jaggedly, as if annoyed that they had been called up. The snow quickly covered all that it touched, and soon the four horsemen emerged.

Their strange bodies and faces looked more sinister in the night. Green Coat stopped his horse inches from Peter's face, and Peter knew he'd made a grave mistake. The flash-frozen grass crunched under his timid backward steps. Before he could tell Green Coat that he had changed his mind, the mummer reached down with his long arm, picked Peter up without much effort, and sat him in front.

Mr. Doyle ran up yelling, "Kidnappers!" His dark amber eyes were focused and ready to transform.

Green Coat kicked Mr. Doyle in the chest, sending him skidding and flip-flopping like a rag doll across the snow-covered ground.

"It's not kidnapping if he wants to go," spat the mummer.

Lying on the ground, Mr. Doyle moaned and made choking and gurgling sounds. Peter called out to Mr. Doyle as he squirmed to get off the horse. Green Coat grabbed Peter by the back of his collar and righted him on the saddle, before kicking the sides of the wooden horse with his heels. Once the galloping horse had gathered enough speed to maintain a certain pace, its body, as hollow as the Trojan horse, remained level while its legs moved fluidly underneath.

Red Jacket rode up to Green Coat. "This isn't the way to the pond. Where are you taking him?" His inhaled speech was barely audible in the rushing wind. Green Coat ignored him and sped up his horse.

Peter knew he was in big trouble. Back at the cabin, Mr. Doyle was lying unconscious, in no condition to call for the wolves. He thought of the other lycanthrope, his twin. Ella had been able to sense his fears in the realm of the pitcher plant fairy. Could she help him again? *I am scared, Ella. The mummers have me and I don't know where they're taking me. Can you see through my eyes like you did before?*

The moon, an enormous silver button on an endless piece of dark blue velvet, followed the riders. Big, feather-like snowflakes descended slowly, and Peter felt like he was gliding through a snow globe.

Green Coat rode the horse out to a headland and stopped near the edge of a cliff that jutted over the ink-black ocean.

Definitely not the pond.

Green Coat jumped off the horse, holding on to the scruff of Peter's neck. The other mummers caught up. The first to dismount was Red Jacket. "What are we doing here?" Red Jacket struggled to be heard above the roar of the waves.

Green Coat replied, "The boy is here to help the old wolf-man take the egg back. We can't let that happen. I am going to throw him over the cliff. If the rocks below don't kill him, the waves will take him out and drown him. It's for the good of Newfoundland."

"No! I won't let you kill the boy." Red Jacket strode forward, reaching out for Peter.

Green Coat motioned to the other two mummers, who rushed forward, each seizing one of Red Jacket's arms. Sneering, Green Coat dragged Peter across the ground, studded with stones slippery with the fallen snow.

Kicking and punching, Peter fought for his life with every ounce of energy he could muster—but he was no match for the seven-foot-tall mummer. As Green Coat dragged him closer to the edge, something pale and fleet-footed caught Peter's eye. The black Lore Isle wolves were harder to make out in the dark, but they were there, running down the hill behind a pale wolf.

Ella!

When the wolves saw the mummers, they barked and picked up their speed. They were seconds away from reaching Peter, but that was all the time Green Coat needed. Green Coat picked Peter up and flung him high over the ocean.

The world became silent and slow-moving. Peter was so high in the air, he thought he could touch the cratered face of the moon. He wondered if the moon orbited closer to Lore Isle than Newfoundland, or if Lore Isle had its own moon, bigger, like everything else here. He looked down and saw the wolves come to a stop near the edge of the cliff. The pale wolf jumped as if the ground was hot. Red Jacket wriggled free of the two mummers, who were laughing.

When Peter began his descent, he passed by Green Coat, who thrust his arms up in a V for "victory." Then

Peter was below the headland, looking at the jagged purple cliffside, and time sped up again. As the deafening roar of the crashing waves assaulted his ears, he flailed his arms and legs uselessly like an overturned insect. He heard Sarracena's angry voice: "You will *not* return to your land with what you came searching for." *Death would definitely fulfill that curse.*

A swoosh of red and white clothes flew toward Peter. Something solid caught him and sailed with him back to the top of the cliff. Cradled in the arms of the fish bone–faced mummer, Peter looked into his eyes. Red Jacket alighted softly, placing him near the pale wolf. Peter's legs wobbled like jelly, and he collapsed. Instantly, the wolves made a protective circle around him.

Enraged, Green Coat stamped his feet and cursed at Red Jacket, who stood there calmly. The other two mummers looked unsure of what to do next. The tight ring of wolves pulled back their lips and bared their long teeth.

"Let's go," Green Coat spat.

The mummers mounted their horses and rode away, disappearing into the night.

Ella took her human form and helped Peter stand up. "Are you alright?"

"I think so." His rapid breathing matched his pounding heartbeat, and he worried he might hyperventilate.

"Can you walk?"

"Yes." He forced himself to take slower breaths. "Green Coat hurt Mr. Doyle badly. He's passed out in front of the cabin."

All the wolves anxiously stepped around the twins.

"Mom and I'll run back first. You're safe with the wolves. They'll take you to the cabin." Ella became a wolf in a leap and, with Nan at her heels, ran back up the hill into the dark forest.

28

Black Wolves

PETER LOOKED AT THE REMAINING SIX WOLVES, whose wet noses came to his shoulders. When none of them moved, he started walking in the direction Ella and Nan had gone. The wolves arranged themselves on both his sides and walked with him. Thoughts about how close he had come to having his head smashed against the wet boulders roiled and coiled his stomach like the waves below. Peter breathed in deeply. The last thing he wanted was to throw up in front of the wolves. *What must these wolves think of me?* Likely that he was the most reckless human they'd ever met, who kept getting into trouble and needed rescuing day and night.

Since the Lore Isle wolves understood human speech, Peter thought he should say something to improve their opinion of him. "I think it's great you're all so loyal to the cause of returning the wolves to Newfoundland."

Peter looked for reactions, but the wolves continued to walk facing forward.

He searched for something he had learned. "Did you know wolves are found all over the world, yet there are no wolves in Newfoundland? Well, unless you count the stuffed one in the museum."

Many wolves turned their heads to look at him.

Why did I say that for? "I mean, the wolf isn't the only one stuffed. There's a whole bunch of other stuffed animals at the museum."

He bit his bottom lip. *That did not sound good.*

"Don't get me wrong. Much of Newfoundland is still pristine wilderness and has lots of wildlife. I think you'd like it there. It looks a lot like Lore Isle, but everything is different."

Several wolves looked at each other.

That just made no sense. Peter thought it might be best to walk the rest of the way in silence.

A wet nose nudged his shoulder. A young wolf, with eyes and nose as black and shiny as licorice, looked into his face expectantly. Peter was sure the young wolf wanted to hear more. Encouraged, he continued to talk about Newfoundland. His heart swelled to talk about the island he loved so much.

By the time the cabin came into view, he had told the wolves about the icebergs in Iceberg Alley, salmon fishing in Exploits River, cod fishing at Fogo Island, the fossil rubbings on his bedroom wall that he made at Mistaken Point, the holidays in Gros Morne, and the place that made the biggest impression on him, the Viking settlement at

L'Anse aux Meadows. Peter realized with a sting in his nose that he had done all those things and seen all those places with Grandpa.

It was the dead of night, and Peter couldn't believe he had yammered the whole way. He wished he could understand wolves, for he was sure they had seen and done amazing, wolfish things and had wondrous stories to tell.

The black wolves settled on the front yard like sentry soldiers. They didn't want to return home without learning their leader's condition.

Peter took a deep breath and opened the door.

On the hooked rug, Nan licked the head wound of the grey wolf to stop the bleeding. The pale wolf watching whimpered. Peter wasn't expecting to see Mr. Doyle and Ella in wolf form. He stood there feeling like an outsider. "Hello."

The grey wolf raised his head and pulled himself up to his feet with great effort and changed into his human form, growling in pain.

The old man, with a deathly pallor, shuffled unsteadily on his feet. "Thank goodness you're alright. Ella told me what happened to you."

"I'm sorry. Calling up the mummers was a stupid thing to do."

"No need for an apology. You were right to be angry."

Ella took her human form and helped her uncle sit in a chair.

Peter looked to Nan. "The wolves are waiting outside for news of Mr. Doyle." Nan padded out the front door.

A kettle hung over the fire in the stone fireplace. Peter made a pot of tea for everyone and joined the two lycanthropes sitting at the table. "I didn't think the mummers were my friends, but why did they try to kill me?"

"Because they've figured out that you're helping me," Mr. Doyle replied, "and you also have a button that will allow you to go back to Newfoundland with the egg."

"Then why didn't they just take me to the pond, push me in, and send me back?"

"You're young. They don't want to risk you coming back. They want to kill you and be done with it." Mr. Doyle sighed.

Ella looked at Peter with serious eyes. "We won't let that happen."

"No matter what you think of me, Peter," Mr. Doyle began, "you can be sure I'll do everything in my power to see that you get back home safely." His calloused hands wrapped around the teacup on the table. "Peter, do you still believe in the quest? Will you help me find the egg and collect your reward?"

Now that his outrage from Mr. Doyle's revelation had subsided and Peter could think more clearly, he again longed to take the wolves in the egg back to Newfoundland and release them from their long slumber. "I want to go on, but..." He raised his voice, "If there are any more secrets and lies, you'd better tell me now."

"What is done is done. I can't change the past. But I promise you, from now on, no more secrets, no more lies."

Peter inclined his head once to show that he would go forward. Mr. Doyle closed his eyes in relief.

"Don't forget about me," Ella said, leaning her head in and looking at Mr. Doyle. "I'm going to help you, too."

"I know, dear girl." Mr. Doyle put his hand out and Ella put hers in his. The knuckles of their firmly held hands turned white. They loved each other as Peter and Grandpa had. Peter's heart ached to talk with Grandpa once more.

Peter's eyelids were heavy, but his mind kept turning. "When I was thrown off the cliff, I thought about Sarracena. She cursed me in her realm. She said that I would not return to Newfoundland with what I came searching for. Pumpkin told me fairy curses couldn't be undone." He looked up. "Is that true? Will I still be able to go home with the gold coins?"

Mr. Doyle weighed two invisible things in his palms. "What you have here is fate versus free will. You've made some interesting choices here in Lore Isle." He gingerly touched a black and green lump on his head. "I believe whether you return with what you came for will be up to you."

The answer made Peter feel better. After being thrown off a cliff, he needed to believe he had control over his future. He vowed to make wiser choices from here on out.

Mr. Doyle's head wound started bleeding again, and Ella retrieved a clean cloth from the kitchen.

"I've only seen four mummers," Peter said. "Are there only four people who have died with unfinished business?"

Mr. Doyle pressed the cloth to his head. "No. There are many. I'm sure you will see scores more before this is all over.

29

Zig and Zag

THE NEXT DAY IN THE FOREST, ELLA, AS EXU-berant as a puppy, circled Peter as they walked. Mr. Doyle, too injured to hunt, had asked Ella to find food. Peter looked at his sister. She had grey eyes like him, but hers were flecked with amber that seemed to glow. Her short hair, now shiny, was the same chestnut colour as his and Mom's.

"Tell me more about your family in Newfoundland," she said.

Peter suppressed an impulse to correct her and say *our* family. He welcomed the chance to talk about their family without the emotion of the night before. "Well, Dad left before I was one, and Mom and I moved in with Grandpa John. He was my best friend."

"Was?"

"He died not too long ago. It's too bad you never got to know him. You know, now that he's not waiting for me at home, I think this is the first time I'm looking forward to school starting up again." Peter's nose tingled because he missed him, but also because Grandpa didn't get a chance to meet Ella, his other grandchild. Grandpa was stubborn, but he was loving. He might have changed his views on wolves because of his love for his lycanthrope grandchild. "Have you ever been to school?"

"Uncle Albert enrolled me in one. I didn't mind learning. I especially liked math and geography, but I just couldn't sit still and got into trouble all the time for sneaking out…and eventually got expelled. Then, Uncle Albert gave me lessons himself and let me run around anytime I needed to move. He knows more than anyone, except for maybe my dad."

"Your dad?" Peter said, surprised.

"My wolf dad. He was good friends with Uncle Albert, and they followed some dangerous leads together, looking for the egg. At first, Dad wasn't sure about having a lycanthrope child, but he saw how happy Nan was with me. He was a kind dad."

"Where is he now?"

"He died when I was still little. He was an old wolf, and Nan was his second wife."

"That's too bad." Even though they had lived in two different worlds and were raised as differently as can be, their situations were strangely similar: Dad out of the picture early, and raised by a single mom with the support of a strong grandfather figure.

"Yeah." Ella rubbed her eyes. Peter felt closer to her knowing they both had holes in their hearts because they had lost someone they loved.

"And your mom, what's she like?"

Peter noticed that she didn't say *our* mom. "She's super. She's magic when it comes to growing things. She has a greenhouse full of all sorts of herbs, flowers, and plants, and she mixes them up to heal wounds. Also, she's an amazing cook—makes delicious suppers and yummy treats." His tummy growled.

"She sounds wonderful," Ella said. Peter was glad Ella had a good impression of Mom, so he was reluctant to continue. "Then…there's this other side to her. She gets sad at times and has a really hard time leaving the house." He plucked a leaf from a tree. "To me, she was always like that, but Grandpa said she was happy until the disappearance of the 'imaginary' twin—you. And all these years, I never believed her. I can't wait to tell her that you're safe and living in Lore Isle. Unless…she'd love to see you. Do you want to maybe live with us in Newfoundland?" He crossed his fingers behind his back.

Ella said, "Er, I don't know. I don't want my mom to feel sad. She's quite old for a wolf now. I love her so much. I want to spend as much time with her as possible."

"Okay." Peter looked away to hide his disappointment. "You'll have to visit Lore Isle often."

"Sure." He tried to sound upbeat.

Ella and Peter had a great time running, pretending, and playing games, even ones that were too juvenile for them. It was as if they were catching up on all the playtimes they had missed growing up. They climbed trees, jumped into streams and kicked water at each other, chased dragonflies, and spied woodland creatures. The forest was their playground.

Ella motioned to Peter to be quiet and pointed in the distance where four grown wolves and three cubs played outside their den. The young furballs jumped on the adults, leaping, pouncing, and biting with their tiny sharp teeth. The grown wolves tolerated it all and gave the cubs affectionate licks. They were social, like humans. Peter recognized two of the adult wolves—they had come to his aid last night and had walked with him back to the cabin. He could now tell apart all the Lore Isle wolves.

"I want to show you my den." Ella bounded ahead, and Peter had to run fast to not lose sight of his sister, who could move swiftly even in her human form.

Ella came to a dead halt. Peter caught up to her and looked in the direction she was staring. Far off, two wolves with stiffened postures argued in front of a cave in a moss-covered mound.

Peter whispered, "Your mom is upset with Mr. Doyle. What are they saying?"

Ella listened, then brushed it off. "I don't know. I can't hear from this far."

"Come on. They're very excited. You must be able to hear them. Why won't you tell me what they're saying?"

"Because it makes no sense." She shook her head. "Mom said Uncle Albert wasn't truthful with her and she doesn't want anything bad to happen to me."

"I'm detecting a pattern here." Last night, Peter's outrage toward Mr. Doyle had thawed when he saw the old man had bruises from Green Coat on top of the injuries from the leprechauns. But now, his head tingled, reminding him that Mr. Doyle had committed an appalling act of betrayal and he must keep his guard up.

Ella stirred to leave. "If you want lunch, I have to start hunting now."

Peter didn't budge and strained to listen to the argument he couldn't understand.

Ella pulled at his arm, eager to get out of there. "Come on. I thought you were hungry." Peter resisted, but she was strong, and they struggled in a tug-of-war.

The wind blew at their backs and carried their scents. The two wolves simultaneously stopped talking, sniffed the air, and stared in their direction.

The twins ducked down.

Peter said, "Okay. Let's go."

Ella led them to a place with shrubs, skinny trees, and tussocks. She instructed Peter to crouch down and not to move or make a sound. She was all eyes, ears, and nose. They waited.

A large jackrabbit hopped into view. Ella transformed with her first leap and ran for the rabbit. It zigzagged, but Ella matched its every move. A part of Peter wanted the rabbit to escape. But he was hungry and thought of his mom's delicious rabbit pie, and he silently cheered on the wolf. The chasee and the chaser were moving far away, and Peter thought he'd be spared from witnessing the kill. The rabbit made a daring, tight U-turn and started to run back toward him.

Figures.

With the young, agile wolf at its heels, the rabbit made a fatal mistake—it zagged when it should have zigged. With one lunge, Ella's big jaws held the head of the rabbit as its body wriggled. She adjusted her bite to the neck and clamped tighter. The rabbit went limp. It was no wonder that Peter had inherited none of the family hunting gene. Every bit of it had gone to Ella to make the wolf half.

Ella, back in human form, held the dead animal up for Peter to see. "Let's head back." She licked the blood on her lips.

At the cabin, Ella set the rabbit down on the kitchen counter and walked over to Peter standing by the table. "What's the matter?"

"I'm still thinking about what Mr. Doyle was doing at your den. What's he up to?"

"He's not up to anything." She threw her arms up in the air. "Stop being so suspicious."

"You're too trusting." Peter pointed a little too close to her face.

She pushed his hand down. "I get that you're angry with him for taking me as a baby, but I am *not* sorry he did."

Peter stared at her, feeling as if she had punched him in the gut.

Ella softened her tone. "I love living in Lore Isle. My life is wonderful here. And I know Uncle Albert. He told you last night that he wouldn't lie to you again. Believe him." She put a hand to her heart. "I do."

Peter held his rebuttal when he saw her eyes glisten.

"Uncle Albert is proud of you for getting the mirror and rescuing me. I can see it in his face when he looks at you. And I am the goof who decided to take a stroll in the realm of an unpredictable fairy. I got myself locked up and caused Mom and Uncle Albert to search and worry when I should've been focused on helping Uncle Albert find the egg." Her face reddened. "And that wasn't the first time I had gone off looking for adventure and gotten into trouble. I'm a disappointment to him. Maybe he wishes he took *you* as a baby and not me."

She laughed like it was a joke, but Peter recognized the heartache buried at the centre. Often, Peter felt he was not enough because he couldn't meet Grandpa's expectations. He had wondered if Grandpa wished he had a different grandchild. At times, Peter wished he was a hunter because it was important to Grandpa, but he didn't wish it for himself because it was not who he was.

Peter said to Ella what he couldn't say to himself: "It's hard to feel like you're always disappointing someone you love, but you can't help what you're interested in. Or, not interested in. You can't change who you are and you shouldn't want to."

Ella looked at him. "You understand me, Peter." She held his hands. "I'm glad Uncle Albert brought you here."

Peter swung Ella's hands out and in like little kids playing, and they laughed.

Mr. Doyle came through the door. "Oh, you two are still together."

I know you smelled us when you were with Nan, Peter thought.

Mr. Doyle saw the rabbit on the kitchen counter. "Thanks, El. Are you staying for lunch?"

"Will it be cooked?" she asked.

"Yes," Mr. Doyle said.

Ella stuck out her tongue. "Yuck, no thanks."

Mr. Doyle said to Peter, "Ella was raised by wolves. I was raised by humans. I enjoy cooked food. Ella, not so much."

"You had the soup last night," Peter said to Ella.

"I was really, really starved. Remember, I had no appetite in the cage because I missed home so much," she replied.

Penelope must be missing her home desperately. "I don't feel hungry all of a sudden," Peter said. "I want to give the dragonfly belt to Penelope."

"Penelope is your tree sprite friend." Ella said remembering from the night before.

Peter nodded. "Will you take me to the mummers' house, Mr. Doyle?"

"That sounds dangerous," said Ella.

Mr. Doyle sat down in a chair. "I don't think it's a good idea either. Now that we're all together, we should be looking for the egg—"

Peter cut him off. "My mind is made up. The magic belt will end her imprisonment. I'm not leaving Penelope in that house another day."

Mr. Doyle looked like he was about to raise more objections when Peter added, "Besides, where do we start looking for the egg, which you haven't be able to find all this time? We need fresh clues, leads, something. Penelope might be able to help us. I'm going to ask her if she's overheard the mummers talking about the egg."

Mr. Doyle considered that angle. "That's an excellent idea." He leaned forward. "Tell her that you'll *only* give her the belt in exchange for information."

Peter prickled. Mr. Doyle was dictating what was to be done with the belt that *he* had gotten at his own peril. "I'm giving her the belt whether she can tell me anything or not."

"Maybe I should go in your place, Peter." Ella interrupted. "I would love to be friends with a tree sprite. Their hidden realm is supposed to have unimaginable-looking trees that make sounds like all kinds of musical instruments." She tilted her head to one side. "You look tired."

"Definitely not you. We'll have to search and find you, again." Mr. Doyle winked at Ella, and she turned red.

After looking at Peter's determined face, Mr. Doyle said, "You and I'll go to the edge of the clearing where we can see the mummers' house and wait for them to leave."

Peter pictured poor Penelope having to cook and clean for her kidnappers and entertain them with the fiddle, to boot. Peter wasn't able to help Sarracena, but he could help a friend who, like him, wanted to go home.

30

the Imprisoned Housekeeper

MR. DOYLE STILL HAD A LIMP AND CONTINUED to use the walking stick, but appeared to be in less pain as they walked toward the mummers' house. "Thank you, Peter, for not quitting. Knowing that you have the same compassion for the Newfoundland wolves as I do has reinvigorated my search for the egg. You may not be a lycanthrope like your sister, but I'll bet there is more than a drop or two of wolf blood in you."

Hearing this, Peter's chest lifted.

A briny odour drifted in from the open water as they neared a yellow brick house with a steeple on the roof. Short stubs of tree stumps littered a large glade that surrounded the building. Mummers had used their magic to chop down the trees, to sever the tree sprite's ability to draw her magical power from them. The front of the house faced a distant forest and the back overlooked the ocean. Peter and Mr. Doyle approached from the side and stopped before the edge of the clearing to stay hidden. The distance from the trees to the house was three times the length of Peter's school's soccer field. In the middle of the open stretch, there was a long washing line tied to two sturdy poles. Near the house, four wooden horses waited patiently.

After several minutes, the mummers came out. Light snow fell around them. Mr. Doyle whispered, "Right on time. The wolves said they leave like clockwork."

The mummers mounted their horses and faced the laundry line. When the mummers squeezed with their legs, the horses broke into a gallop. The moment each mummer touched the line, they disappeared as if they had entered a different dimension.

"Whoa. Where did they go?" Peter said.

"I have no idea. The wolves tell me that they disappear at noon and return for supper at the exact same time every day." Mr. Doyle stood up from his crouched position. "Well, shall we go knock on the door?"

"No." Peter got to his feet. "I want to go by myself." He didn't want Mr. Doyle to bribe Penelope with the belt for any knowledge about the egg. He wanted her to see that he got the belt for her, no strings attached.

Mr. Doyle furrowed his forehead, but said, "Alright, if that's what you want." He pointed down. "I'll wait for you right here until you come out. Be careful."

The old man wore the same tender expression of concern that Grandpa had worn when he looked at Peter and Mom. At that very moment, Peter decided that he'd let go of his distrust for Mr. Doyle, for his own sake. He wanted to enter the mummers' lair with a clear mind and focus.

He knocked on the front door. The anticipation of seeing Penelope again quickened his heartbeat. When she opened the door, he almost didn't recognize her. She had dark circles underneath her doleful eyes, and her skin looked pale and papery. Her face was the shape of a thin heart, and her pointy ears poked out of her long hair, the colour and texture of green cornsilk. Under the apron, the pink dress she had worn to the wedding was faded and stained. She did not recognize Peter, for as a waiter, he had worn a mask.

"Hi, I'm Peter. Do you remember me? I was a waiter at George and Sarracena's wedding. You touched my arm to tell the truth about why I needed the enchantress's mirror."

Penelope examined him more carefully. "Oh, yes! Peter." She reached out to touch his shoulder, but her hand hit an invisible barrier at the opened doorway with a bang. "Ouch!" She shook out the hurt hand, then she motioned him to come in. "I'm the only one cursed." And he stepped through the doorway.

"When will the mummers come back?" Peter wanted to make doubly sure that he would not encounter them on their home turf.

"Not 'til suppertime. They're creatures of habit."

The house smelled of cinnamon and fruit baking. To the right was a kitchen with a wood-burning stove, near the middle of the room a square table was surrounded by four large chairs, and pressed against the short wall to the left sat a cot, extra-long and deep to accommodate a seven-foot-tall mummer. An open space for dancing was left between the cot and the table.

"Do you want a partridgeberry tart? They just went in the belly of the stove."

"There's no time for tarts." From his rucksack, Peter pulled out the magic belt and gave it to her.

"The dragonfly belt! Queen Meliss gave it to Sarracena. Why did she give it to you?" Her face broke into a big smile. "She must've already used it to rescue Cousin George! Are they together now? Did my undoing spell help?"

Peter hesitated. "I think you should sit down."

Penelope, no longer smiling, braced for bad news as she sat with Peter at the table. "Sarracena let me take it because she doesn't need it anymore. She found out that George has died in the barrens."

Penelope wept for her cousin and his widow, and Peter didn't know what to do but tap her back. Between gulps of air, Penelope recounted how nice George had been to her and how he had included her in group conversations at family reunions even though she was his youngest cousin.

She calmed down somewhat and wiped her eyes on her apron. Peter said, "At the wedding I told you I needed to find gold to take back to my mom. I still don't have it. The gold is with an enchanted egg the mummers have stolen. Have you ever heard the mummers talk about an egg with a pair of wolves inside?"

She thought about it and said, "No, never."

"Oh." He couldn't hide his disappointment.

Penelope tilted her head. "Tell me about this egg containing wolves."

"Ok. Well…" He blew air out between his lips. "I might as well start at the beginning." Peter told her about how the Newfoundland wolf became extinct.

Penelope raised her brows. "There are no wolves at all where you're from?"

Peter nodded.

"If it wasn't for the black wolves in Lore Isle, the blue-eared deer would multiply rapidly and cause serious consequences. The deer devour plants and tree saplings, especially in the spring." She turned her head and looked out the window. Peter followed her gaze to the distant wooded hills. "If there were too many deer, not enough saplings would get a chance to grow into mature trees, then we wouldn't have flourishing forests." Penelope looked back at Peter. "We tree sprites need many healthy trees for our magical powers and well-being."

Peter nodded. "That makes me like the wolves even more."

He told her about the magic egg and Mr. Doyle's belief that the mummers had it. "We want to find it so we can take the egg back to Newfoundland to restart the wolf population."

Penelope became quiet staring at the dragonfly belt in her hands.

"Well, we can leave anytime you're ready," said Peter.

"No. Not yet."

"Why not?"

She looked into his eyes. "I really want to help you. There must be a way to get the mummers to tell us what they know about the egg."

"Okay then, let's think."

In their brainstorming session, Penelope came up with a brilliant idea to find out where the egg is hidden. But in her plan, she would be taking a lot of risks—she was smart and brave. *Who was rescuing who?* Peter wondered.

After the details were worked out, Peter helped Penelope prepare supper for the mummers, as everything must seem as usual to them when they returned. As they washed, peeled, and chopped, they confided in each other like old friends. Penelope listened wide-eyed, crunching on a carrot, as Peter told her that just the night before, he had been thrown off the cliff by Green Coat and rescued by Red Jacket.

"Green Goat yells and complains that my cooking is terrible," Penelope said. "I know he's lying because he always demands seconds. And when he is in a fouler mood than usual, he stands over me and makes me clean and scrub every inch of the house when everything is already spotless. Tree Bark and Goat Face always snicker and agree with Green Coat like mindless henchmen."

Peter felt sorry that she had endured such mistreatment.

"Red Jacket tells Green Coat to leave me be, but he doesn't listen to anyone."

"Red Jacket looks different from the others," Peter said, chopping the peeled potatoes.

"His body hasn't disfigured yet. It means he came to Lore Isle recently. Mummers' bodies change more the longer they stay in Lore Isle."

He came recently. Peter held the knife above the chopping board.

"Are you okay, Peter? You look like you've seen a ghost."

"Yes, I'm fine." He went back to chopping.

When all the ingredients were simmering in the pot, Penelope put one of the tarts on a plate.

Peter, who was already seated at the table, said, "I saw you get carried off by the mummers that night. I'm sorry I couldn't help you." It was easier to confess such a thing when there was no eye contact.

Penelope put the tart in front of Peter. She sat down and put her elbows on the table and rested her chin in her hands. "If only I had kept near the trees."

She recounted the harrowing tale of what had happened next.

Out in the ocean, away from the trees, I knew my powers were limited. I couldn't summon any new magic, but I could alter spells I had already conjured. The wooden gift box I was holding already had magic inside—it was full of rare butterflies that would have danced in beautiful patterns around the bride and groom when it was opened.

So, I recast the spell:

Metamorphose again, my butterflies
Ugly outside, fill with poison inside
Bite them with your venomous fangs
Fill the sky with their agonizing cries

The mummers looked frightened, and I unlatched the box. But all that came out was an army of carpenter ants. Far from the trees, my magic was weak.

Green Coat laughed and snatched my beautiful box. Oh, how I despised him.

By the time the ship sailed within view of this yellow house, the carpenter ants had chewed big holes in the

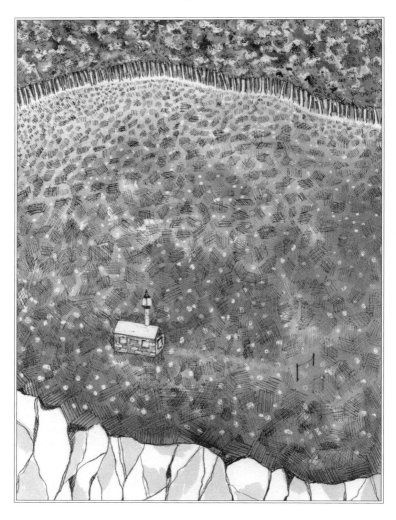

ship, and it began to creak and list to one side. The mummers used their magic to strip their property of trees—the source of my powers. Then they put a spell on the house so I could never leave.

Red Jacket carried me to shore, alighted weightlessly as a small bird, and set me on the ground. We all watched as the wooden railings of the ship disappeared with a noisy bubbling of air escaping from the ruined hull. Then, the dark, cold water dragged down the single square sail. The groaning and gurgling subsided, and the water became smooth on top exposing only the tip of the mast, like a pitiful tomb marker. And I was glad it was my magic that sent their ship to its watery grave.

The mummers marched me through the naked glade to this house. I squeezed Goat Face's arms and said, "Tell me how to undo the spell so I may go home."

He answered, "We mummers cannot undo our own spells." I cried then, for I knew he was telling the truth. No one can lie while a tree sprite is touching them.

I crossed the threshold of the door into their house, my prison.

"You're a great storyteller. I saw everything." Peter looked into Penelope's sad eyes and thought of his mom. Mom was a prisoner of the house too, even if she didn't want to leave it.

"It's so nice to have someone my own age to talk to," Penelope brought Peter another tart. Not having had breakfast or lunch, Peter gladly accepted.

After Penelope and Peter cleaned the house of all traces of Peter being there, she hid him under the over-sized cot. The light from the kitchen did not quite reach the other side of the room, and underneath the cot it was as black as a starless night. She walked all around the room, making sure he couldn't be seen from any angle. No sooner had she completed her inspection when the sound of hooves reverberated outside.

31

Mummers' Dance

SNOWFLAKES BLEW IN AS THE MUMMERS CAME
through the door, but it did not snow inside the house.
The air became cool.

Lying on his stomach with his head craned to one side,
Peter had a good view.

The four mummers went straight to the dining table.
Penelope set their supper—salt beef with potatoes, carrots, and parsnips—on the table. When she placed the
bowl in front of Red Jacket, he looked at her face and said,
"Your eyes are puffy. Have you been crying, girl?"

Green Coat growled, "A sook, always blubbering about missing her family."

"Boo hoo, boo hoo," Goat Face mocked. Tree Bark snickered.

Green Coat sniffed the air. "Something doesn't feel right. I smell wolf blood." His inhaled speech sounded like wind scraping through a narrow opening. Red Jacket looked around the room.

Penelope placed the last bowl on the table. "Don't be ridiculous. You're fixated on wolves."

Red Jacket stood up, took off his coat, and turned it right side out so it was red on the outside and the fleece lining was on the inside. He hung it on the back of his chair. Peter caught his breath when he saw that it was missing one of its red buttons.

"When are you going to learn to cook? Your suppers are not fit for eating," Green Coat said as he shovelled food into his flappy, wide mouth.

When it was time to eat dessert, they saw that there were two partridgeberry tarts instead of the usual four.

"What happened to the other two tarts?" growled Goat Face.

"I ate one and dropped one in the fire in the stove," she lied. "Besides, I made them extra big today." She cut the two tarts in half, producing four pieces.

Way to think on your feet, Penelope, Peter silently cheered.

After he devoured his piece of tart, Green Coat stretched and moved toward the cot.

"Where are you going?" Penelope asked in an alarmed voice. *If he sits down on the low cot, he is sure to feel that something or someone is under it.*

"I want to lie down, maid."

She opened her fiddle case. "But I'm ready to play."

"Later. I need rest."

As Green Coat bent to sit down on the cot, Penelope began fiddling, and all the mummers, as if they couldn't control their own bodies, stood up and jigged. Amazingly, the monumental figures were light on their feet, able to step and leap with agility. The fiddler played fabulously, as only a magical being could. Overcome with the desire to dance to the bewitching music, Peter struggled to remain under the cot.

After a marathon of lively jigging, one by one the mummers gravitated back to their seats and fell asleep with their arms and faces on the table, exhausted. Penelope quietly put the fiddle back in its case.

At the table, she shook Tree Bark's shoulder and kept her hand there. She lowered her head close to his chicken leg earring. "Where is the egg with the wolves?"

"On our ship that you sunk," he replied with his eyes closed. "You can still see the tip of the mast sticking up from the back of the house." With those words, he started snoring.

Penelope moved on to Green Coat, his face on the table like a rumpled sheet. She touched his arm. "How can I retrieve the egg?"

He clamped his lips, but unable to fight the sprite's touch, he mumbled stiffly, "Swim to the mast, dive down, and turn the ship's wheel counter-clockwise to raise the ship." He chuckled in his sleep. "The water is too cold for any person to swim in." He started snoring.

Next, Penelope walked around Red Jacket and stood between him and Goat Face. She rested her hand on the draped goat hide on his humped back. "Where is the egg on the ship?"

Goat Face's backward feet twitched. "It's in the wooden box we took from you. Once the ship is raised, it will appear."

Red Jacket sat up and grabbed her arm. His eyes were still closed. "Tell your friend not to trust a wolf in any form." His head flopped back down on the table and he joined in on the snore-fest.

His words jarred Peter. *Does Red Jacket know I'm in the room?*

Soon the mummers were snoring so loudly, the legs of the cot began to tremble.

Peter crawled out from his hiding space with his rucksack. He and Penelope tiptoed to the kitchen cabinets.

"So, they hid the egg in your box on their ship," Peter whispered.

"Apparently, but I didn't know that's what they were doing when they took it."

"Then, you didn't see the egg or the gold coins be put into the box?"

She shook her head. "No, they took the box and went to the other side of the deck." *But it must be true, because they confessed while the hand of a sprite was on them.*

"I hope what you've heard helps."

"I think so. Thanks so much, Penelope." Peter looked at her with admiration for coming up with a clever plan so quickly, then executing it so well.

Penelope took off her apron, revealing the dragonfly belt around her waist. "Goodbye, Peter. Best of luck to you." Her face was bright with the joy of knowing that she was at last free to go back home.

After Peter closed the door behind him, he watched the sprite, with a fiddle case in one hand, bound toward the trees where branches were spread like open arms.

32

Sunken Ship

LATER THAT NIGHT AT THE CABIN, PETER TOLD Ella, Nan, and Mr. Doyle (who had worriedly waited for hours outside the mummers' house) what the mummers had said.

"So, the bottom line is that the egg and the gold are in a box, in the sunken ship. No person will be able to swim in the cold water to reach it." By Penelope's account, Peter estimated that the mummers' ship sank pretty far from shore. "Even if the water weren't so cold, that's a long way, and I'm a terrible swimmer."

"Not a person, but a wolf can swim in the cold water," said Mr. Doyle.

Nan and Ella both stood up and spoke at the same time. Ella said, "I'll go!" And Peter was sure Nan had said the same thing in wolf language.

With her ears tensed, Nan took a step toward Ella with her chest out. She spoke to Ella in a stern tone.

"I'm as good a swimmer as you are," Ella said, but she sat back down, looking defeated.

Mr. Doyle said, "Nan, you'll reach the mast without too much trouble, but I imagine that a mast even on a small ship is quite tall. Wolves aren't designed for deepwater diving. And besides, you need hands to grip and turn the ship's wheel."

Ella leapt to her feet again, and said in one breath, "I can swim to the mast as a wolf and dive down as a human and turn the wheel."

Nan pressed her ears back, obviously not liking the idea.

"That's not a bad thought," Mr. Doyle said. Then a second later, he shook his head. "In your human form, your body temperature would drop to a hazardous level in no time. By the time you reach the steering wheel, hypothermia would have set in, and you'd be in no condition to do anything, much less turn the heavy wheel of a ship."

Ella's face contorted with disappointment.

We're so close. Come on, think. What's the answer? Peter yelled out, "I have something." All eyes focused on him.

"When I escaped from Sarracena while Ella was still in the cage, somehow Ella entered my body, taking on all my pain. I wonder if it could work the other way around. Could I take on the coldness of the water for Ella, so she could move freely and do what she needed to do?"

Ella turned to Mr. Doyle, her eyes wide.

"Hmm. I think that will work. You two need to practice to make sure you can master it." He looked worriedly at his goddaughter. "Ella's life will be at risk."

Nan dropped her head and whimpered. Ella hugged Nan. "Don't worry Mom, I'll be careful."

Peter wondered if he had spoken too soon. He hated cold water. On the rare hot days in Newfoundland, kids from the neighbourhood went to the pond for a swim. Always the last one in and the first to come out shivering, Peter spent most of the time basking on a warm rock like a lizard. But he was determined to keep Ella safe. He found strength in the fact that he and his sister would work together to get the box with the egg and the gold.

Early the next morning, they started their training. Ella tapped herself with a stick while Peter tried to feel what his twin was feeling. By the afternoon, Peter started to have some success. Although not consistently, he could feel what Ella felt and could see what she saw. Peter learned he had to focus his mind a certain way; it was kind of like when he daydreamed, and his eyes didn't focus near or far but somewhere in between. He had to do that with his mind—focus somewhere inside his head on the one sweet spot that could plug into Ella's mind and body and take on her physical pain.

It worked best when there was nothing solid between them, like the trees or the cabin. There were times when Peter became unfocused, and the connection switched directions. Of course, this would be a disastrous thing to happen while Ella was submerged in water, for she'd be exposed to the icy cold temperature and become immobile in no time. However, by the end of the third day, Peter easily found the sweet spot and confidently held his focus for as long as he wanted.

The following day, in the afternoon when they knew the mummers would be out, Mr. Doyle, Ella, and Peter approached the yellow house from the side. In the clearing stood the mysterious washing line that made the mummers and their horses disappear when they crossed it.

Peter wondered what had happened when the mummers woke up to find their housekeeper gone. The brains in their scary heads must have gone into overdrive trying to figure out how she had broken the spell.

The three scouted the waterfront, which dropped down from the mummers' property, to find the best place to see the ship's mast poking out of the water. Waves lapped the beach, which was studded with massive grey- and ochre-mottled rocks that blocked the sightline to the mast. The twins decided the best spot for Peter would be the rooftop of the house. Thinking there was no time like the present, they decided to immediately get to work.

Mr. Doyle said, "El, do not open the box on the ship. We don't want the egg and the coins to fall out." Peter was buoyed by his words. Finally, he was going to get gold coins he would be allowed to keep and take back to Mom.

Ella walked down to the rocky beach. As Peter and Mr. Doyle walked up to the yellow house, Peter said, "I don't want to sound like a wimp, but what if the water feels so cold to me that I can't concentrate?"

"Nan and I've been thinking about that. We have an idea. She is waiting for my signal."

With interlocked fingers, Mr. Doyle gave Peter a boost. From the top of the wall, he climbed up the roof and wrapped his arms around the steeple.

Ella reappeared, swimming in wolf form. Once the pale wolf reached the mast, she looked toward the mummers' house, treading water. Peter waved to show that he was ready.

With great concentration, he found the sweet spot.

The moment Ella turned into a human, the bone-chilling temperature of the water shocked Peter. He could've never imagined that being cold could be so excruciatingly painful. Every part of him shrank. He saw what Ella saw. In the dark water, Ella swam down, following the mast to the hulking wreck. From the big holes on the sides and the deck of the ship, silvery fish darted in and out.

Fearing he might lose consciousness and put Ella in grave danger, Peter hugged the steeple tighter and stomped his feet to get warmer. But soon, his toes fused together, and his legs slipped out from underneath him.

He clawed at the steeple with his icy fingers and managed to hang on. Still concentrating on the sweet spot, he saw a blur of grey run past the side of the house to face the woods. The grey wolf howled an impassioned captain's cry. Within moments, dozens of black wolves ran out of the forest, led by Nan.

She led them to the ocean-facing back of the house. The wolves looked up at Peter, positioned themselves around the yellow structure to get the correct angle, and started to huff and puff, as if they wanted to blow the house down. Their powerful breaths enveloped him, and he understood what they were doing. They were warming him up. He felt like he had slipped into soft flannel pyjamas. A grateful sigh escaped his lips. Slowly, but surely, his body temperature climbed back up to normal.

He saw through Ella's eyes that she had reached the ship's wheel and was trying to turn it, but it wasn't budging. She was worried about how Peter was holding up on the rooftop.

Cool wind blew in, snowflakes fell gracefully, and Peter knew the mummers had heard the grey wolf's howls too. The sound of galloping horses emanated from the clothesline. Never losing the connection to the sweet spot, he turned to the side and watched the clothesline vibrate. As Peter dreaded, the opposite of what he had witnessed the day before happened: the four mummers appeared on horseback on this side of the clothesline and sharply steered toward the back of the house.

Green Coat, Red Jacket, Goat Face, and Tree Bark manoeuvred their horses in between the wolves and the house. The mummers faced the wolves, tall on their horses. They spoke in ingressive speech, inhaling the warm breaths of the wolves. "Mummers allowed, mummers allowed…"

Peter saw four more wooden horses with four different mummers come through the washing line. This happened over and over. The new mummers stood alongside the first four, swallowing the wolves' warm breaths. As less and less of the warm breaths reached him, once again Peter shivered uncontrollably.

The wheel gave, and Ella turned it. The mast of the ship rose. A carcass of a ship surfaced, creaking and complaining like a waking giant. Water rushed out from the holes on the sides of the hull. Ella hung onto the wheel as the ship groaned, listing to one side then the other before righting itself on the water.

Now that she was out of the water, her hide clothes hung wet and heavy. The bitter wind that brushed against Ella's face and hands felt like a thousand paper cuts shredding Peter's. It was pure torture. Peter no longer had control of his body parts. He ordered his useless fingers to keep a grip on the steeple, but they would not obey. His

legs slipped out from underneath him. As he fell, he saw in his peripheral vision that Red Jacket, who was right under the steeple, was turning his horse around to face the house. Peter's head collided with the edge of the roof, and a vision of green fairy dust exploded in his eyes. Just then, Ella changed into a wolf. Peter knew this because it felt like a warm quilt had been thrown over him. Relieved, he closed his eyes and let go of the sweet spot.

33

In the Box

"PETER, CAN YOU HEAR ME?" SAID A FARAWAY voice.

Peter could hear something pounding. *Is that Pumpkin, hammering on his anvil?*

A pair of blurry faces stared at him through a cobweb of light and shadow.

"You bumped your head hard before you rolled off the roof," said the second face.

Peter managed to move his mouth, "Who caught me?"

"A mummer," said a voice that he recognized now as Mr. Doyle's. He didn't need to say which one, Peter knew. Mr. Doyle continued, "They're gone for now, but I'm sure we're not finished with them yet."

Peter tried to focus. When Mr. Doyle's face became clear, he turned to the other one and saw worried grey eyes flecked with amber. Ella was safe! Peter sat up on his cot and hugged his sister—her hide clothes felt cool and a little damp. Then he regretted moving so quickly; the pounding was in his head.

He looked around. His cot had been moved from his room to the kitchen near the stone hearth with a roaring fire. Mr. Doyle put a second blanket around Peter like a shawl.

"We did it! Here's the box!" Ella placed it on Peter's lap. "We didn't want to open it 'til you woke up."

Mr. Doyle wiped his mouth then looked over at Nan, who was sitting in the corner.

This was it. The moment Peter had worked so hard for. With trembling hands, he touched the inlaid wood design on the top of Penelope's box and undid the delicate latch—with some difficulty due to the lingering numbness in his fingers. He drew in a deep breath between his smiling lips and opened it. Inside the velvet-lined box, there was an ordinary looking egg—the size of a goose egg—and nothing else.

"Where are the gold coins?"

"Peter," Mr. Doyle began. By the tone of the old man's voice, Peter knew something was definitely wrong. "There was never any gold."

Gold, gold everywhere, but none to keep, Sarracena had cursed. His heart thudded down to his stomach.

"What do you mean?" he and Ella said at the same time.

"Uncle Albert, you didn't lie," Ella continued. "You promised."

Mr. Doyle said, "We will *only* take back the wolves in the egg, nothing else."

Peter wrapped his hands around his head like he wanted to prevent it from bursting. "No, no, no! There must be a mistake. I can't go back without gold. Think of my mom, please!"

Mr. Doyle said, "I understand your disappointment, but the egg cannot be opened until it's returned to Newfoundland. That means no gold, nothing, can be put inside the egg. And you saw that the portal would not let you cross with your lucky red button in your pocket. Only the magic egg can cross, it and its contents, undetected."

The cogs in Peter's thinker moved up a gear. "What if we release the wolves in Newfoundland, come back with the egg, and…go to the smithy! Pumpkin will give me gold to take back."

Ella patted Peter on the back. "Brilliant!"

Mr. Doyle shook his head. "Once the egg goes back to Newfoundland and the wolves have been released, it will turn to dust. It will have completed its mission."

Peter's face contorted in disappointment. He shut the box and stumbled out of his cot, tripped over the hooked rug, and knocked down a chair. He shot out of the cabin.

With the box in his hand and his breathing ragged, Peter was surprised that it was already close to twilight. The Lore Isle wolves Peter had seen from the rooftop were there, sitting or lying down in the front yard of the cabin as if they were waiting for him to come out. He screamed and screamed until his voice was hoarse, then wept tears full of anger, disbelief, and humiliation. The wolves watched him in silence.

A breeze rippled the wolves' black fur. Snowflakes.

The four mummers rode out from a slow, white swirl. The wolves sprang up with their hackles raised and tails straight out. Mr. Doyle, Ella, and Nan came out of the cabin.

"What do you want?" Mr. Doyle shouted.

"Our business is with Peter." The mummers weaved through the wolves and rode up to Peter.

Red Jacket said, "Wolves are not the only ones with good hearing. Doyle has misled you again. It is true that the egg will turn to dust once opened in Newfoundland, but the egg *can* be opened here. You can change its contents." He held out a coin pouch, the same one that was offered to him at the smithy.

"I can't open the egg," Peter said. "It can only be opened by someone with wolf blood."

"You share your twin's wolf blood," Red Jacket said. "Open it, let the wolves evaporate, and pour all the coins in the egg."

"What do you mean 'let the wolves evaporate'?" Peter said.

Mr. Doyle rushed up beside Peter. "The wolves will only survive if the egg is opened back in Newfoundland. I beg you, do not take the gold. Your destiny is to take back the wolves."

Red Jacket said, "It's only your destiny if you choose it. The choice is yet to be made."

Mr. Doyle moved around to face Peter. "You said you'd be proud to bring the Newfoundland wolf species back to life."

Peter's face burned. "And you said no more lies. I trusted you."

Red Jacket said, "The sheep's clothing has come off. See him for what he is. You owe him nothing. Put your money in the egg, go home back to the Rock, and save *our* house." Did Peter hear him right?

Mr. Doyle pushed Red Jacket's horse's face, and the horse whinnied, showing its nail teeth. "Peter, if you take the gold and sacrifice the wolves, you'd be no better than the bounty hunters and the government who brought the wolves to extinction."

Peter's eyes flashed. *How dare he preach morality?* Mr. Doyle had known all along that, in the end, Peter would open a box that had no gold. *Surprise, chump!* For almost five weeks, Peter had been in Lore Isle, risking his life for nothing—a literal empty space in the box. He wanted to take the mummers' gold just to spite Mr. Doyle. But he remembered that the last time he had acted with revenge in mind and called the mummers, he had almost ended up dead.

Red Jacket raised his voice. "Newfoundland has been without wolves for a hundred years. If you take them back, you're taking back a Pandora's box."

Peter knew the Greek myth about Pandora, a curious girl who opened a forbidden box and all the evils of the world escaped. Red Jacket was saying the egg contained a similar disaster, but Peter knew that Pandora's box contained one other thing—hope. And Peter had great hope that this time, humans would figure out a way to coexist with wolves. Wolves deserved a second chance in Newfoundland. At the same time, he couldn't bear the thought of going back to Mom without the gold coins and losing the house, the place where he grew up and the only place where Mom felt safe.

Ella put an arm around him. Peter turned to his sister, the only one he trusted at that moment, and said, "What am I going to do?"

"I support whatever decision you make," she said.

The wolves, shaggy with snow and devoutly loyal to Mr. Doyle and his cause, watched him. The thought of opening the egg and abandoning the Newfoundland wolves to dissolve into the air made Peter feel like he'd be destroying a big part of himself.

If he didn't bring back the gold to pay for the house then, without a doubt, his aunts would sell it to the first person who made an offer and send him and Mom packing with a third of the proceeds.

Peter knew, no matter where they lived, he and his mom could bank on each other for love and support. He had to give Mom credit for trying—the trip to the grocery store was far from a success, but she had taken the initiative to go. She was also willing to find a job to support them. There were organizations that could connect her with professional help. Peter looked down at the box he was holding. For the wolves, there was only one way for them to go back to Newfoundland.

Red Jacket watched him intently. Sacrificing Grandpa's house to bring the wolves back to Newfoundland would be an act of betrayal. The thought didn't make Peter feel good, but he knew the decision was the right one.

"I'm taking the egg back to Newfoundland. Just the way it is."

Mr. Doyle had to hold on to Ella to keep from falling down. Rivulets of tears flowed through the creases on his cheeks. The wolves wagged their tails. Their long, journey to return the Newfoundland wolves was coming to an end.

Red Jacket shook his head, put the purse in his pocket, and turned to leave.

All this time, Green Coat had been silently inching his horse closer. As quick as a seasoned pickpocket, he reached down and snatched the box from Peter's hand.

From behind a veil of snow, a slew of mummers who had been hiding and waiting, rode out on their horses chanting, "Mummer's stick, mummer's stick." In each mummer's hand, a long and sturdy stick appeared. Then the sticks grew spiked balls, sharp spearheads, or curved blades.

As fast as lightning, Ella turned into a wolf, leapt up, and clamped her big jaw around the box before Green Coat knew what had happened. The pale wolf landed sure-footed on her thick pads and turned her head so Peter could grab the box from her mouth. Mr. Doyle rushed Peter toward the cabin, then pushed him through the door. He closed the door from the outside before turning into a wolf.

34

Battle

MORE WOLVES CHARGED OUT FROM THE FOR-est and more mummers emerged from the snow, which was really coming down now.

Placing the box on the windowsill, Peter watched the scene with horror. The wolves leapt up with their powerful legs, knocking the mummers off their horses before attacking with their long, lethal teeth. It was obvious when a mummer was "killed." As soon as the body became lifeless, it shimmered and rippled like the air above a hot paved road and vanished, along with their weapons. The mummers used their sticks to stab or wallop the wolves.

The black wolves stood out against the snow, but the mummers appeared hazy and nebulous. The mummers steered their mounts, backing the wolves into tall snowdrifts where their horses, with long legs, moved more freely than the wolves. The wolves—who had inherited their battle instincts from their ancestors—fought back undiscouraged. Unable to leap in the deep snow, the wolves stood on hind legs and clamped their jaws on the legs of the mummers. Then, shaking and twisting their great heads, the wolves dragged the riders off their mounts in such a way that the mummers landed in the drift with their bellies up. Sometimes the wolves ripped the shirts and jackets off the fallen riders with their teeth, before sinking their teeth into the exposed bodies. These clothes on the ground did not disappear when the mummers died, only the clothes on their bodies.

Ella, noticeably smaller than the black wolves, was constantly challenged. As soon as Ella defeated one mummer, another lined up. Peter gasped when a particularly large mummer with a veiled face grabbed Ella by her furred throat, slammed her back to the ground, and held her there. With his other hand, the mummer flipped his stick over, so the blade pointed down.

"Stop!" Peter burst out the door, yelling at the top of his lungs to be heard above the cacophony of the battle. Ella twisted, and the mummer stabbed her in the shoulder. The mummer took a firmer hold of Ella and raised his weapon, aiming for her heart. Peter threw himself against the mummer with a battle cry and got in a right hook to the back of his head. The mummer didn't lose his balance, but, annoyed by the interruption, he let go of Ella, grabbed Peter by the shirtfront, and threw him down. Peter's head hit the ground and he saw everything in twos. Ella took the window of opportunity to stand up and positioned herself between Peter and the mummer.

Blood soaked through the fur on her shoulder above a tenderly raised paw.

"Alright then, wolfie, you first." The mummer readied his sharp weapon.

Out of nowhere, Nan jumped on the mummer, bit his face, and knocked him down. The two rolled around in the snow, fighting ferociously and so entangled it was difficult to see where one ended and the other began. Her wide jaws snapped. His keen weapon stabbed. There were sickening sounds of ripping and crunching. The mummer slumped forward, his limbs twisted in unnatural positions. He shimmered and disappeared. Nan lay in a broken heap.

Ella hobbled over. She licked her wolf mom's face to wake her up, but the fierce yellow fire in her eyes had already extinguished. Ella let out a howl so agonizing that her sorrow echoed inside of Peter, who felt like he'd lost Grandpa all over again.

Through his tear-filled eyes, Peter saw a blurry image of a mummer riding toward them, as slow as a dream, gracefully swinging his stick. The mummer hit Ella with the spiked end of his stick and sent her sailing toward a thick tree, aiming for a bull's eye crash against the trunk. The tree moved sideways, and Ella landed with a thud in a powdery snowbank. Peter rubbed his eyes; he must've bumped his head hard and was seeing things. Yelling, "Ella," he ran to her. The pale wolf moaned before losing consciousness.

Peter wanted to take his injured sister into the cabin where she would be safer, but he couldn't figure out how to carry her. Ella was too big and heavy for Peter to carry in his arms or on his shoulders. He thought about dragging her, but the ground was peppered with sharp rocks, the cabin was far away, and Ella's shoulder was bleeding profusely. He pressed on the wet fur with his palm to stem the bleeding.

Blasts of white snow eddied around them. He looked up helplessly at the raging battle, which was looking grimmer and bloodier against the deepening crimson sky. It was just a matter of time before another mummer noticed their vulnerable situation.

Unfortunately, the mummer he dreaded the most spotted them. As Green Coat, with Tree Bark close behind, rode toward them, Peter yelled for help, but all the wolves were fighting for their lives and did not hear him. The two mummers dismounted, picked up one twin each in their big arms, and billowed deep into the forest.

They set down the twins under a tree. Peter slipped an arm under the head of his motionless wolf sister.

"Did any wolves see us?" Green Coat asked.

"No."

"Are you sure?"

"Yes. I looked with the eyes in the back of my head."

Green Coat's shoulders relaxed. "Then we kill them, now."

Peter hugged his sister and leaned into the tree. The knock on his head made the tree sound like it was humming.

Tree Bark looked at his feet. "I'm not sure anymore."

"What are you saying, wooden head? You know we can't destroy the egg ourselves. Let's get rid of these young ones helping the old wolf-man. With some luck, the wolf-man may be killed today as well."

Tree Bark shifted his weight from one foot to the other and played with the chicken legs hanging from the sides of his tree trunk–shaped head.

Green Coat jabbed at the air with his weapon. "I'm tired of 'living' here in Lore Isle. I've been here for a very long time. I want to move on. I can go in peace if I know the wolves won't be returning to Newfoundland."

"I can't do it. I can't kill a boy," said Tree Bark.

"Then you kill the wolf. I'll kill the boy."

"No," Tree Bark said quietly.

"Why not?" Green Coat sounded exasperated. "You killed wolves while you were alive in Newfoundland."

"The boy loves the wolf."

"Aargh! You disgust me! I'll kill them both." Green Coat spat saliva when he spoke. Holding his weapon like a javelin, he moved sure-footed toward the twins.

Peter tried his best to cover his sister.

Green Coat screamed and arched his back as the end of a spear burst forth from his chest. He dispersed into shimmery heat waves and vanished, revealing Red Jacket standing behind him. His weapon had just ended Green Coat's stay in Lore Isle.

Red Jacket walked up to Tree Bark. "I won't let you hurt them."

"I got no desire to do that," Tree Bark said. "I don't believe in what I'm fighting for anymore. I'm leaving Lore Isle."

Then Tree Bark rippled into shimmering particles and vanished.

Red Jacket bent down and picked up the unconscious wolf, cradling her in his arms, then spoke to Peter. "Get on my back and hold on."

Peter climbed onto the seven-foot mummer's back and clung to the jacket.

Red Jacket's body dematerialized, but Peter could feel that he was still there, not in his solid form, but still present and strong. The clothes billowed through the forest like a gentle breeze, sidestepping trees until they were at the back door of the cabin, where Peter could see all of the mummers again.

Once inside, Peter pointed to his bed still in front of the hearth. Peter was glad the fire was still burning. Red Jacket gently placed the wolf on the cot, then stationed himself a few steps away. Battle sounds seeped into the quiet room as they watched the faint rise and fall of the wolf's chest.

Ella began to stir. Peter gently shook the wolf. "I don't know what to do, Ella."

All the fur should have turned into uniform, quill-like white lights as Ella transformed, but the lights appeared only in some places and started the transformation, while other parts did not change. Except for the beginning and the end of her transformation, Ella looked like a monster—the product of an experiment by a mad scientist gone terribly wrong. The air crackled.

At one point, she looked like a gigantic naked mole rat with patches of fur. As her bones lengthened and shortened, Ella made unearthly cries that sounded neither wolf nor human.

Desperate to ease his sister's suffering, Peter focused his mind on the sweet spot and tried to take on her pain, but Ella refused to relax her mind and blocked him out. All he could do was hold Ella's hand, which still had paw-ish qualities, and lightly squeeze it to give her support.

When it was finally all over, Ella gave a faint squeeze back. Peter looked over at Red Jacket, who had watched in silence.

The wound on Ella's shoulder started to bleed again, making a dark circle on her hide tunic. Ella said, "My back..."

Peter carefully pulled up the back of her tunic. He gasped at the map of marks made with the mummers' sticks on her back. There were circular-shaped bruises filled with puncture marks, long, oozing welts, and an assortment of cuts and lesions.

"I wish Mom was here." He hurried to the cupboard and got a bowl and filled it with water. With a cloth, he cleaned the wounds as best as he could. The arm below the wounded shoulder, where Peter was able to staunch the bleeding, was definitely broken. It was unnaturally bent.

Ella fell into a restless sleep on her side with the good shoulder. Red Jacket came over and covered her with a warm blanket, just as Grandpa had done many times for Peter. Red Jacket's fish bone face was impossible to read.

Peter said, "I could've never imagined in a million years I'd come to a place called Lore Isle and be your enemy. I'm sorry."

"Don't be sorry. I love my enemy—a particular one, anyway. I want you to do what you believe in." Red Jacket spoke normally, not inhaling his speech. For the first time in Lore Isle, Peter heard his grandpa's voice rather than a mummer's voice.

"Thank you. Again." He remembered how Grandpa had let him off the hook from future hunting trips the night he died. Now he was absolved again, this time for the guilt of taking back the wolves.

"Are you ever stubborn," Red Jacket chuckled.

"I'm like my grandpa that way."

The mummer started to shimmer, and he spoke hurriedly. "I can't stay in Lore Isle any longer. I'm at peace. Goodbye, son."

"Wait!" Peter reached out to touch Red Jacket, but his hand went right through the rippling figure. "Why did you change the will to leave the house to Aunt Bea and Aunt Agnes?"

"I never changed the will."

The shimmering waves dispersed and disappeared.

The room darkened as if a cloud had covered the sun. Sadness seeped into Peter's bones. He would miss seeing Red Jacket in Lore Isle, even if he was just a shadow of Grandpa.

With no trace of Red Jacket having ever been there, Peter, wanting to return to Newfoundland with ease of mind, wondered if he had imagined the conversation. Listening to the sounds from outside, he wasn't sure if he'd be returning at all.

35

Escape Plan

WELL INTO THE NIGHT, MR. DOYLE CAME INTO the cabin, bruised and battered. When he saw Peter, he said, "Thank God you're in here, safe." But when he saw his goddaughter lying on the cot, so gravely hurt, he had no words. He sat by the cot holding Ella's hand, while Peter cooled the patient's forehead with a cold cloth.

"The mummers have retreated for now. I need to go back outside and tend to the injured wolves and," Mr. Doyle swallowed hard, "see to the dead." He left again.

The mournful bays of the wolves that had survived the battle resounded from the forest. Ella ran a high fever. Peter suspected her wounds were infected.

Once in a while, Ella awoke from an agitated slumber to the nightmare of reality and sobbed, "Mom, don't leave me."

As Peter stood up to make some tea for his sister, he noticed the box with the egg sitting on the windowsill near the front door. He must've left it there when he saw Ella getting thrown down by the big mummer and ran out to help. He took the box and placed it under the cot Ella was sleeping on.

Peter held Ella's hand and said, "I'm going to take you with me to Newfoundland. If I leave you here, you'll either die from your wounds or the mummers will kill you. I told you before that our mom has a magical way with herbs. She'll know what to do to make you well again."

A weak voice said, "Alright."

Later, after Ella had managed to fall into a deeper sleep, Peter sat at the table trying to figure out the next step.

Mr. Doyle came in with his fingernails encrusted with soil and sat at the table. "I buried Nan." He covered his face with his hands and wept. "She was like a daughter to me."

Peter looked over to his wounded sister to see whether she had heard, but she was still sleeping deeply. He looked Mr. Doyle square in the eye. "I'm taking Ella back with me to Newfoundland. Her wolf mom is dead. Ella will die here too if she doesn't get help. I know our mom will be able to heal her wounds."

Mr. Doyle was quiet for a long time. "I wonder if she could stay and live with you and Lily." He wiped his tears on his sleeves. "At last, Lily can have her daughter back, and Ella will be part of a loving family again."

Peter's eyes became moist. "Mom and I would love that."

Mr. Doyle exhaled deeply. "Ella will have to go to school like the other kids; it'll be difficult for her to fit in. You'll help her."

Peter worried his sister would go stir-crazy in her human body when she was used to spending most, if not all, of her days as a wolf. Ella had told him how she couldn't sit still in the school she had briefly attended. But an uncertain new life in Newfoundland was infinitely better than a certain death in Lore Isle.

"Peter, I'll do everything I can to help you, but it's a long way to the pond. The mummers are determined to… stop us." Peter knew that Mr. Doyle had checked himself from saying "kill us." "Ella has serious injuries. How do you propose we take her to the pond?"

Peter hadn't worked out the logistics. "We need something to move her in. If we found a cart, could the wolves pull it?"

"Yes, but that would attract the mummers' attention. We need to go quietly. Unnoticed, if possible," Mr. Doyle said.

Peter rubbed his eyes and stood up. "I need to go for a walk. I need to think."

Mr. Doyle also stood up. "Don't wander far from the cabin. The mummers will regroup and return by sun-up. About an hour from now."

Peter should've walked out the back door, but he went out the front. With the mummers gone, all the snow was melting. His boots squelched in the mushy glop of softening snow and mud. Dark, wet, crimson splotches puddled on the ground mixed with tufts of black fur. His stomach lurched. The battle scent of rust permeated the air. Peter stepped over the mummers' clothing, ripped off by the wolves, and ran around to the back of the cabin and into the woods.

The cogs in his head were idle. He was too tired to figure out how to get Ella and the egg to the pond. It was hopeless. The moonlight shone on one tree brighter than the rest. Peter went to the beacon, touched it with both his hands, and prayed for ideas. "I need help."

Knobbly contours of a face appeared on the tree and said, "I'll help you."

Peter almost jumped out of his skin, stepped backwards, tripped over protruding tree roots, and fell down. Penelope emerged from the tree. Instead of a stained party dress, she wore a simple, cream-coloured dress, fresh as a flower petal. Her greenish yellow hair, smooth and shiny, cascaded down her shoulders. Peter felt like a klutz sprawled on the ground. He flushed when she took his arm to help him to his feet.

"I've been watching you, Peter. I can see from any tree. I moved the tree so your wolf sister wouldn't hit it when the mummer threw her. And I called Red Jacket when I saw that Green Coat was going to kill you."

"Thanks." Peter felt less alone, knowing he had a friend who was looking out for him. "It's so good to see you again."

She clasped her hands. "I'm eternally grateful to you for rescuing me from the mummers. The dragonfly belt is safe in the realm of the tree sprites. Tell me what you need."

"My sister is hurt, and I have to transport her to the portal pond. I need to carry her in something." He rubbed the back of his neck and mumbled, "Go unnoticed. Blend in."

"What did you say, Peter?"

The answer popped in his head: "I need a mummer's horse."

Penelope guided him deeper into the woods, and they came to an open space where there were dozens of wooden horses walking or sleeping. "This is where the horses who've lost their riders wait for new mummers to come to Lore Isle."

Peter selected a horse that appeared to be docile. It became spooked and whinnied when Peter reached for the bridle. Remembering that the horses were used to the speech of the mummers, he spoke in an ingressive voice and the horse calmed down. He put a foot in a stirrup and pushed himself up on the leggy horse better suited for a much taller rider. Once in the saddle, his feet did not reach the stirrups. Penelope climbed up effortlessly and sat behind him. Peter took hold of the reins and squeezed the sides of the horse with his legs, as he had seen the mummers do. Instead of going where Peter wanted to go, the horse walked in a big circle. Peter felt he was making a fool of himself in front of Penelope.

She said, "Relax, Peter. The wooden horses are intuitive to their rider."

It was true. The horse quickly learned the awkward signals of the novice rider, and Peter managed to get back to the cabin without difficulty as a sliver of light peeped above the horizon.

Peter left the horse in the back with the tree sprite. He grabbed a few pieces of mummers' clothes strewn near the front of the cabin before he went inside.

Mr. Doyle looked up with a cold cloth in his hand. "Where have you been? I was so worried. It's almost sun-up."

Peter motioned to the kitchen window.

Mr. Doyle turned and looked to the back of the cabin. "How did you get a mummer's horse? Is that the kidnapped sprite?"

"Yes. She helped me find a horse."

Mr. Doyle looked confused. "We need all the help we can get. But why the horse?"

Peter explained eagerly, "When the mummers came to the smithy to get their horseshoes replaced, I saw the horses were hollow. Ella can be carried inside."

Mr. Doyle raised his brows, as if it was news to him that the mummers' horses were hollow.

Peter continued, "The wooden horses move very smoothly, it's like they glide. I noticed that when I was on Green Coat's horse. If we line the inside with blankets, Ella should be comfortable." Mr. Doyle nodded.

Peter held up the colourful mummer's clothes. "I'm going to wear these. They need a few stitches. Hopefully, even if they notice me, I'll be far enough away that they'll mistake me for one of their own and won't come after us."

Mr. Doyle dabbed his forehead with the cold cloth meant for Ella. "They'll never expect anything like that. It just might work. You must leave as soon as possible."

From his room, Mr. Doyle brought the pillow and sheet, and pulled off the pillowcase. Peter tied the pillow around his chest with strips of bedsheet and slipped the mummers' outfit on top. Mr. Doyle retrieved his sewing kit and loosely stitched up the front. Then he cut two holes in the pillowcase, to be worn over Peter's head.

Mr. Doyle woke Ella up, who was delirious from her high fever, and gave her water to drink. Then they half walked, half carried her out the back door.

When Penelope saw them, she told the wooden horse to lower its body. Peter inserted his fingers into the indented handle and lifted the door on the side of the horse. After lining the hollow space with blankets and a pillow, they helped Ella inside. Once reclined inside the horse, Ella closed her eyes, exhausted from the short walk.

"Peter. I'm going to let the wolves know what you're up to," Mr. Doyle said. "Go east and find the road that goes toward the village. When it splits, take the right one. It leads to the hill that overlooks the smithy. I'll catch up with you."

"I hope I can find it." Peter's head steamed up with worry; he couldn't recognize every tree and rock like Mr. Doyle.

"Don't worry, I'll lead you," Penelope said.

"Thank you," said Mr. Doyle, "but I don't think a mummer should be seen with a tree sprite."

"I won't be visible. I'll use the trees," Penelope said.

Mr. Doyle bowed and disappeared into the woods.

Peter turned to go back into the cabin one last time to get the box with the egg. Leaning against the wall beside the back door was Red Jacket's spear-tipped mummer's stick. It hadn't disappeared with Red Jacket. Grandpa had left it for him. Could he have known Peter would need it? *Mysterious to the end.*

When he came back outside, Peter took the egg out of the box, nestled it between Ella's arm and waist, and closed the hinged door. Then he gave the inlaid box to its owner, who was glad to have it back.

Penelope hugged him tightly. "Goodbye, Peter. You won't see me again, but I'll stay with you in the trees for as long as I can."

He pressed his cheek to the side of her head and smelled the fresh sent of new leaves. "Thanks, Penelope. You're a great friend."

Peter slipped the pillowcase with the cut eye holes over his head and saw the tree sprite walk to the nearest tree. Just before she touched the tree and disappeared, she said, "I shortened the stirrups for you."

As the colour of blood orange smeared the horizon, Peter rode eastward, following the trees that seemed brighter than the others. He knew it was Penelope's subtle and clever way of directing him.

He had been unsure if he could manage the reins with one hand while holding the mummer's stick in the other, but the horse almost seemed to read his mind. With the slightest, awkward one-handed pull on the rein, the horse understood where it had to go. It climbed and stood at the spot, just outside the edge of a forest, where Peter had first gazed down at the smithy and the village on his second day in Lore Isle. The big doors of the smithy were closed. Pumpkin had not started his workday yet.

Peter had left Newfoundland filled with the hope of returning with the gold coins to pay for his house. Now he was going home with no gold, but with two things he hadn't even known existed—the magic egg containing the Newfoundland wolves, and his twin.

When he heard a rustling behind him, he snapped his head around and peered into the shadow-filled forest. To his relief, he spotted Mr. Doyle in wolf form. The grey wolf led him to the path in the woods that he needed to follow, and vanished into the thick foliage so Peter, disguised as a mummer, wouldn't be seen with a wolf.

Anxious to get to the pond, Peter squeezed his calves and heels around the horse's barrel, and the horse accelerated smoothly. He hoped his sick twin was resting comfortably and the air wasn't becoming stuffy in the chamber.

He was bringing Ella back to Mom. The baby heartlessly snatched at birth. The baby who had grown into a girl, so full of life and fun. The girl who looked so much like her. The other twin she had longed for, for more than thirteen years. *Will she love her more?* Peter couldn't help but wonder.

Deep in his thoughts, he didn't see the few flakes of snow falling stealthily about him. As he followed a bend in the path between two hills, he saw two mummers on their horses up ahead blocking the way. Peter was sure they saw him and couldn't turn back without causing suspicion. He slowed down his horse and stopped in front of the mummers, keeping a certain distance.

36

Moving Trees

THE MUMMERS DWARFED HIM. THEY COULD surely see he was much smaller than all the other mummers.

One had huge breasts and a belly, and wore a long, yellow dress with black and white flowers, inside out. She had a face of woven straw and barred the path with a blood-encrusted, scythe-tipped stick. In a deep inhaling speech, the mummer said, "Why aren't you at your post on the lookout for the boy?"

The second mummer, hunched over and clad in a plaid robe, had a face like he was wearing a Cyclops mask. He leaned his rotund head in to have better look with his one eye and blinked.

Peter needed to answer right away, but he felt tongue-tied. He had spoken in an ingressive speech to the mummers' horses to calm them down, but could he speak their tongue well enough to convince the mummers themselves that he was one of their own? He had to give it his best shot. His and Ella's life depended on it.

"I was told to check the path for unusual signs," Peter replied, inhaling.

The mummers' faces remained impassive. The silent seconds ticked on like hours.

Peter adjusted the grip on his mummer's stick to bring their attention to it. He didn't have a prayer of passing for a mummer if he wasn't in possession of a stick. Finally, they parted to let him through. Peter sat up tall as he passed between them.

When he had ridden quite a way from the two mummers at the checkpoint and thought it was safe to have a look, he turned around and was alarmed to see the two mummers tailing him at a distance. Their horses broke into a smooth gallop. Peter's did the same, but he wasn't an experienced rider, and they gained on him.

More snow. More mummers.

They didn't need to stay on the path as Peter did, for they were able to drive their horses with precision, manoeuvring them between the trees. Many mummers rode beside him, their gruesome mouths twisted in mocking smiles.

One of the checkpoint mummers caught up to him. Cyclops swung his spike ball–tipped stick. Peter clumsily blocked the blow, then jabbed his stick wildly and managed to stab the mummer's beefy thigh. Cyclops swore and swung his stick again in a big arc. The wooden part of the stick thwacked Peter across his back and almost knocked him off his saddle. He braced himself for the impact of the metal tip.

A familiar voice whispered from the trees, "Keep going, Peter. I'm with you."

A tree smoothly slid sideways, directly in front of Cyclops, and his horse rammed into it with a wood-meeting-wood *thunk*, and the mummer fell off his mount.

Beside and behind him, the trees skated sideways to block the mummers. Sometimes, they managed to manoeuver their horses around the trees, but most of the time they hit the tree or had to come to a complete halt, their horses rearing, before steering around it. This slowed them down greatly.

A mummer who deftly guided his horse around the moving trees caught up with Peter. It was Goat Face, the only one of the original four mummers who was still here in Lore Isle. With sharp horns poking out from his head and a scythe-like stick in his gloved hand, he looked like a demonic beast set on dragging his victim back to the underworld.

Goat Face shouted in his ingressive voice, "Stop your horse and open the egg and you'll return home, unharmed."

"Never!" Peter's horse picked up speed, but Goat Face kept pace.

"After I am done with you, you'll be begging to open the egg."

"You wish!" Peter sounded much more confident than he felt.

The mummer steered his horse closer and kicked the side of Peter's horse. "Perhaps I'll start by breaking all the

bones of your wolf sister. That'll change your saucy tone, boy."

Cold fear ran through Peter's body. *Goat Face knows Ella is inside the horse.* Fear was a strong emotion that often mushroomed into fury. He thrust his stick and made contact with the mummer's arm. The shallow cut fuelled Goat Face's animal eyes to burn more savagely.

Goat Face swung his stick like he wanted to cut Peter in half. Peter blocked it, but somehow his spear tip and Goat Face's scythe tip became locked together. Goat Face yanked, trying to pull Peter off the horse. Peter just wanted his weapon to be untangled. With one smooth movement, Goat Face unlocked his weapon and swung it down. The powerful blow split Peter's stick in two.

With a splintered half of a stick gripped in his hand, Peter feared the next blow would knock him off his horse and Goat Face would trample him to finish him off. Then his wounded sister would be defenceless.

Up ahead, another tree was sliding to get ahead of Goat Face. The adept horseman focused his attention on steering around the tree, leaning into Peter's side. Peter seized the two seconds of opportunity. With all his strength, he plunged the broken, jagged end of his stick into Goat Face's side, under his ribs. His beastly eyes stared at him, his mouth open in frozen shock. He rippled and vanished. His wooden horse veered sharply, likely heading to the open field where the riderless horses waited.

The trees continued to shift and block until all the mummer riders were far behind.

In an open area up ahead, Peter could see the same purple and yellow wildflowers he saw on his first day in Lore Isle. That day seemed like a lifetime ago. With no trees there, the tree sprite would not be able to help him. But he must ride through the open space to get to the next forest that circled the pond.

From the dark forest, he charged into the bright morning light and saw hundreds of Lore Isle wolves gathered there. Many had new battle scars where fur would never grow again. Peter pulled off his pillowcase mask and threw it away. The wolves divided like black waves to let him through. The young wolf—who had listened to his stories while accompanying him to the cabin from the cliff—stood on his hind legs when Peter went by. Sitting tall, Peter turned and waved to the young wolf.

Soon, the grey wolf ran beside him, and they raced to the portal. Briefly, Peter looked back to see the wolves fighting in a snowstorm, holding back the mummers who had reached the clearing.

In the next woods, Peter slowed down when he saw the familiar pond. Once dismounted, he took off the mummer's clothes and pillow, which he was wearing on top of his own clothes. He and Mr. Doyle, now in his human form, helped Ella sit up and get out from inside the body of the kneeling horse. Ella put her good arm around Peter to keep herself from falling down.

From the hollow of the horse, Mr. Doyle fished out the egg and firmly placed it Peter's hand. Then Mr. Doyle took off his button and put it around Ella's neck. That's when Peter realized that there were three of them and only two crossing buttons. "Oh, Mr. Doyle…"

Mr. Doyle would not be able to return to Newfoundland with them. He was sacrificing himself so Ella could go back with Peter. The dream of retirement in Newfoundland faded from his amber eyes.

"That's okay, Peter. I'm an old man, and you have helped me achieve my lifelong goal. You were instrumental in allowing me to have a legacy. Thank you. My story ends here, but I think yours is just beginning."

With his self-sacrificing act of giving up his button so his goddaughter could have a future, Peter's hatred for the man with a single-minded focus dissipated. *How could I hate someone who loves my sister?* he realized. He didn't want to leave Mr. Doyle thinking that he despised him. They had gone through so much together.

The sounds of wolves barking and the hooves of the mummers' horses were getting closer. It was obvious the wolves couldn't hold back the mummers any longer, and Peter knew he didn't have much time to say what he wanted to say. "Goodbye, Mr. Doyle. Thank you for taking care of me in Lore Isle and saving my life…twice. We are allies when it comes to the future of the Newfoundland wolves." He tapped the egg, now safely in his pocket.

Mr. Doyle looked at Peter gratefully.

Peter propped up Ella, who drooped her head and leaned on him heavily. "I'm glad to be reunited with my sister and take her home to Mom."

The old man looked many years older than he did the first day in Lore Isle, when he had briskly led the way to the wedding. "I told myself that what I did wasn't so bad because Ella was thriving in Lore Isle with Nan. You made me face what I had buried deep in order to live with myself. If I could do it all again, I would not have taken Ella. My legacy is the return of the wolves, but it's also the suffering I caused your family. Please tell Lily I am sorry. I pray that one day she can find it in her heart to forgive me."

With glistening eyes, Mr. Doyle stroked Ella's head. "Goodbye, my dear girl. Take good care of yourself."

With effort, Ella took her arm from Peter's shoulder and reached out to find the wrinkled hand. "Uncle Albert, is there no way for you to come with me?"

Peter couldn't bear to see Ella, who had lost her mom, suffer the loss of her beloved uncle, too. "What if I take Ella to Newfoundland, then I wear both buttons, come back, and give you one?"

"No! You mustn't do that. One button per being. You don't know how the pond will react to two buttons and only one body. At best, it may not let you through. At worst, you may be trapped forever between the two worlds."

Behind them, a snowstorm blew in between the trees as fierce as an avalanche, and the mummers rode out.

"There is no more time. Go now, Peter, and don't come back! The mummers won't forgive you." Mr. Doyle became the grey wolf, and ran toward the mummers.

Peter led Ella to the edge of the pond. This time, he didn't shut his eyes as he had done when he came to Lore Isle. Holding on to Ella, he fell into the water that had no wetness. As he and his sister slowly turned upside down, he saw the skies of the two worlds. Again, invisible hands gave him a pat-down. Suddenly, he stood beside the pond with his sister. His breathing slowed as he looked around at the familiar surroundings.

37

Return

A RAVEN CAWED AND FLEW ACROSS THE POND. Peter returned to Newfoundland one month and eight days after he had left, according to Lore Isle calendars; just over a minute, according to clocks on the Newfoundland side of the pond. Peter guided a feverish Ella on the puddled path through the woods on this Saturday morning.

Once in his house, Peter helped Ella to Grandpa's room and laid her down on the ornate iron bed. He placed the egg in a drawer in the oak desk and ran downstairs.

"Mom!" Peter charged outside and startled her. She was still repairing the greenhouse after the storm.

"What is it? You look so serious." She put down her hammer and looked at him with concern.

"I need you to come upstairs, now." His voice was urgent.

She took hurried steps toward the house. "Is it Mr. Doyle? Is he alright?"

Rushing up the stairs behind Peter, Mom said, "You really need a haircut…and a shower."

In Grandpa's room, Peter pointed to the figure in bed, not knowing how to introduce to Mom her long-lost baby who was now a teenager.

Mom went to the girl, bruised, cut, and broken, wearing clothes made of hide. "What happened to her?" She leaned in and scrutinized her face. When the girl opened her eyes, Mom covered her mouth and took a step backwards. Mom's eyes were wild and confused as tears ran down her cheeks. But when she took her hand away, she was smiling.

"Her name is Ella," Peter said.

"Ella," Mom repeated softly. "It's perfect. Ella is short for Helen." Then Peter understood why Mr. Doyle had named her Ella—she was named after Peter and Ella's Grandma, the woman Mr. Doyle had adored.

"What happened? Where were you? How…" Mom wiped the tears from her cheeks. She exhaled through her lips. "It can wait."

Mom sat at the edge of the bed and bent over to gently hug Ella. Mom extended an arm to invite Peter into the hug. With his arms around Mom, Peter said, "I'm sorry I didn't believe you."

After a couple of days of Mom's attentive nursing, Ella was looking much better. The bruises had faded a good deal, the infections had cleared, and the cuts were healing nicely. Her broken arm (which could only be healed with time) was in a cast.

The twins had filled Mom in on all that had happened in Lore Isle, how Ella got there, and the business of the quest to return the Newfoundland wolves.

When Peter, who did most of the explaining, told Mom that Mr. Doyle had taken Ella because she was a lycanthrope, Mom looked at Ella in astonishment.

Ella said, "I'll show you when my cast comes off." Mom nodded with her mouth agape.

When everything had been explained, Mom shed pearl-sized teardrops, mourning the fact that she didn't get to see Ella grow up. "Was your adoptive mother kind to you?"

"Yes. She loved me so much."

And when Ella started to cry while describing Nan and how she had died in battle and saved Ella's life, Mom enfolded Ella in her arms. She said, "I am sorry that I cannot thank Nan for taking such good care of you."

Mom was over the moon to have Ella back, but Ella's return did not lessen her anxieties. In fact, her fear of leaving the house grew stronger—she became agitated when her children went out of the house as well. But she wanted them to grow up to be confident and independent young adults. So, for their sake, Mom did what she couldn't do just for herself: she decided to seek out professional help. She was going to start seeing a therapist. Peter hoped that the therapy sessions and his support would make the transition to another house bearable for Mom.

On Monday, true to Aunt Bea's word, the aunts returned with a For Sale sign for their lawn. The aunts came inside to get Mom's signature on some paperwork and were baffled when they saw Ella and Peter sitting together. Mom, thinking on her feet, conjured up a story about Ella living with her estranged husband in another country all these years.

To Mom and Peter's dismay, their house was sold a day after it was listed. It sold to the Parks, the couple Aunt Agnes and Bea had shown the house to before Peter's adventure in Lore Isle. The buyers wanted to move in one month later, and the aunts badgered Mom to agree, but Mom held firm on closing at three months. Peter was proud of Mom for wanting to leave on her terms, and helped her search on the internet for prospective places they could move to.

Later that week, Peter and Ella went for a walk so Ella could get to know the neighbourhood. She complained that her sensitive ears felt assaulted by the constant sounds of household appliances, lawn mowers, cars, sirens, and so forth—technology that didn't exist in Lore Isle. As they were coming back to the house, they saw Ben sitting on his porch with his dog, Willow. When Peter climbed up the steps of the porch, Willow stood and wagged her tail, and Peter petted her head. "Have you been on one of your adventures lately?"

"Willow's been keeping to the house since John passed away. It's like she knows I need her company," Ben said.

When Ella came up the steps, Willow seemed to be extra happy, doing little jumps.

Peter said, "Ben, this is my sister, Ella."

They shook hands. Ben said, "Nice to meet you. Lily told me you'd been living with your dad."

"Yes." Ella said awkwardly.

Ben looked back and forth between the two faces. "Boy, you two really look alike."

Peter and Ella looked at each other and smiled.

"Have a seat," Ben said, taking one of the comfortable deck chairs. Willow sat between Peter and Ella.

Ben thumbed toward Peter's house. "I'm sorry to lose such good next-door neighbours. Really going to miss you folks."

Peter was sorry, too, because he had known Ben all his life. "Mom and I are going to miss you, too. But we'll always keep in touch."

"I hope so." Ben, looking sheepish, rubbed the nape of his neck. "I still feel that I played a part in your aunts forcing Lily to sell the house, because I changed the will for John."

Ever since Red Jacket had said he did not change the will, Peter had wanted to ask Ben a question: "Did Grandpa look different that night?"

Ben adjusted his cap. "Are you asking if he looked unwell because he died later that night?"

Peter nodded, even though that's not exactly what he meant.

"No, he looked the same, but his voice was kind of high-pitched and crackly."

"Crackly?" Peter said.

Ben rubbed the armrest of his chair. "Yes. Kind of buzzy. Didn't sound like him, but he had a sore throat from a cold, he said."

"Grandpa did have a sore throat that night. Mom made him herbal tea for it," Peter said.

They chatted pleasantly about this and that for a while, then the twins stood up to return next door.

Standing on the porch, Ben called after them, "Let me know if you need any help with the move."

Ever since they had returned from Lore Isle, Peter and Ella had spent a lot of time discussing where the wolves should be released. It was an important decision that needed careful consideration.

Late one night, they had one of their brainstorming sessions in Peter's room. Ella, sitting cross-legged on Peter's bed, looked up from a travel magazine and said, "I can't stop thinking about Uncle Albert. I hope he's alright."

Peter, who was studying an aerial map of Newfoundland on his computer, leaned back in his chair. Something about the business of the portal buttons had been bothering him. "When Mr. Doyle took you as a baby, he used Grandpa's button for you to cross into Lore Isle."

"Yes."

"Then, he left you with Nan, came back to Newfoundland, and returned Grandpa's button. Which must be true because I used that button to go to Lore Isle and Mr. Doyle had his own."

"Okay." Ella seemed unsure of what he was getting at.

Peter swivelled his chair to face Ella. "How's that possible, when he insisted only one button could be worn by a person? How did he bring both buttons back after he left you in Lore Isle?"

"Oh, yeah. I see what you mean." She closed her magazine.

There was one possible explanation, but Peter was reluctant to say it out loud. "Someone from Lore Isle wore the second button back to Newfoundland for Mr. Doyle so it could be returned to Grandpa."

"Then how did that someone go back to Lore Isle without a button?"

He drained the glass of water on his desk. "Can't go back without a button. I think that someone is still here."

"You think someone from Lore Isle has lived here for over thirteen years?" Ella gave Peter a doubting look and stood up to stretch.

Peter nodded. "And I think that someone is a shape-shifter."

Ella stopped mid-stretch with her arms in the air, then slowly lowered them. "What makes you think that?"

"Because I asked Red Jacket—that is, Grandpa—why he changed the will and left the house to all of his daughters, and he said that he didn't. Only a shape-shifter could have fooled Ben, his best friend, into changing the will."

Ella sat down again and dangled her long legs over the side of the bed. "Ben told us Grandpa John sounded different. Shape-shifters can't disguise their voices."

Peter felt sure that his theory was right.

There was no time to continue brainstorming about the button and who was here from Lore Isle when they had a more immediate question to answer: where should they release the wolves from the egg? Poring over a map on the computer screen, the twins considered the Avalon Peninsula (too populated) and the national park on the west coast (too far), but eventually decided on a pristine wilderness reserve with plenty of game in the central part of Newfoundland. They asked Mom if she'd like to make the long drive with them or if they should ask Ben, who would only be told that Peter wanted to show Ella the reserve. Mom considered it briefly and said, "I want to be the one to drive you two and be part of your amazing mission. We'll go in the morning."

38

Curse Breaker

THE SANDPAPERY SOUNDS OF DRAWERS SLID-ing in and out from the next room half woke Peter and he thought Mr. Doyle was looking for the button in Grandpa's room. But that was a month and a half ago according to the Lore Isle calendars, or six days ago according to the calendars on this side. *I'm imagining things*, he thought and rolled over.

But there was that sound again. Peter pushed off the quilt and tiptoed to Ella's room, opened the door, and quickly found the light switch. Under the bright ceiling light, Ella woke up, squinted her eyes at Peter, and pulled out the earplugs she used to block out the sounds that kept her awake. "What's going on?"

Then she saw a strange woman standing by the oak desk with her hand in the opened drawer, and Ella sprang up into a sitting position.

For a moment, no one said anything. The woman, who looked to be in her mid-thirties, slowly took her hand out of the drawer, looking guilty. Under her thick bangs, she had a round, freckled face. She wore a patterned pastel blue and brown dress in the same style Peter had seen in Lore Isle.

Peter asked, "Are you looking for the button?"

"Yes." She seemed relieved that Peter knew. "I must return to Lore Isle as soon as possible." Her voice crackled and buzzed.

"You've been in Newfoundland for a long time."

"Fourteen years on your next birthday, but I think you've figured some things out."

"Are you a shape-shifter?" Peter said.

"Yes, I am." Her brows completely disappeared under her bangs, impressed.

"You changed Grandpa's will?" It was an accusation more than a question.

The shape-shifter opened and closed her mouth. She turned the desk chair around and sat down. "About two and a half weeks ago, I was walking in the woods by the pond and overheard Albert talking with John."

Peter was shocked. *That must've been shortly before Grandpa died.* "Are you sure?"

"Yes." Her eyes followed Peter as he moved from the door to sit down on the edge of Ella's bed. "Earlier that day you hobbled home from the pond with bloody knees."

The last time I went fishing with Grandpa. "The day Grandpa and I saw the grey wolf." He looked at Ella. "I mean, Mr. Doyle as a wolf."

The woman crossed her legs and wrapped her hands around the top knee. "I remember it was a cold and misty evening. Albert told John that Peter had a twin who was a lycanthrope and was missing in Lore Isle. He asked John for his permission to take Peter to Lore Isle because Peter, being her twin, could possibly help locate her."

Peter held his breath for what he guessed would be an explosive response from Grandpa.

The woman whistled. "John lost it on Albert. Accused him of somehow finding out about Lily's imagined twin and using it to take his grandson to Lore Isle for some nefarious prank. John could not be convinced even a little that Albert was telling the truth.

"When John stormed off, I spoke with Albert. Albert said he was going to Lore Isle to look for Ella for a few days and would return to have another talk with John, hoping he would have calmed down enough to entertain that what Albert was telling him might be true."

"Wait," Peter said. "Have you been in contact with Mr. Doyle all this time, for thirteen and a half years?"

"Not for the first eleven and a half years, because I lived all over Newfoundland searching for a rare plant, but in the last two years I've seen my Lore Isle friend several times because I've been living next door."

Next door? Peter's house was at the end of the lane, so Ben's house was the only one next door. Ben had lived in that house for decades. Peter's mind whirled, then landed on the stray that Ben had adopted two years ago. "You're Willow?"

"Yes. My real name is Greta. You give good scratches under the collar." Greta smiled. "The morning after John and Albert's meeting, I followed Ben when he came to your porch and asked you and Grandpa to go to his cabin."

The day I was tricked into going caribou hunting.

"When I saw John, I knew he would pass before the next sunrise. Shape-shifters like me are born from the earth, so we know when someone is about to go into the ground and become dust. I knew Albert would not get a second chance to talk to John."

Greta lowered her head, and her eyes were hidden behind her bangs. "That evening, I shape-shifted into John and asked Ben to change the will. Over the last two years, I have seen John so many times, I could replicate him perfectly. Living next door and listening to John and Ben talk, I knew your aunts would not be generous. And with Lily's…condition, I knew if there was a monetary incentive, Peter would have no choice but to go to Lore Isle."

"So, Uncle Albert doesn't know it was you who changed the will," Ella said brightly.

"That's correct. When Albert found out about the change in John's will at the funeral reception, Albert thought John had believed his story and wanted Peter to help find the twin. He thought John was letting him know by making it easy for him to offer Peter a reward to go to Lore Isle."

"See, Uncle Albert is not nearly bad as you think." Ella opened her hands like a magician who had made something appear.

"But he still lied about the gold coins." Peter made a zero with his hand. "*No* gold coins." Peter shook his head at Ella for always wanting to present Mr. Doyle in a favourable light. Then he glowered at Greta for manipulating the situation to send him to Lore Isle…but he *had* found and rescued Ella, and here she was in Grandpa's room. And he was so happy to have a sister.

"Why did you help Mr. Doyle in the first place?" Peter asked.

"I needed the egg to come to Newfoundland," Greta said. Peter thought Greta must want the wolves to return to Newfoundland and his feelings toward her mellowed.

"You wore the portal button to Newfoundland for Mr. Doyle over thirteen years ago. Why?" Peter said.

"It's bit of a story." She stuck out her lower lip and blew up at her bangs. "Let me start by telling you I have three brothers. And as with all shape-shifters, we were born from a witch's garden. Witches make wonderful parents."

Ella nodded as if this was common knowledge.

"Our sweet mother raised us all the same and taught us right from wrong, but Jacob and William became notorious thieves, while Hans and I became bakers.

"Fifteen years ago, Jacob and William tried to steal vials of potions from the fairy of the berries."

"Racem is the fairy of the berry realm," Peter said, remembering the intricate gates Pumpkin had made for him. The apprenticeship seemed like years ago.

"Yes, Racem." Again, Greta looked impressed. "The most volatile of all the fairies." She crossed her arms. "Why my hare-brained brothers took such a risk, I'll never understand.

"When Racem found them with the stain of his prized berries around their mouths, and the potion vials in their rucksacks, he cursed them to become a two-headed insect always searching for food for grubs that never grow up."

Peter gasped, and Ella looked at him wide-eyed.

The shape-shifter rubbed her eyes, and her voice began to break. "They were banished to a mine in Whale Island for one hundred years, for the one hundred vials of potions Racem found in my brothers' rucksacks." She paused briefly. "When our mom found out, she was very upset. She has special powers as a witch, but no one can undo a fairy's unbreakable curse."

Peter nodded sympathetically.

Greta blinked and tears rolled down her face. "They're thieves and they've done some awful things, but they're still sons and brothers who are loved. Mom, Hans, and I searched for a way to break the unbreakable curse and we discovered a drawing of a plant called Black Infractus Braya. It can break a fairy's curse and restore the condemned to exactly as they were.

"When we learned that the curse breaker only grows in Newfoundland, Hans and I immediately thought of Albert, our friend, and his mission to take the magical egg back to Newfoundland."

"I met Hans," Peter said. "He gave us delicious bread and cider on a day Mr. Doyle and I went fishing."

"That sounds like him. I miss him and the bakery," Greta said. "When Albert told Hans and me he was bringing a lycanthrope baby from Newfoundland and needed someone to wear the portal button back for him, I volunteered right away." She let out a small laugh. "But I was the not prepared. Newfoundland is a futuristic world compared to Lore Isle."

Ella nodded. "So true."

Greta continued, "It was a huge learning curve at the beginning, but my shape-shifting ability really helped." She brought her folded hands onto her stomach and leaned back. "And, after eleven and a half years of searching, I found it, Black Infractus Braya, on the northwest coast of the Great Northern peninsula in the limestone barrens."

"Where is the plant now?" Peter asked.

"In your mom's greenhouse. I planted it in one of her pots. I was sure Lily would take good care of it, but I've been living next door for the last two years to keep an eye on it." She stood up. "Now, I need the egg to put the plant in and the portal button to wear."

Ella got out of the bed, opened the bottom drawer of the desk, and reached to the back. She gave the portal button to Greta. "Here is a button for you to go back. As for the egg…" She looked over at Peter.

He said, "We're going to release the wolves from the egg this morning."

"That's great," Greta replied.

Peter hesitated. "The egg was specifically made for the wolves. One-time use. It will turn to dust after the wolves are released."

Greta sat back down slowly. "Oh, Albert didn't tell me that."

"Mr. Doyle has withheld information more than once to get what he wants," Peter said. "He wanted you to bring back the button baby Ella wore, so he didn't tell you that the egg couldn't be used again. He knew that could be a deal breaker."

Greta's face turned crimson with anger. Ella looked miserable. "I'm sorry, Greta."

After a long silence, Greta spoke with new resolve, clutching the button to her chest. "I have heard there are other portals to Newfoundland that are not so restrictive with what passes through. As soon as I get back to Lore Isle, I will search. I found Black Infractus Braya, I can find another portal."

Greta spoke bravely, but her chin wobbled. "My plant is in the planter with the fern hanging from the rafter. It's a small and fragile plant with black blossoms attached to a bit of limestone. Could you make sure that it goes with you when you move? I don't know if the portal will open up where the plant grows in the Great Northern Peninsula, or near here, or somewhere else altogether."

Peter and Ella promised they would.

Ella asked timidly, "When you are in Lore Isle, could you find Uncle Albert and give him your button?"

"He's still in Lore Isle?" Greta said.

"Yes. There are only two buttons and there was a terrible battle with the mummers and Uncle Albert stayed behind."

Greta whistled. "It's unlikely Albert would have survived the vengeful mummers."

When Ella whimpered, Greta continued. "I will give it to him *if* I see him, but my quest is for another portal.

Outside Ella's bedroom window, the pale light of early dawn rolled out. Ella and Peter watched Greta hurry across the street and disappear down the wooded path toward the pond.

39

Once Upon a Time

MOM HAD PUT ON A BRAVE FACE WHEN SHE got into the truck, but she had not been so far from the house since she moved in, and her white knuckles gripping the steering wheel showed her true feelings.

Peter looked over at his twin sitting in the back. A newly purchased T-shirt, windbreaker, and jeans hung loose on Ella, as she was losing weight while trying to get used to cooked food she did not enjoy. Ella wore a serious expression, her head full of sorrow for Nan and concern for Uncle Albert. Peter worried that when her cast came off in seven weeks and she was able to run on all fours again, she would risk her life by going to Lore Isle to find out what happened to her uncle.

They parked the truck and hiked along the trail that led to the edge of the wilderness reserve. Once deep in the boreal forest, Ella said, "Here. I think they'd like it here."

Peter crouched on the ground and brought out the egg from his pocket. His radiant face looked up at Ella. This was it, the culmination of all they had been through. He pressed the sides, and the egg split neatly in half.

I did it! I do have wolf blood!

Beams of golden light poured out and took the shape of two wolves.

Mom gasped. "Beautiful."

The adolescent wolves, with dappled grey fur, stretched fully with their tails in the air. They yawned, sticking out their long red tongues, and shook their heads. They had slept for a hundred years. The wolves became tense when they noticed the three humans staring at them. Together, the two wolves bolted and ran deeper into the woods, never looking back. Ella took a couple of steps as if to follow them, then stopped, staring longingly at the disappearing wolves.

Mom took Ella's hand. "Let's go home." Ella nodded. The two started to walk back to the trail.

In Peter's hand, the empty eggshell crumbled into dust. The magical vessel had fulfilled its purpose. He clapped the dust off and reached in his jacket pocket.

He pulled out the red button from the Santa jacket. The day after his return from Lore Isle, he had gone to the pond and searched the spot where Mr. Doyle and he had left for Lore Isle. When he saw the red button, he was

joyous as if he had found a long-lost treasure. He rubbed the smooth button before putting it back in his pocket.

Peter took his time looking around before catching up to his mom and sister. The forest felt changed—greener, fuller, richer—whole. There were wolves in Newfoundland again, just as there had been once upon a time.

Acknowledgements

I EXTEND MY GRATITUDE TO EVERYONE ON THE Nimbus Publishing team. Thank you to my extraordinary editor, Claire Bennet, whose insights and feedback were invaluable; to Emily MacKinnon for critiquing and believing in *Lore Isle*; and to Jenn Embree for the beautiful layout.

My deep appreciation to the established authors Paul Butler, Trudy J. Morgan-Cole, Jessica Grant, and Ed Kavanagh for reviewing drafts as *Lore Isle* developed.

I am thankful for my supportive family: my wonderful sisters, Sooin and Haein; my sons, Timothy and Matthew, who were in elementary school when I started writing *Lore Isle*; and my husband, Tony, my rock.

My creativity is owed to my parents who brought their young family to Canada and worked tirelessly so their children could grow up dreaming. I miss you both.

Lore Isle received financial support from Arts NL (Newfoundland and Labrador Arts Council) and WANL (Writers' Alliance of Newfoundland and Labrador).

And finally, thank you, dear reader, for taking the magical journey to *Lore Isle*.